AUCILLA BONES

BILL LIGHTLE

ISBN: 9781686162596

Published by Bill Lightle
285 Kari Glen Drive
Fayetteville, GA 30215

This is a work of fiction.

For the two best boat captains on the Florida Panhandle:
Lon Sweat & Leonard Lawless

You must speak the language of justice.
Joy Harjo, Muscogee Nation, U. S. Poet Laureate, 2019-2020

CHAPTER 1

A giant sea turtle emerged a few feet from our boat and stuck its greenish head above the saltwater, rolled its eyes at us and then dropped back into the flats below. Then a stingray quickly darted away as the turtle prodded forward and kicked up sand and brown slender grass along the way. Two bald eagles landed on top of a tall, jagged cypress tree along the water's edge and near a cluster of reeds. Those powerful raptors mate for life. Their black and white bodies sat above the vibrant colors of the water and below those of the sky. These bountiful waters were their hunting grounds.

I'd caught three speckled trout, each around fourteen inches. They were now covered in ice inside the red and white cooler that also contained a twenty-inch redfish Abby had caught. Her first one ever. She fought hard to land him, and the fish fought hard, too.

We'd left the *Albany Chronicle,* about a three-hour drive north in Albany, Georgia, for a few days of fishing, boating, sunning, and anything else we wanted to do along the Florida Panhandle, one of the most beautiful places in the world. I hadn't seen much of the world, but I was convinced of that.

I'd met Abby Sinclair a few years earlier during her first day on the job as a feature writer for the *Chronicle.* She was hired not long after I started working there as a general assignment reporter in the newsroom.

We'd just graduated from college in the early 1980s and were both idealistic about how newspapers could be a force for good. Abby'd studied English and journalism at Valdosta State, while I'd studied political science and history at Georgia Southwestern College in Americus. Soon Abby was moved to the newsroom, and we became a writing and reporting team. About the same time, we fell in love with each other.

We came to the Panhandle to forget about writing news stories, sometimes about violent and tragic events, and just have some fun.

That was our plan anyway.

*

We were tied to an oyster bed in the Gulf of Mexico near the mouth of the Aucilla River, when something we couldn't identify floated in our direction. The October afternoon had stayed clear with a few small cotton-ball clouds over blue-green water, the sun warm but not punishing.

"What is that? Do you see it? Can you tell what it is?" I pointed to a fairly large object in the water a few hundred yards away and north toward the mouth of the brackish Aucilla.

It appeared to be drifting toward us.

We continued fishing near the oyster bed and along a small island of three-foot tall reeds swaying with the tide. The light breeze felt good on my face. My eyes now alternated between our fishing lines and what we had seen in the water but couldn't identify. Two minutes passed before we spoke again.

"Look over there," I said. "Whatever it is got stuck in those high reeds not far from the eagles. You see it? You see what I see, don't you?"

Abby reeled her line all the way in, attached the yellow and red-tail grub to her rod and leaned it near the engine of the nineteen-foot Boston Whaler we'd rented that morning at Shell Island Fish Camp, where we were staying for three nights.

We looked at what we couldn't identify. It wasn't a boat cushion, too big for that. It wasn't an ice chest, too big for that as well. Nor was it a buoy, like the orange ones that lead boaters to open water. Much too long for a buoy.

A squadron of pelicans, probably fifteen or twenty, flew V-shaped overhead, going south and away from the mouth of the Aucilla. In the direction they were headed, the few clouds had cleared and it was all blue.

We kept looking at the object. Then we saw something flop in the water next to it, like a large fish jumping from water into air. The way a mullet does. Or a big tarpon.

The movement and the noise caused the two eagles to leave their perch in the cypress tree and fly, side by side, north toward the Aucilla. I watched them fly a hundred yards or so and land together near a big piece of driftwood.

The object of our interest remained motionless.

"Was that something jumping out of the water?" Abby said. "A school of fish?"

"Probably. We've seen a bunch of them. Big fish chasing little ones. Gator trout, sharks, tarpons, dolphins, and redfish. It's tough out here. Beautiful but tough. There are killers in the water. Everywhere."

A few seconds passed, and Abby kept her focus on where we'd seen the splash. And that object we couldn't identify. I turned to follow the pelicans as they became smaller and smaller in flight.

Abby broke the silence. "What's happening over there?"

"Could be a big trout waving at us," I said. "Or a redfish doing the same. Giant tarpon. They get six feet long. Something keeps moving over there, but I don't think it's a fish."

She pulled in the anchor that was tied to the oyster bed, I turned the key once and started the Whaler. We slowly headed to what was lodged in the reeds. The thing we couldn't identify.

When we were about thirty yards away, we saw something just above the water. Now there was no doubt what we were seeing.

CHAPTER 2

It wasn't a big redfish, a mullet or a tarpon. Or a school of bait fish. We knew now what we had earlier seen but couldn't identify.

It wasn't a trout waving at us, because trout don't have arms. People have arms.

I eased our boat a few yards from whoever it was in the reeds. Now we were pressed against the thick reeds and close enough to see clearly what we had seen from a distance.

Blood ran from the man's forehead onto his face and the green shirt he wore. His left arm was entwined with a red boat cushion. That was what kept him afloat and his head above water. His eyes were closed. He wore tan khaki pants and high black rubber boats, the kind oystermen wear.

As our boat came to a stop, he turned his head toward us and held up his right arm as if he was trying to signal us, or call for help. He didn't fully extend his arm but held it up halfway for a second or two before it splashed in the water. Then he became motionless again.

"Let's get him in the boat!" I said. "He's not dead."

I jumped in the water and placed my hands under his armpits and pulled him toward our boat. He looked to be around six feet, solid chest and arms. A man used to a lot of exercise or hard physical work. Probably in his late thirties, early forties.

"Bring him to me, and I'll hold him while you flip him in," Abby said. "Easy with him. He's hurt."

She leaned over the side of the boat and placed her hands under his armpits, the same way I had done. She held him steady and above water. His eyes remained closed. I stood chest-deep in the water and lifted his legs, and together both of us were able to get him into the boat. He was still unconscious as I jumped back in.

"Lay those cushions down," Abby said. "We'll put him on top."

I placed two blue life-saving cushions on the floor of the boat, and we laid the man on them. We propped his head on a rolled-up blue and gray beach towel. Abby got another beach towel from one of the storage cabinets and covered the man from his neck to his black boots. Then she found a smaller towel in the same place and gently wiped the blood from his forehead and cheeks.

"Look at his head," she said.

Two inches above his right ear was a bloody gash about a fourth of an inch deep and three inches long. It was not actively bleeding.

"Bullet wound?" I said.

"You think someone tried to kill him?"

"Could be. Or could be an accident."

"Knife? Hatchet? Bow and arrow?" Abby said.

"Bow and arrow?"

"Something cut into him."

"Maybe he was drunk and fell out of his boat."

"Boat? What boat? I don't see a boat," Abby said as she looked toward open water and then back into the mouth of the Aucilla. Not a boat in the area. She refocused on cleaning the man's face.

"I don't see one either, but maybe it's up the Aucilla. He fell out of it, hurt his head and lost consciousness and floated with the tide."

"What about the boat cushion he was on?" Abby said.

"Probably came from his boat. He grabbed on and passed out."

"You think it was an accident?"

"Yeah, I've been down here a lot and never heard of anyone being shot in the head while fishing. People have accidents on the water all the time."

"That's surprising."

"What is?"

"You talking like that." Abby finished cleaning the man's forehead and face and put the bloody towel in a plastic bag and stored the bag back in the cabinet.

"What does that mean?"

"How long have you worked for the *Chronicle*?"

"Same as you. About four years. You know that."

"Then you should be wiser now."

"What do you mean?"

"Stop thinking things are going to be as they always have been," Abby said. "The world doesn't work that way."

The man slowly moved his head from side to side, said something we couldn't understand and raised his right arm again as if he attempted to wave. But two seconds later, his arm fell back on his chest.

"We've got to get him some help," Abby said. "Get us out of here and let's get him to a hospital."

"There's a boat dock up the Aucilla. It's a lot closer than the ride back to Shell Island."

"Let's go." Abby remained next to the man. "I don't see any other wounds. Just the head wound. That's all I see."

"Good. I think there's a pay phone at the dock up there. We'll get help."

I jumped back into the water and pushed our boat out of the reeds and mud. Then I got back into the boat, started the engine with one turn of the key and full-throttled toward the dock on the Aucilla. The 150 HP Evinrude ran smooth, like the water we were on.

Three minutes later we saw a marker for the no-wake zone as we approached the dock. I knew there were large rocks in that part of the river just below the surface but no markings to warn boaters. I'd once fished with a friend from Albany who damaged his boat on the rocks just below the surface. I went slow heading toward the dock. I knew the dangers.

There were no homes or marinas or any human-built structures along this part of the Aucilla. These tannic waters gave life to alligators, egrets, pelicans, eagles, and water birds whose colors surpassed rainbows. Cypress, oaks, swaying pines, tall reeds along the water's edge, all of it unchanged for centuries and centuries.

The poet says "beauty is truth, truth beauty." The Aucilla made you believe it.

When we were about a hundred yards from the dock, Abby said, "He's awake. His eyes are open."

*

As I guided the Whaler closer to the dock, I looked at the man on the floor of our boat. Coal-dark eyes wide open. Thick black hair, almost shoulder length. A dark face and high cheekbones. He'd yet to move or speak. A few seconds later, that changed.

"Who are you?" the man said. "Where are you taking me?"

"We're going to get you some help," Abby said. "We're on the Aucilla River and headed to the dock. You need to see a doctor."

"I do not need a doctor, but I do need to get away from this river," the man said, then he tried to stand but couldn't. He was obviously weak. Then he moaned. "Bad things happening here. They see me, they will try again."

"Try what again?" Abby said. "Who are *they?*"

"Tried to put a bullet through my head. Missed the first time. Not by much."

"Who?" Abby said.

"I can't give you names. I do not know who. They've been following me for a few days now. Watching me. I could feel their eyes all over me. I could see their guns."

The man put his right hand on his wound and gently rubbed it. He swung the towel off of himself and sat up and looked in all directions.

"Why would someone want to kill you?" Abby said.

He kept looking across the dark waters of the Aucilla as if he anticipated more bad things to happen. No reply to Abby's question.

"Tell us your name," Abby said. "At least tell us that."

"Have you seen any other boats since you picked me up?" he said. "Any airboats?"

"No, nothing since we headed up the Aucilla," I said. "We found you a couple of miles toward the Gulf. There are some boats on the flats, far out, but nothing around here."

"Good, that is very good," he said. "But we can't stop here. We can't get out on this river. Not now. We have got to get to open water. Get away from here."

"What do you mean?" I said. "Why can't we dock here?"

"They are still on this river," he said. "I know what they came for. If they think I am dead . . . I want them to keep thinking that."

The man stood up and held on to the side of the boat and looked north, up the Aucilla.

"I'm going to stop here and use that phone and get you some help," I said, as I was about to make a right turn toward the dock, about fifty yards away. "I don't see any trouble around here."

"I don't need help from a doctor," the man said. "My head will heal on its own. If we stay here and they see us, there will not be anything a doctor can do for us. They will kill us."

Then we heard an airboat up-river, about a half mile away, heading toward us.

"That will be them," the man said. "I recognize the flag on the back. The United States of America flag. Those are the men who have been following me the past week or so. Probably same ones who shot me."

"John, listen to what he's saying," Abby said. "We can't stop here."

"You have guns on this boat?" he said.

"Nothing but fishing poles," I said.

"No help," he said. "You can't outrun that airboat but you must try."

"Let's go," I said.

CHAPTER 3

The no-wake zone and the big rocks be damned. I full-throttled the Whaler and headed away from the dock and toward the Gulf. I couldn't outrun the airboat over long distance, we knew that. But I needed safer water, if there was such a thing.

Picking up a man in the water who said he'd been shot in the head ended our day of fishing. If the wounded man was right, whoever was in the airboat still wanted to kill him. If they were willing to shoot him again, they'd likely do the same to Abby and me. Those were my thoughts, anyway.

What if we were wrong? What if it was the wounded man who had done some evil deed and the good guys were in the airboat? Sympathy is not without its cost.

We'd find out soon enough.

I pressed hard on the Whaler and figured I could beat the airboat to the mouth of the Aucilla and open water, but it'd soon catch us after that, if it wanted to. We'd have to get lucky.

Maybe the presence of other boats would convince the men in the airboat to end their pursuit and go back up river. Or maybe they'd kill anyone who got in their way to get to the man we'd saved. I didn't feel lucky.

But thirty seconds later, I did. I weaved around a big rock in the middle of the Aucilla that was unmarked and just below the surface. I knew it was there, because on an earlier fishing trip my friend Lanny Saunders from Albany, after a couple of beers and a joint, cracked his propeller on it. The men in the airboat apparently didn't know what I knew, but they were about to find out.

I looked back the moment they struck it. Their airboat lifted out of the water several feet, flipped to its right and the three men tumbled into the Aucilla. The airboat landed upside down next to the big rock. The flag pole snapped in two, and the flag floated off in the water and then disappeared. We're lucky for now, I thought.

Over the roar of the Whaler, we heard our passenger say. "They hit Thunder Rock. Either did not know about it or forgot it was there. Maybe they don't know this river. This land. They know greed and violence. That I know they know."

I slowed the boat some. The men who flew into the water represented no danger to us. Not now anyway.

"Thunder Rock?" I said. "Didn't know these rocks had names."

"If a thing is important to you, you must give it a name," he said. "Sometimes two or three names, if you love the thing a lot. The Creator said a turtle placed it there so my people could stand on it, wait long, and throw their nets for fish. The turtle put it there during a storm. Thunder Rock. A good rock."

"Thunder Rock," Abby said. "I like it."

"What's your name?" I said.

"Joseph Threadgill. My people called me 'Quiet Bird' when I was young. Some still do. My mother was all Seminole. Father was half. Both are gone now."

Abby and I introduced ourselves.

*

During our thirty-minute ride west back to Shell Island Fish Camp, we listened to Joseph's story and learned why those men in the airboat might've shot him.

"My mother said when I was young and sat along the lake or near trees, I became like a quiet bird. Eyes everywhere. Watching everything that moved. Spiders even. Saying nothing while the other children played games. She said I was different. Mothers are right most of the time."

He was born on the Brighton Seminole Reservation in South Florida, along the northeast shore of Lake Okeechobee. He went to a mostly-white high school where he was taunted by white boys into fist fights because he was an Indian. A proud Indian. Never lost a fight, he said. Joseph dropped out after his junior year. Two years later he was in the Army. A year after that, 1968, he arrived in Vietnam in time for the Tet Offensive. A quiet bird no more.

He served three tours in 'Nam, all "to make the Seminole people proud." Wanted to prove his manhood, like his ancestral warriors who once walked this land. "It was a selfish reason to kill people who had not threatened my way of life. I did it anyway."

After he left the military in the early '70s, he met a woman in a bar in Miami. She convinced him to move to Tallahassee where she worked as a postal clerk. Her name was Alberta Shingler, and she was half Seminole. He moved in with her, but he was drunk and useless most of the time back then. Sometimes he used heroin and had nightmares of the war. Made her life hell in just a few months.

She ended the relationship and he came to the Aucilla, bought a couple of acres of land along the river from the money he saved when he was in the military. And over time he made money harvesting oysters, catching and selling mullet and sometimes repairing boats for other fishermen. He said his home was a couple of miles up the Aucilla from the dock, the direction the airboat had come from.

"Why did those men shoot you?" Abby said. "What's all this about? What did you do?"

"It's not what I did, it's what I found."

"Found?" Abby said. "Found what?"

Here's how he told it. A few weeks ago, he was scuba diving in the Aucilla not far from his home and looking for arrowheads, pottery, and other artifacts from when the Seminole had lived in North Florida, before the Seminole Wars and the Trail of Tears. He'd started diving about three years ago, about the same time he quit drinking and using drugs.

"The diving helped me. I replaced the bottle and the needle with the river. The things I have found down there help me remember the old ways. They were good ways. There were warrior clans that once walked and lived along the Aucilla. The highest praise you could give a male Seminole who showed courage in battle was to call him a man and a warrior. Before the white man showed up here, warfare was not for conquest. Only honor."

On that particular dive, he found a thirty-five-foot deep hole in the middle of the Aucilla, a couple of miles upriver from his home. The hole was in an area he hadn't been in before that day and looked to be about two hundred feet wide, with steep banks. He had never seen anything like that hole and what he found there. He called it the Big Hole.

Surprised by the depth and width, Joseph could see clearly with the thousand-watt light he used underwater. But the things he saw in the Big Hole surprised him even more.

"I saw an object around six feet long that reminded me of elephants I had seen in Thailand," he said. "I travelled there years ago with a couple of guys from my platoon. One married a girl from Bangkok. But that thing I saw was lying at the bottom of the Aucilla. Not attached to an animal in Thailand."

"Elephants?" I said. "In Florida?"

"The universe is a mysterious and beautiful place," Joseph said. "Many Seminole elders reminded me of such thinking when I was a boy. Many times."

"What was it?" Abby said.

"I did not know. Looked identical to a tusk. I took it to archaeologists at Florida State. They examined it. Looks like mammoth, they said. They wanted me to take them to the spot on the river where I found it. I told them no. They wanted me to leave it with them so they could further test and examine it. I told them no again. I got the big tusk and left."

"How old?" I said. "Did they have any idea?"

"They said maybe thirteen thousand years old," Joseph said. "Maybe older. My people were here then, too. Seminole ancestors."

"I didn't know they were once in Florida," Abby said. "Mammoths that is."

"Same thing the scientists in white jackets said at the university. They said this tusk could rewrite the ancient history of Florida and the Southeast. Museums all over the world would be interested. Private collectors, too. Many people would want to know about the Big Hole and what is in it."

"Why didn't you tell him where you found it?" I said. "Maybe they could send some divers and see what else is down there."

"No. I have been pulling my *life* from the bottom of that river during the past few years. Staying alive and away from the bad things. Away from most white people. I will keep what I find to myself. It's all part of myself now."

"Did you go back down there?" I said. "To the Big Hole. Did you dive again down there after you went to FSU?"

"Next day. Found other large bones, stone tools, knives. Several knives. It looked like an ancient hardware store on the bottom on the river. I could tell there was more down there, but it would be harder to excavate."

"Did you show any of the other findings to the scientists at FSU?" Abby said. "Did you go back to see them?"

"I didn't plan to. Now I could not do it even if I wanted to."

"What do you mean?" I said.

"Everything I found in the Big Hole I placed in a storage shed next to my house. Same place I have kept my arrowheads and pottery the last few years. One morning, about a week ago, I saw that someone had come at night or early morning, cut the padlock and stolen everything I'd found in the Aucilla. Gone. All of it. Every arrowhead. Probably had three hundred. All the bones. Big and little. That beautiful tusk. Gone. Old knives and tools. Gone."

"The men in the boat did it," Abby said. "That's what you think?"

"Those are my thoughts now. I knew somebody had been watching me on the river for the past few days. I could not see them, but I could feel them. It's the same feeling I had in the war. You never saw the VC in the jungle until they wanted you to. I could sometimes feel them hiding and knew exactly where they were. Others in my platoon could not do such a thing. Growing up Indian has its advantages sometimes."

"Here's my question," I said. "What's the point of trying to kill you if they already stole those bones and ancient hardware?"

Joseph turned behind us and looked at the Aucilla we were leaving behind. "That's what I want to find out."

CHAPTER 4

After we listened to Joseph tell his story and asked him questions for a few minutes, again I pushed down on the throttle, and we left the Aucilla farther behind on our way to Shell Island Fish Camp.

This part of the Panhandle is defined by the St. Marks Wildlife Refuge, nearly seventy thousand acres of land and wildlife, including forty-five miles of coastline. The federal government set aside the refuge in the 1930s. No high-rise condos. No expensive resorts. No goofy golf or titty-bars. If you want those things, go farther west to Panama City, the Redneck Riviera.

This area seemed timeless in its natural beauty.

Conversation stopped when the engine got loud. We wanted off the water by dark.

Abby gave Joseph a can of Coca-Cola she pulled from one of the two ice chests. The largest contained the fish we'd caught. He was sitting on top of that one, his back to us, looking into the fading sun. Joseph was still wrapped in the big towel that Abby used to cover him when we got him into the boat. He needed dry clothes.

She gave me a can of Budweiser, a Coca-Cola for herself, and took the white-cushioned chair next to me. I felt relaxed for the first time since we pulled Joseph from the water. That's the only feeling I'd ever known when I came to the Gulf. Until today.

I saw a big tarpon, looked half as long as our boat, jump three feet out of the water about two hundred yards to our right toward the shoreline. There were only a couple of other boats in view and they were both green flat-bottom aluminum. I didn't see any airboats. There were three fishermen in each boat probably working for trout in the same grass beds where I had caught one earlier in the day.

The calmness of the water ahead indicated not even a slight breeze. Blue and green stillness, above and below. It only took a few moments before it all became hypnotic, if you allowed it. We could see the brown grass beds sway below us as the Whaler passed over them.

* *

At the dock, we secured our Whaler near a yellow Shell gas pump and a wooden platform and water hose used for fish cleaning. We made two trips getting things out of our boat and into our cabin. Dark was coming.

"You stay with us tonight, Joseph," I said. "We'll figure out things in the morning. We'll take you back to your house or wherever you need to go. It'll be safer with us tonight."

Abby answered before he did. "Don't you think we need to go report what happened to the police? Somebody in law enforcement needs to know. Maybe the Florida game and fish folks. Somebody needs to know you can get killed on these waters."

"My answer to you, is no. To your question, John, yes is the answer. I can sleep here and then return to my home in the morning. I would be grateful for that. But no police. Not yet."

"You sure?" Abby said.

"Certain. Too many times I was drunk around here. Got in fights because I would not walk away from the hateful mouth of a white man. Deputies came and took me off. I did not always act like Quiet Bird. It's been a while since then, but they remember like I do. What I once was, I am not now."

"Okay, I understand," she said. "We'll figure all this out later."

"No, no police. I will see to this my way," Joseph said. "For now, no police."

"We understand," she said.

"Then you stay with us," I said. "It's a one-bedroom, but there's a big couch that should fit you. We got some extra blankets and a pillow. We'll all feel better about things tomorrow, I hope. Rested anyway."

"John's got some extra clothes you can wear," Abby said. "You'll need to get out of those wet ones."

"Should you ask John about that first?" Joseph said.

"She just did," I said.

That was the first smile we'd seen from Joseph. Big, beautiful white teeth.

"You change, we'll get cleaned up and cook some food," Abby said.

"I accept the clothes," he said. "Thank you for your kindness. For sharing what you have with me."

Joseph changed into a pair of my jeans and gray Atlanta Braves T-shirt. He took my fillet knife and the fish we caught to the dock to clean them. Abby showered while I started preparing the kitchen to cook fish, hush puppies, cheese grits, coleslaw, and iced tea. When she got out of the shower, I took a quick one and returned to the kitchen to help.

The small gray wooden cabin had a screened-in front porch with a green wooden swing and two white wicker chairs. We placed our rods and reels, tackle box, and the ice chest with the Cokes and beers in one corner of the porch.

There were about fifteen cabins at the camp, and several areas to set up tents and park RVs. Our cabin had no television or telephone. There was a pay phone near the office and a marina where bait, food, beer, and ice were sold. I'd probably been to the camp ten or twelve times since I was a high school student in the early '70s. On one trip with a group of friends, we had enough money for gas, beer, food, and bait but couldn't afford a cabin. And didn't have a tent.

We slept on the dock and in the back of a black Ford pickup truck that belonged to Leonard Walters. He and I grew up in the same neighborhood and first fished together when we were twelve. That night on the dock we boiled shrimp and drank beer, and fought off mosquitoes, but in the end they won. We were some fishing team that weekend with nicknames such as Bad-Eye, Skinner, Hatchet-Head, Lover Boy, and Tubby. Those you love, like Joseph said, usually have more than one name.

I thought about that trip from high school and grinned as I was helping Abby prepare our meal. Then Joseph entered the front door carrying our cleaned fish in a plastic bag. We cooked the fish and ate off big white paper plates on a small wooden table covered with a red-checkered table cloth. We drank iced tea from red plastic cups.

During dinner Joseph told us what he remembered before being shot. Around one that afternoon, he'd left his home in his johnboat to check a couple of crab traps at the mouth of the Aucilla. After he pulled the second trap into the boat, his memory stopped until we plucked him out of the water.

"I have been shot before. Happened in 'Nam. One through my shoulder. One right below the knee. Stayed awake when it happened. Today I must have fallen out of my boat and lost consciousness. I must have hit my head on the boat. Got a lump back there." Joseph rubbed the back of his head with his right hand. "Somehow the cushion ended up with me. Lucky that way, I guess."

"I don't remember seeing your boat today," I said. "Did you see it after we picked you up?"

"No. But I wasn't looking hard. It could be stuck anywhere along the bank. In some weeds. Those reeds are thick. Hard to look for a small boat when you are running like we were."

"Guess so," I said.

"Any idea where the shot came from?" Abby said.

"No to that question, too. Lots of places to hide along the banks. As I said, somebody has been watching me. This thing was planned. I saw an airboat with the United States flag several times. I did not see it before I was shot today. Whoever was in that boat shot me. Or they know who did."

"I got one more question," Abby said.

"You're good at it," he said. "What is it?"

"How did you know that airboat was coming after us? They were too far away to recognize you, don't you think?"

"Binoculars. A couple of days ago I saw them using binoculars up and down the river."

"How could you see them today?" she said.

"I didn't see them clearly today but assumed they saw us with binoculars. I think I was right."

We finished the meal around eight and went to the front porch to relax and talk. I opened a bottle of Chardonnay and poured Abby and me a glass. We sat together on the swing. Joseph made himself a cup of coffee and sat in one of the white wicker chairs next to the ice chest. His thick dark hair with a few strands of gray was now dry, it almost touched his shoulders and was parted down the middle. He reminded me of how Beatle George Harrison looked in the late 1960s. Striking with a quiet confidence, and my clothes seem to fit him just right.

He took a slow drink of coffee and said, "Both of you work for the same paper, right? *Albany Chronicle*. I've heard of it. I've seen it in stores in Thomasville. Never bought it. Never read it. But I know about your paper."

"That's right," I said. "We both do. The paper covers most of Southwest Georgia. We started working there about the same time. Around four years ago."

"Southwest Georgia is your coverage area, but looks like you found a good story in Florida."

"Looks that way," I said, and nodded my head and looked at Abby.

"Abby looks at you, you look at her," he said. "It is the same way. That way from the beginning?"

Abby put her left arm across my neck before she spoke. "We're just fishin' buddies, right Johnny Boy?" She smiled and kissed my cheek. She hadn't called me that in a while. I'd missed it and still liked the way she said it.

"That's right," I said. "It happened the first time I saw her walk into the newsroom. When I saw her, beautiful dark hair and dark eyes, I forgot what I was writing. Forgot my name for a week. She started working there not long after I did. Been fishin' buddies ever since."

"Here is a Seminole blessing to fishing buddies," Joseph said as he raised his cup of coffee for a toast. We did the same with our wine glasses. "May you be fishing buddies forever and the Creator protect you from all the bad things in the world."

"That's a real blessing?" I said.

"Must be, I just made it up." He nodded toward us and sipped his coffee.

We all drank together, then Abby said, "I like your blessing, Joseph. 'From all the bad things in the world.' It's not always possible, but I like it. Especially in our business."

Joseph walked to the screen-door and looked out at the dark and the quiet of the fish camp. There were a few boats on trailers and a handful of pickup trucks and cars. The fall air felt good coming in through the screened-in porch. The wind rustled the top leaves of a big green magnolia tree next to our cabin. That kind of soothing sound, with the smell of saltwater, was perfect for sleeping.

He stood a few feet away from us, and I saw long scratches on his left arm, from above the elbow to the wrist. They were thick and scabbed and looked like racing stripes.

"Joseph, your arm," I said. "Did that happen today? If it did, they healed quick."

"No, not today."

Now Abby saw the scratches. "You hurt yourself diving?"

"No, not that way either."

"Are you going to tell us or is it a secret?" I said. "Those scratches look awful. Someone cut you? You got into a fight?"

"Someone did." Then he said nothing for several seconds.

"Okay, we give up," I said. "You don't want to tell us what happened, we understand."

"That someone was me."

"You?" Abby said. "They look like a big cat got you. There are panthers around here, right?"

"No, Co-wah-chobee did not make these marks on my arms."

"Who?" Abby said. "What did you say?"

"Co-wah-chobee. Seminole word for panther. He is the Creator's favorite animal. Co-wah-chobee was created first on top of a big mountain. Then came the rest of the animals. They spread all over the world as the Creator told them to do. A much better creation story than Genesis."

"There are panthers still around here?" I said.

"Yes, not as many as there once were but they are still here. Protected in the St. Marks Refuge. My family — we belonged to the panther clan." He ran his right hand over the long scratches on his left arm. "Co-wah-chobee did not do this to me. I did it to myself. It was intentional."

"What?" I said. "Explain that to us."

"I do it every year in the fall. Just like my people on this land once did."

"Why the fall?" Abby said. "Why do it at all? How'd you do it?"

"Green Corn Dance." After he said it, he took another drink of coffee and looked toward the outside. We waited.

"Tell us what that means," Abby said. "The Green Corn Dance."

He held his cup in both hands as if it was something sacred and could easily be broken. As if it needed protection. "Every year the most important event for the Seminole is the Green Corn Dance. Comes with the corn harvest. A time of ritual and renewal."

"You cut yourself during the Green Corn Dance?" I said. "Purposely?"

"Yes, I did. Just a few weeks ago. I do it every year. I take six needles and attach them to a wooden block. Then I take the block and scratch the back of both of my legs and my arms until I bleed." Joseph set his cup on top of the ice chest next to his chair and held both arms up so we could see them.

"But why?" Abby said. "Why are you hurting yourself when it looks like, after today anyway, someone's trying to kill you?"

"I speak of scarification and purification. Seminoles have been doing this a long, long time. It's a reminder that life is hard. We are renewed through personal sacrifice and suffering. My Catholic Army buddies took the bread and wine, Jesus's body and blood, as they say. I shed my own blood. I started doing it when I quit drinking a few years ago. It helps me. Makes me stronger."

We were slowly swinging and Joseph remained at the door. Several seconds passed, and we heard an owl in the nearby woods. Then a second owl from another direction.

"Okay, I understand now," Abby said. "The self-discipline of it gives you strength. Courage. That's the purpose, right?"

"Yes, you could say it that way and it would be true. The Green Corn Dance usually lasts several days. Always thankful to the Creator, Master Breath, for a good corn harvest. Games, rituals. A realignment of relationships each year to remind you what is important in this world. Family. Love. Caring for one another."

"Courage. Strength. Self-discipline," I said. "You had it all today after being shot and surviving in that water until we got to you."

"You two proved you have it, too," Joseph said. "The courage to help another."

Joseph returned to his chair and a quiet minute passed. We heard the breeze sway the magnolia, crickets chirping, and the two owls again.

Then we saw headlights, and a vehicle drove up and stopped in front of our cabin. Two people got out and walked toward us.

CHAPTER 5

"Looks like we got some visitors. They're a little late for dinner," I said.

Two security lights lit the fish camp. The closest one was fifty yards or so in front of the cabin.

The two figures came closer, and they appeared to be wearing uniforms.

I looked toward Joseph but didn't see him. Then I turned and saw him through the open doorway that led inside the cabin, out of sight from the two people approaching us. He must think our visitors are looking for him, I thought. Maybe here to finish what they tried to do to him on the Aucilla.

The men stopped a few feet from the steps after they saw Abby and me on the swing. Both wore short-brimmed Stetson hats and had badges on the top left side of their shirts. I saw that for certain. Jefferson County Sheriff's Office? We stayed seated in the swing.

"Evenin' folks," one of them said. He was closest to us, about six feet tall, a little taller than his partner.

"It is a good evening," I said. "Is there trouble around here tonight? Any problems?"

"No, no trouble at all," the man said. "Nothin' our office can't handle. But I gotta ask you two a question, if you don't mind?"

"How can we help?" Abby said.

"Well, ma'am, we do need your help," the tall man said. "We're lookin' for a fellow who robbed a store over on Apalachee Bay. It was Mr. J. W. Wingfield's store. J. W. ain't never been robbed 'fore. Been on these waters some thirty-five years. He's a little bit pissed right now. Everybody loves J. W. 'round here."

"We don't know anything about that," I said. "We've been out on the water most of the day. Got down here early this morning. Drove

28

down from Albany."

"Looky here, now," the man said. "We're lookin' for a man about my size, thick 'round the shoulders, dark hair, wears it long, dark eyes. He's an Injun. We know he did it. Got eye-witnesses. Last name Threadgill. Like the fish *bluegill*. First name Joseph. His momma called him Quiet Bird, they said. He's meaner than a wildcat. We got witnesses, like I say, that he robbed J. W. He's Seminole, but it doesn't matter what kind of Injun. You can't trust any of 'em. You seen anybody like that?"

"No, sir," I said.

"How 'bout you, ma'am?"

"No, sir, I haven't either. We were fishing all day."

"I heard they were breakin' lines out there today," he said. "People catchin' lots of big uns."

"We caught a few nice trout and one big red," I said.

"Where'd you go?" the man said.

"Just out by the lighthouse," I said. "Stayed around the St. Marks River. No need to go far from the fish camp."

"Didn't go over to the Aucilla River?" he said. "Pretty good ride from here, but it's worth it. That's where the Injun lives. The one who robbed J. W."

"We like it around here," Abby said. "The lighthouse is just beautiful."

"Was that a yes or a no?" he said. "Did you go to the Aucilla?"

"Oh, no, we didn't go that far," I said. "Stayed in this area, like Abby said. We hope you find who you're looking for."

"Okay, now. I thank you for your time. We'll be goin', but if you see that Injun or anybody that you think might be him, call the Jefferson County Sheriff's office. Would ya?"

"We will," I said. "Thanks for letting us know. Sounds like a fellow we wouldn't want to be around. We'll make sure we lock the cabin tonight."

"You bet," he said. "Can't trust a thievin' Injun. They'll take everything you have and then some more, if you let 'em. That one has been causin' trouble 'round here for too long. Good night now." Both men tapped the top of their hats, walked to their car and drove away.

After the car disappeared from sight, Joseph returned to the porch. He walked to the door and looked through it. Several seconds later he sat back in the wicker chair, we waited for him to speak, but he didn't.

"Did you?" Abby said. "Did you Joseph?"

"Rob J. W.'s store? No, of course I didn't. I was home repairing a mullet net. I got into some drunken fights around here over the years. Did a lot of things I regret but never robbed anyone. Never will."

"Why did you leave the porch?" I said. "If you're innocent, you could've told them somebody's trying to kill you."

"Remember today? You and Abby pulled me out the water after somebody shot me. I am not inclined to trust anyone right now. Especially some of these local boys. When I see some of these cops now, I can see in their eyes they would like to hurt me. I have seen that look for years. If they don't see me, they can't hurt me. Those two men lied. There has to be a reason for their lie."

"Okay, I understand that," I said.

"Did you recognize them?" Abby said.

"The one who didn't speak, no. The one who did was Dwayne Leach. Deputy sheriff for Jefferson County. I know him. He has arrested and handcuffed me a few times back when I was drinking. I deserved it. *Injun* was his favorite word around me. Haven't seen him for a year or so."

"You didn't rob a store last night and now the sheriff's office is looking for you after someone tried to kill you," Abby said. "Makes you think, doesn't it?"

"It does lend itself to full concentration. That's why I disappeared into the cabin. I trust you two. You saved me. I can't trust others right now."

"What do you know about Deputy Leach?" I said. "What's his reputation? How long has he been with the sheriff's department?"

"Probably around ten years. Born here and grew up here. Never left. In his mid-or-late-thirties. Before the sheriff's office hired him, he shucked oysters at the Eat 'Em Raw Bar in Panacea. Then he got the judge's daughter pregnant and married her. Right after that, he got hired by the sheriff's office. And not because of his great law enforcement skills. The judge did not want his new son-in-law shucking oysters. Not a respectable career. People would talk."

"Has Leach played by the rules since becoming a deputy?" Abby said. "Up until tonight?"

"I don't know if he has ever broken the law as a deputy. Before becoming one, he sold enough pot to fill up a football field. Being a racist asshole is not illegal. He's the kind of guy who would knock you unconscious while you were sleeping and say he whipped you in a fair fight. He smacked me around pretty good once after he handcuffed me."

"You think Leach has something to do with you being shot today, don't you?" Abby said.

"As soon as I heard his voice, that thought did occur to me. Why else did he show up here? Everyone is suspect. Except you and your fishing buddy."

"Now what?" I said.

"I will stay away from Leach and away from anyone else in a uniform. *Any kind of uniform.*"

"How long can you do that?" Abby said.

"Until I get some questions answered. I am not going to run away from my home. I could. I got an Army buddy in Oregon — Harney County, I believe — who asked me to come out and work on his ranch. But I like it here. This is where I belong. I am going to find out who stole the bones I found in the Aucilla, and who wants me dead."

Joseph returned to his chair but continued looking outside as if he anticipated the return of Deputy Leach. "Maybe you two should go back to Albany in the morning. If they find out you lied for me, you could get yourselves in trouble. Or worse."

"You may be right," I said. "It's hard to think about having fun after what happened on the water today."

I looked at Abby and knew exactly what she was thinking. She was concerned about Joseph and curious about who stole what he had found in the river and why. We'd fished our way into a big story while on a three-day getaway from work. She wasn't going to turn away from that, me neither. Her instincts as a reporter had taken over. Mine too.

The Florida Panhandle wasn't in the *Chronicle's* coverage area, but this story had national and international implications. "It could be a helluva goddamn story, Maynard!" as our editor Mickey Burke would say. "Above the fuckin' fold!"

We weren't leaving in the morning.

"What do you think, Abby?" I said.

"We planned to stay three nights and I think we should."

"I agree."

"Joseph, you tell us how we can help you," Abby said. "We'll do what we can, but you need to know this. We're going to write this story for our paper. It needs to be told. There's been a major scientific discovery on the Aucilla and your life has been threatened. There is something happening here people need to know about."

"Understood. You want what you want. I want what was taken from me. I want to be the one who decides where those old bones end up. Not whoever stole them from me and shot me. This will be dangerous, but that is something we already know."

"We'll be all right," Abby said. "Comes with our job sometimes. Don't worry about us."

"We need a plan," I said.

"What about it, Joseph?" Abby said. "Do you have one yet?"

"I do."

"Tell us," Abby said.

"I'll do more than that."

"What do you mean?" I said.

"I'll show you. Are you two up for a night hike in the woods along the Aucilla?"

"We are," Abby said. "That's the reason we pulled you out of the river."

CHAPTER 6

About twenty minutes after Deputy Leach and his partner drove away, we left our cabin for a hike in the woods along the Aucilla. Joseph said those responsible for shooting him might dive the Big Hole tonight searching for mammoth bones. We agreed to go.

As he stood near my car, Joseph said, "They kill me and then there is no one to stop them. That plan failed. They may know I am alive but believe I will stay away from the river, fearful for my life. Now is the time to look. When they do not expect it. A quiet bird is patient and wise. That's an old Indian saying I just made up." He smiled after he said that.

He sat in the back of my four-door brown Buick, with Abby up front. He explained his plan as I drove away from Shell Island Fish Camp. It was simple.

He'd lead us through the woods on the westside of the Aucilla close enough to see the Big Hole. To see if there were any night divers. Joseph said we'd take back roads to the spot near the river. The thirty-minute drive ended at an old railroad line a few hundred yards from the Aucilla. The place was dark, heavily wooded. A three-quarter moon and a million and one stars cast light upon us. I gave Joseph the flashlight from my glove compartment.

"Good. Very good," he said. "This will allow us to see our way through. And to see Stikini."

"To see who?" Abby said.

"Not who. What."

"What?" I said. "What is *what?*"

"*Stikini,*" he said again.

"What in the hell are you talking about?" I said. *"Stikinicky?"*

"No, it is called Stikini."

Then we heard an owl, clear and nearby. Another hoot and another.

"That could be Stikini," Joseph said.

"An owl?" Abby said.

"Evil witches that transform themselves into owls. Some are nine feet tall. Sinister monsters. They eat humans alive."

"I'll wait in the car," I said.

"I'm with John."

"It is only a story. An old, old story. I will not let Stikini harm you. Or Stikinicky. I promise you that."

"All right, all right," I said. "Just protect us from all the monsters. Whatever their names are."

"Stay behind me. There is a trail up ahead animals take to the river. It's not far. Let me handle the monsters."

We walked single-file over the trail with me in the middle. Moss-draped trees, ferns, and big palms lined both sides of the trail. Joseph used the flashlight for the first couple of minutes, then turned it off. "Getting close now. They will not see us," he said. My eyes adjusted, and my vision was good for about twenty-five feet all around the trail.

In a couple of minutes, we came to a cypress tree, hollow at its base but big enough for one of us to hide inside of and not be seen by someone from the opposite side. We stopped at the tree.

"The Aucilla is about two hundred yards over there," Joseph said pointing east. "You two stay here. No need for all three of us to get close. I will see what it is I can see." Then he handed me the flashlight. "Take this. I won't need it."

I didn't take the flashlight. "We're not staying here," I said. "The owl monster may get us. We want to see what you see."

Joseph looked at Abby. "We're together," she said. "Just keep the monsters away from us."

"It appears I'm outvoted. Is that what people say in a situation like this?"

"Sometimes they do," I said. "Not all the time."

We continued along the trail in the same walking order and less than a minute later we stopped behind a tall tangle of vines and underbrush. I smelled honeysuckle.

"It's not far now," Joseph said. "We will move but stay behind trees. If there is anybody diving the Big Hole tonight, we will soon see their lights. If no lights, no divers."

*

Slowly, we walked farther into the woods but after several more yards we stopped and saw lights from the river, just as Joseph had suspected. "Follow me," he whispered. "There is a clearing near the bank next to some big water oaks. We'll stay behind the trees and look. We won't stay long."

We reached the water oaks and concealed ourselves behind them. Like quiet birds we looked intently toward the river. I saw the slow-moving Aucilla and other things, too.

There were three aluminum flat-bottom boats and one person in each. I couldn't see any markings or numbers on the boats. Overhanging lights were attached to each boat and they formed a triangle in the middle of the river, over the Big Hole. I saw a light in the middle of the triangle moving toward the boat along the east bank and farthest from us. A scuba diver surfaced and gave something to the person in the boat, but I couldn't tell what it was. On one boat I saw ropes and pulleys being used to bring up large objects.

"Looks like the kind of bones I found. They're about the same size. These are the men who shot me. Or had someone else do it. That I believe."

We didn't hear any talking from the men at the Big Hole. We continued watching for the next couple of minutes as divers brought up objects from the bottom of the Aucilla. Some were small and we couldn't identify them, but some of them would've reached across the trunk of my big Buick.

Joseph motioned for us to return to the trail, and we walked west toward where I'd parked. We started talking after a couple of hundred yards, certain it was safe to do so.

"Joseph, any idea who we just saw?" Abby said.

"No. I recognized no one. The three divers could be people I know. Could not tell unless they took their masks off."

"The men in the boats?" I said.

35

"Same answer. No. Never seen them, that I can recall anyway."

"You were right all along," Abby said. "They wanted to kill you, dive the hole, and take what they found."

"Why?" I said. "What will they do with it? Sell it?"

"Yes, that is exactly what they will do," Joseph said. "It is always about the selling of something. Greed makes people crazy. And violent."

"We're going to have to get some help," I said. "I think the Jefferson County Sheriff's Office is not the place to ask after our visit from Deputy Leach. What about the game and fish folks around here? Is there any one of them you know? Anybody you can trust?

Joseph's reply came quickly. "No. No. We will not contact anyone in uniform for now. Deputy Leach is not the only one involved. He would not come to your cabin looking for me unless someone told him to. Someone wearing a uniform most likely. Everything he does someone must tell him to do. That's the way he is."

"I understand about not trusting the sheriff's office," Abby said, "but why not contact the game and fish folks? You *really* think those two law enforcement agencies have conspired to kill you and take what's at the bottom of the river?"

"Conspired? Maybe. Maybe not. I only know right now in these woods, I trust no one wearing a uniform. I'm Seminole. I have good reason not to."

"You served in the Army," Abby said. "Did the same rule apply?"

"Yes. I served in the military to serve myself and my people. No one else. Even when they put medals on my chest, I did not trust them. There were only a couple of white boys in my platoon who accepted me. All of the black guys did."

"What you're saying is that it's just us right now?" I said.

"Those are my words. For now."

*

We were about twenty yards or so from leaving the woods when Joseph stopped, turned around and held his open hand up in front of my chest. I stopped and so did Abby. We heard what sounded like a car door shut but I couldn't be certain.

I whispered to Joseph. "Now what? The owl monster? Stikinicky?"

Joseph whispered back. "You mean Stikini."

"I don't know what the hell I mean. I'm just ready to get out of these woods and back to our cabin."

"It may take longer now. There are people at your car. I can see them by the inside light. Someone opened the door. They are looking for us."

"Who is it?" Abby said. "Could you tell?"

"Could be Leach. I see two wearing big hats. Like Stetsons. And two who are hatless. There may be more but I see four now."

We were still whispering. "*Leach!* How did he find us?"

"That is not the most important question we face right now," Joseph said.

"They must've followed us from our cabin," Abby said. "They suspected we were lying. Maybe they saw Joseph's clothes drying on the picnic table. They waited somewhere and followed. Wouldn't be hard to do with all these dirt roads and trees around the camp."

"Again," he said. "That's not the most important question."

"You're right," Abby said.

"What're we going to do?" I said.

"That is the question most pertinent," he said, whispering lower this time.

Joseph took five steps toward the clearing that led to the railroad tracks and my car. He stood behind three tall pine trees. We were still hidden by the darkness and a thick river-bed forest. One of the hatless men near my car had a flashlight turned on, and then I saw four people in all, two wearing hats. Leach and his partner must've gotten help.

Thirty seconds later, the two hatless men walked toward the woods and the trail we were on. The lead man carried the flashlight, and its strong beam illuminated several yards in front of them. The second man was about ten paces behind the first. They kept a steady pace. They kept coming toward us.

They weren't out hunting mushrooms or owl-monsters. They were looking for us. That seemed certain.

Joseph hurried back to us. "Hide. You must hide yourselves."

"We can help," Abby said.

"You already have. Now please do what I ask. Go. That way . . . *NOW!*"

He pointed north and off the trail. We jogged in that direction and stopped after about twenty-five yards and hid behind a circular mound of large palm plants and ferns. Some were five feet tall. We hid behind them and watched Joseph and the trail.

"John, if he needs us, we got to go," Abby said. "I don't like this. He's all alone out there. One against two."

"This is his home. His fight. I think we need to trust him on this, but if he needs us, we'll go."

The two hatless men entered the woods on the trail. The lead man with the flashlight remained about ten paces in front of the second man. Joseph positioned himself behind a cluster of water oaks and cypress trees off the trail to the south and several feet into the forest. The two men couldn't see him, that much I knew.

What happened next took about as long as it does to put a live shrimp on a hook.

Joseph was unseen as he moved behind the second man. He got closer and closer and came hard with his right hand at the base of the man's back. The man cried out, then turned to face Joseph. Big mistake. Joseph extended his right leg and kicked him hard on his forehead. He fell to his knees and Joseph knocked him out with a blow to the base of his neck. Another loud moan from the man before he collapsed on the trail.

The lead man, the one who held the flashlight, attempted to pull a pistol from his side holster, but Joseph kicked him in the face like he did the first man. Then a blow to his midsection forced the man to double over. He cried out in agony, too. Another blow to the back of his neck, and he was on the ground just like his partner.

We ran to where the three of them were. Both appeared unconscious on the trail as Joseph stood over them.

"They'll be awake soon," Joseph said. "We must move quickly." He picked up the flashlight and gave it to Abby. Then he took pistols from both men and gave one to me and kept the other. "Carry this until we get out of here. I want to make sure we do not have to use them."

Joseph walked west several yards, staying along the trail as we moved closer to the clearing, to my car, and who we believed to be Deputy Leach and his partner. We followed Joseph. He stopped within a few yards of the clearing and looked toward the other two men near the railroad track, not far away. They were standing on the opposite side of the squad car and both appeared to have pistols pointed in our direction. The moaning from the two men on the trail appeared to have alerted them, I thought.

"What now?" I said.

"Co-wa-chobee."

"What?" Abby said.

He cupped his hands around his mouth and what came out of him was a high-pitched, frightening sound. The sound a large cat might make. A panther. The sound came from him louder and louder, as if death itself were calling out. At times it seemed as if there were more than one big cat. Joseph was masterful, operatic. I didn't think it was possible for a human to sound like that until that night along the Aucil-la River. It startled me, and I knew what was happening.

Co-wa-chobee.

His plan worked. Two minutes after the first screech from Joseph, Deputy Leach and his partner were in the squad car and driving away.

CHAPTER 7

We waited in the woods a few minutes after they drove away from the river and Co-wa-chobee. Then we got into my car and left.

Joseph-the-panther had saved us. Here's what he told us. "A couple of years ago, a big cat jumped Leach, who was hunting near here for wild hogs. It was a momma with two cubs, so the story goes. They are protective to the death if need be, like all good mothers. Leach was lucky that morning. She scratched his neck and back. He took a lot of stiches. He has been scared of panthers ever since."

"Good reason to be," Abby said.

"I don't know how a human could make the sounds you did," I said. "But it worked."

"I was taught that when I was a boy by my grandfather. Like a white grandfather teaches his grandson to throw a baseball."

"Leach didn't seem to be too concerned about the two men who came after us on the trail," Abby said.

"They will wake up soon and find their way out of there," he said. "Leach was too afraid to help."

"Where to now?" I said.

"We shouldn't go back to our cabin tonight," Abby said. "It's not safe there. They'll be watching it. Leach and others."

"There is a place nearby we can stay," Joseph said. "We will be safe there."

"Your home?" Abby said. "Don't you think they'll be watching it, too?"

"Bad idea," I said. "Abby's right."

"Not my cabin near the Big Hole. We won't go there. I have a hunting hut I use a few times a year. We'll go there. It's safe for now."

"Hunting hut?" Abby said. "Like a Holiday Inn?"

"Better. Much better."

"Where to, Joseph?" I said. "Tell me how to get there."

His instructions took us west about three miles from where we were parked, away from the Aucilla. We went down a couple of dirt roads and finally turned onto one not much bigger than an oversized hiking trail, passable for only one vehicle at a time. Trees and thick underbrush lined both sides. No artificial lights. Darkness and more darkness. This was the home of Co-wa-chobee, wild hogs, deer, bear, and other animals we couldn't see. And Quiet Bird.

The ride had me thinking, not of the men who shot Joseph and who now were tracking us, but the experience of being attacked by a panther. What that must be like. The fear that must swell inside you when it's happening. The mother cat was ferociously protecting her cubs that she was fearful of losing, Joseph said. Leach chose the wrong spot to hunt.

"You will have to stop here," Joseph said. I parked in an area off the road where the underbrush looked to have been flattened by other vehicles. "This is where I park when I come into these woods."

Joseph grabbed the two revolvers from the back floorboard, the ones he took from the men on the trail. He gave Abby and me the guns. He still had my flashlight and turned it on as we started walking up a trail on the east side of the road. The trail reminded me of the one we were on earlier, the one that took us to the Big Hole and divers taking bones and other things from the bottom of the river.

"This your land?" I said.

"It is not. It belongs to a man named Walt Gosser. We fish together. Used to drink liquor together. Now when we drink together, I have coffee or Coke. He is a good man. A friend. The one man around here I can trust."

"What does he do for living?" Abby said. "Does he know about the Big Hole?"

"I haven't told Walt about what I found. Told no one but you two and those at the university. Have not seen him in a few weeks. Walt owns a couple of hundred acres and does what he wants to do. His family has been around here for several generations. He served in the Army like me. Battle of the Bulge in '44. Different war, same kind of killing."

"How far is the walk?" Abby said.

"You will soon see a sign that says HOLIDAY INN."

"Can't wait," she said.

"Only another couple of minutes. There is a big swimming pool and Tiki bar."

"I love these Florida resorts," I said.

Then we came to a clearing in the woods about as big as a basketball court and saw the small hut.

"Never seen a Holiday Inn like this," Abby said.

Joseph called it his "chickee," the Seminole word for house. He built it himself with cypress logs and a palmetto-thatch roof, he said. He opened the wooden door with a leather latch, and we lowered our heads to keep from hitting the doorway and walked inside. He shined the flashlight throughout the hut. There was one single bed on a wooden frame and a couple of sleeping bags, extra pillows and blankets on top of the bed.

In the middle of the hut was a simple wooden table without paint or varnish, a couple of black folding chairs, boxes with a few food items and a few plastic jugs of water. No indoor bathroom, no running water. He lit a lantern and we could see in full.

"Out back is an outhouse. I have toilet paper, but be mindful of snakes and other things."

"I look forward to that," Abby said.

Joseph found three red plastic cups and poured water from one of the jugs into them. He handed us cups of water. "Drink. Whether you think you need it or not. Then we'll sleep."

We each drank, then Joseph and I spread two sleeping bags on the floor, Abby took the single bed. We were exhausted and didn't know how much until we lay down.

"Just a day fishing, that's all we wanted," I said. "Right, Abby?"

"Got more than that. Tomorrow we need to see some people and ask a few questions."

"What people?" Joseph said.

"We need to talk to the same folks you did at FSU," she said. "Maybe even the guy who owns the store Leach said you robbed. What's his name?"

"Wingfield. J. W. Wingfield. The Bearded Clam."

"The Bearded Clam?" she said.

"That's the name of his business," Joseph said.

"Fascinating name," she said. "We need to see what we can find out. Don't you agree, John?"

"Yeah, I do. We need to interview these people and tell them we've heard about the discoveries on the river. See if we can pull some information out of them. Find out who tried to kill you, Joseph. Who's diving the Big Hole. We'll do all of this without using your name."

"That's right," she said. "Maybe we can go by the cabin and get our things. I don't think we need to stay there."

"I agree," I said.

"You do those things tomorrow, and I'll wait here," he said. "But you're right. Do not stay another night at that cabin. Better look hard before going inside to get your belongings."

"Okay, that settles it," Abby said. "I can't keep my eyes open any longer. Good night."

"Hope Stikini doesn't come tonight," he said. "There are big witches all over these woods."

"I don't believe in monsters," I said. "Not the animal kind anyway."

He turned off the lantern and we slept.

*

We'd probably been asleep for a couple of hours before I heard it. I'd been in a dream I couldn't get out of, one in which I was late for an eight o'clock class at college and the professor gave me a hard, squint-eyed look for being late. Even forgot my notebook and pen. Probably hungover from a keg party. It was one of those helpless feelings from my subconscious. The mind is a mysterious mechanism. Then I realized what I heard wasn't part of my dream.

I woke up the same moment Abby did. Joseph's loud, painful cries reminded me of his imitation of Co-wa-chobee along the Aucilla earlier in the evening. He was having a nightmare. I grabbed the flashlight next to him and turned it on. I kept the beam from hitting him directly, but I could see him clearly shaking his head and crying. A cry of deep sorrow. Then he stopped, and he talked clearly while still asleep.

"I am sorry I let you die. I promise I will get you home. Back to your people. That is my promise to you."

Then he cried again and violently shook his head.

I shook his right shoulder. "Joseph! Joseph! It's a bad dream. Wake up. Wake up."

No response. He was still sobbing, eyes closed. Sweat on his forehead. Overcome by sadness.

I shook him and repeated myself. "Joseph! Joseph! It's a bad dream. Only a dream. Wake up."

He kept still for a few moments. Then with the palm of his right hand, he slapped the wooden floor twice. More sobbing, louder even.

Now Abby tried. "Wake up, Joseph. Wake up." She shook his left shoulder.

We waited as Joseph was silent for a few more seconds. Eyes still closed.

Then with both hands he grabbed my shirt and pulled me close enough to him that I felt his breath on my face. I couldn't escape his powerful grip.

"Let go, Joseph! Let go of me!" I wrapped my hands around his wrist and tried to break free of his hold but couldn't. I'd seen his strength earlier that night on the river when he knocked out the two men who were coming after us. Now I felt it. He was a man of great strength.

A few seconds passed before his eyes opened and he released me. I moved away from him and he sat up, looked at me then at Abby.

"You're okay now," Abby said. "Just a bad, bad dream. You're okay."

"Did I hurt you?" Joseph said to Abby.

"No."

He looked me and said, "Did I hurt you?"

"No, we're both okay. You had a helluva grip on me, though. Nobody's hurt."

"I am sorry. That dream has been away for a long time. It came back tonight. There have been others, but this one is the worst."

"Do you want to tell us about it?" Abby said.

*

February 1968. He was a private in the Army's First Cavalry Division in Vietnam during the Battle of Hué. The Tet Offensive was underway. His platoon was in action near the Citadel, an ancient fortress in the center of Hué held by the Vietcong.

Dead American soldiers lay in the streets, civilian atrocities, mutilations, committed by the Vietcong. He'd seen the same kind of things done by Americans. Sometimes the fighting was "eyeball-to-eyeball," he said. It went on for weeks that way.

It was the same year as the My Lai Massacre and riots and assassinations in America. The year of death and destruction.

"I held him in my arms," Joseph said. "I promised him, as I tried to keep his intestines from spilling out on the ground, I would make sure he got home. That his body got back to his people. That was all I could do. I could not save him."

Joseph said the soldier was with the First Calvary but in another platoon. He was from Pine Ridge Reservation in South Dakota. "He was Oglala Sioux. His name was Johnny Kicking Horse. There is much power in his name. I had gotten to know him a few days before he was killed. We talked for a few hours when the fighting stopped one night and shared cigarettes. I have not dreamed about him for a year or so. Nothing goes away forever. Nothing."

He lay on his back on the floor telling his story and staring at the chickee's ceiling.

"I'm sorry you had to go through that experience," Abby said. "I'm so sorry for your loss."

"He fought for the same reasons I did. For himself. For the Indian. Not for the *United States of America*. He invited me to Pine Ridge to meet his family. I told him I wanted to come visit. One day maybe I will."

Joseph then covered himself with a blanket, turned to his right side away from us.

I turned the flashlight off and tried to sleep. When the sun came up, I was still awake.

CHAPTER 8

The next morning Abby and I left Joseph in his hut and headed to Tallahassee to interview the archaeologist he'd shown the mammoth bone to. Joseph said he'd stay near the chickee and out of sight from those who were likely still looking for him. For now, anyway.

On the way to the city we stopped at Shell Island Fish Camp and drove through it a couple of times looking for Deputy Leach or anyone else that might be looking for us. Things looked safe.

I parked in front of our cabin but kept my car running. We went inside and quickly gathered our belongings, including Joseph's clothes, and loaded them in my car. I drove to the office, we bought coffee and honey buns, paid the bill, and left. The drive would take us about an hour.

We'd both been to Tallahassee a few times and together we saw a Bob Dylan concert on the FSU campus in '82. And we'd gone down to watch a couple of FSU football games with friends from Albany. We knew how to get around in the city and where the university was located. Big oak trees draped with Spanish moss lined the downtown streets. There were great bars and good live music, and Tallahassee was also home to Florida A & M, an historical black college. On the way there, we talked about Joseph and this thing we'd gotten ourselves into.

"You havin' fun on our little getaway, so far?" I said.

"Oh, yeah, lots of it. Just like the other times when we were chasing news stories and people were chasing us. At least then we were supposed to be working. We came down here for some fun, didn't we?"

"That's how I recall it. Does it bother you that we've chased some news stories together that've almost gotten us killed the last few years?"

"That is one of the most all-time foolish questions I've ever heard. And I've heard a lot of foolish questions."

"Figured you'd say that."

Thirty seconds passed, then Abby said, "I've never seen anyone have such a terrible, terrible nightmare like Joseph had last night. I just can't imagine what he experienced over there during that war."

"What waste that was. Our government ruined the lives of thousands — here and there. A couple of million people killed. For what? Not a goddamn thing."

"He was suffering. He survived that war and now someone on the river is trying to kill him. He's still suffering. Did he get drafted?"

"No, remember, he said he enlisted. They stopped the draft in the early '70s. I was in junior high watching that war on the evening news with my father. God, it was awful. Bodies stacked on top of bodies. The 'body count' war."

"That's right. I remember what he said now. Fought for himself and his people. For the Seminole, not for the country. That's what he told us."

We drove north on U. S. Highway 319 as a white Ford pickup pulling a Boston Whaler passed us headed toward the Gulf. The boat looked similar to the one we'd rented yesterday. We'd planned to have that boat three days. Those plans changed, but the weather hadn't. The morning sky was blue, the air crisp, clean. Another great day to be on the water. Not us.

"How do we approach this?" I said. "What are your thoughts?"

"I think we tell what we know but, of course, leave Joseph out of it for now."

"Okay, I like it. How do we do that?"

"We tell them we have a source who told us about an important scientific discovery on the Aucilla. We want some comments for the story. Since they saw the mammoth tusk, the scientists, they should be able to comment. How's that?"

"It might work, but they're going to know who Joseph is. Unless he lied to us about coming to FSU."

"Yes, they'll know, but we still won't use his name," she said. "We won't admit to knowing him. No, he didn't lie to us."

"But we lie to them?"

"You don't have to say it that way."

"How would you like for me to say it?"

"We're protecting a source. We've done it before."

"Who was the head guy Joseph spoke with?" I said. "The guy in charge of the department. The one who examined the tusk. What's his name? Joseph told us, but I don't remember."

"I remembered to write it down," she said and pulled a reporter's notepad from her purse. "Dr. Zibe Growdy. That's his name. G . . . R . . . O . . . W . . . D . . . Y."

"Zibe Growdy. Shouldn't be a hard name to forget."

"But you did."

"I knew you'd write it down." I said. I smiled and she did the same.

A few minutes later we were on the FSU campus and followed the roadside directory to the Department of Anthropology. We found one of the few empty spaces near the building, parked the car and went inside. A directory listing inside the building said Dr. Growdy's office and lab were on the fourth floor. We took the elevator up.

Two minutes later we walked into his office. The door was open that led to his secretary sitting behind her desk. On her desk was a maroon and white — FSU colors — electric typewriter, a black push-button telephone, a stack of brown folders, a maroon and white coffee cup, and an ashtray with one unlit cigarette in it. The name plate on her desk read "Mrs. Mary Ann Shanks." She wore a pale white button-down blouse and a silver crucifix around her neck. She had auburn hair, bright red lipstick, and olive skin. Mrs. Shanks was pretty and looked to be in her thirties but wore too much lipstick, way too much.

It was around nine-thirty when we introduced ourselves to her. Dr. Growdy was in his lab down the hall. He had a ten o'clock class to teach but would be happy to speak with us, she said. He always likes meeting new people, especially reporters.

"Go to the end of the hall," Mrs. Shanks said. "You'll see the big door, the entrance to the lab. He's in there. He'll answer your questions. He just did an interview recently with the *Tallahassee Democrat*. He's also the director of the Florida Panhandle Archaeological Society and has been for ten years now. He likes people to know that. Loves talking about what he does. Go ahead now, he's got a class coming up soon."

"Thank you for your help," Abby said.

"Happy to help y'all. That's why we're here." She took the unlit cigarette and put it her mouth but didn't light it. She smiled big, red lips glowing, nodded her head twice, and we left.

We walked into the lab unannounced and saw a long room with white metal storage racks about six feet tall on both sides of the room. There were large plastic containers on the racks with writing on them. You could see objects inside the containers but not clearly enough to identify them. They probably contained research material, I thought. Bones, pottery, and tools from centuries ago.

Dr. Growdy was in the middle of the room standing near a microscope that was sitting on a big, black countertop, probably ten by five feet. We saw no one else in the room.

"Excuse me, Dr. Growdy," Abby said. "Mrs. Shanks sent us down to see you. I hope it's okay."

"Why shouldn't it be?" he said. "Whatever Mrs. Shanks says is always okay with me. I can't function without her. My whole department would fall apart."

"My name is Abby Sinclair and this is John Maynard. We write for the *Albany Chronicle*."

"Good to meet both of you." We shook hands standing near the microscope.

He took off his black horn-rimmed glasses and set them on the countertop. Growdy was probably mid-fifties, five ten, slender, hair graying but thick. Blue eyes and dimple in his chin and a welcoming smile. Not an unattractive man.

There were objects lying on the countertop that appeared to be old bones, most about five or six inches long, some more than a foot. Next to the bones, were a couple of the large plastic containers with more objects inside them. I couldn't tell what they were. The containers were marked with white labels, probably giving the dates and places where the artifacts were found.

"We've got just a couple of questions to ask you," I said.

"*Albany, Georgia*. How about that."

"That's the one," Abby said. "Right up the road."

"Right on the Flint River and about an hour from the Kolomoki Mounds near Blakely," he said. "I've researched both areas over the years. Lots of great arrowheads and pottery from along the Flint. It's still rich grounds for research."

"Sounds like you know the area pretty well," Abby said.

"We've researched the Kolomoki site recently," he said. "It's the oldest and largest Woodland Indian site in the Southeast. People lived there about three hundred years after the birth of Jesus of Nazareth. There are fascinating artifacts from that place. It still holds mysteries. We hope to take a team of students back there again. You two ever been?"

"It was one the first places my parents took us when we moved to Albany in '66 from Indiana," I said. "Been back a few times since. I love that place."

"What about you, Miss Sinclair? Have you been there?"

"Same as John. But we moved to the Albany area a few years after he did. We're from Alabama. My parents took me to the Kolomoki Mounds, too. I was probably thirteen or fourteen."

"Is that what you want to ask me about? I'd be happy to answer your questions about the Kolomoki site, if that's what you're writing about. Don't have much time right now with my class coming up."

"No, Dr. Growdy, we're actually here for something else," I said. "Won't take long. We know about your class. Mrs. Shanks told us."

"That's right. I got time for a few questions, though. I just did an interview with the *Democrat* recently. The reporter did a piece for the tenth anniversary of the Panhandle Archaeological Society. I'm the director. The Society gets a lot of support in Tallahassee. You interested in the work we're doing down here? A lot of great people involved in the organization."

"Yes, we are," Abby said. "Our paper covers the Georgia-Florida line. Our readers have a lot of interest in the Panhandle. Sometimes we stretch out. We're doing a series of stories on the Panhandle — how it has changed but, in some ways, is still timeless. It's fun for us to get away. Especially to Tallahassee. We heard about your work."

"I understand. I'm always happy to talk about the good work this department and the university is doing. I'm awful proud of our work for the Panhandle Society."

"Great," Abby said. "We're interested in what's happening on the Aucilla River. On the new discoveries there." She pulled a brown reporter's notepad and a black pen from her purse. I didn't bring a pen or notepad on the trip. Didn't think I'd need them.

"The Aucilla?"

"That's right," I said.

"There's not any research going on at the Aucilla. If there is, I'm not aware of it."

"We were told there've been some mammoth bones found there," Abby said. "They were found just in the past few weeks, a few miles from the mouth of the river."

"Was his name Joseph Threadgill?" Growdy said.

We hesitated for a few moments, then Abby said, "Yes . . . that's who we met on the river. He told us he brought a large bone, looked like an elephant tusk, here to the lab. Did you see it?

"I did," Growdy said. "After a preliminary review of the artifact, my conclusion was that Mr. Threadgill may have made a new scientific discovery. I wasn't able to do a conclusive carbon-dating test. I asked him to leave the bone and he wouldn't, but it looked promising."

"So, you think it could be a mammoth bone?" Abby said.

"Could be," Growdy said. "If it is, it'll rewrite the history of the Panhandle. I asked him to take me to the spot on the Aucilla where he found it. He refused that, too. If I knew where it was, I'd research that area of the river right now. I got a group of hard-working graduate students who'd dive the river immediately, if we knew where."

"All right, Dr. Growdy," Abby said. "Another question for you. Let's say mammoth bones are being found in the Aucilla along with human tools. What might that mean?"

"Human tools? That would rewrite our history here, like I said. It could mean that humans settled in the Panhandle fourteen thousand to fifteen thousand years ago. Much earlier — maybe by fifteen hundred years — than what we accept today. Could be the earliest site of humans in the Southeast, if what you're saying is true. If there were tools found in the same place as the mammoth bones."

"Who would want those bones and old tools?" I said.

"Museums, private collectors," he said. "That kind of finding would get international attention. We would want them here at FSU. Almost any university would be excited to have them. To study them and allow the public to see them."

"Okay, it would have a great intellectual value," Abby said. "We understand that. Would the discovery be worth a lot of money?" She was taking notes the whole time he was talking.

"Of course," he said.

"On the black market?" I said.

"Yes, that's why I said *private collectors*. Rich people, super rich people, the kind that own yachts and original paintings by Picasso, might spend millions for such discoveries. It's not unheard of."

"You'd rather see the bones in a museum, right?" I said.

"Of course, I would. That kind of discovery needs to be shared with the world. Not used for profit. Shared and studied."

"I agree with that," Abby said.

"Now I got a question for you two."

"Go ahead," I said.

"Where did you meet Mr. Threadgill?"

"We just happened to run into him at the Shell Island Fish Camp," Abby said. "We were spending the night there. Met him at the marina with some of his fishing buddies."

"I see. Then he told you this story about the mammoth bones?"

"He did," I said. "We were just interviewing some other folks for our stories at the marina."

"I suppose he didn't tell you where on the Aucilla he found the bone, did he?"

"We asked, but he wouldn't say," Abby said.

"Same with me," Growdy said. "It's been good talking to you two, but I've got a class coming up in just a few minutes. If you talk to Mr. Threadgill again, please tell him I'd love to bring a team of divers out to the Aucilla. What a discovery this could be for FSU and the whole area."

"I doubt we'll see him again," I said. "We didn't even get a phone number or address. Just a few quotes from him."

"I understand," Growdy said. "He seemed like a fine man. Quiet and reserved, but a fine man."

"We thought the same thing," I said.

"Maybe he'll change his mind and come back and see me," Growdy said. "Or maybe I ought to go find him and try to persuade him to show me the site."

"Good luck with all that," Abby said.

"Thanks, I'll need it."

CHAPTER 9

Growdy's lab door was still open. We said our goodbyes and he stood next to it and watched us walk back down the hallway toward the elevator we'd used earlier. His office door remained opened.

"Y'all take care, now," Mrs. Shanks said as she saw us go by. She still had the unlit cigarette in her mouth. Her way of trying to quit, I thought.

We stopped long enough for Abby to respond to her. "We will, Mrs. Shanks. Thank you for your help. We had a good talk with Dr. Growdy."

"Oh, I knew you would. He loves talking about his research. Proud of it, too." She took a drink of whatever it was in her coffee cup.

"Take care," Abby said.

"Both of you do the same."

"Thank you, Mrs. Shanks," I said.

We drove away from the campus, discussed our interview with Growdy and planned our next move.

"Looks like Joseph told us the truth about going to FSU," I said. "So much for protecting our source."

"Yes, that changed in a hurry, didn't it?"

"It was all your call."

"Dr. Growdy would love to know where the Big Hole is, wouldn't he?"

"You could see his eyes light up."

"Joseph doesn't trust people," Abby said. "Especially white people."

"He's got good reason not to."

"Yeah, but I agree with Growdy. This kind of thing — such a scientific discovery — needs to be fully researched by experts and the knowledge shared with the world."

"You convince Joseph of that."

"Right now, Joseph is focused on staying alive and trying to find out who's after him."

We drove near the capitol, past big oak trees, and clean redbrick walkways in downtown Tallahassee. Then headed south back on U. S. Highway 319 toward the Aucilla, and the Gulf. It was a few minutes after ten, Growdy's class was supposed to be in session by now. Maybe the topic was the extinction of the mammoth.

*

Joseph had given us directions to J. W. Wingfield's business near the Apalachee Bay, the one Deputy Leach said that Joseph had robbed. The Bearded Clam. We didn't believe Leach, of course. The truth in the Panhandle was as murky as the bottom of the Aucilla.

Traffic was light and the drive easy. Soon we hit the fresh aroma of saltwater again.

The Bearded Clam was a few miles west of the Aucilla off U. S. Highway 98. Joseph said that Wingfield bought the store about twenty-five years ago. Wingfield often hired himself out as a fishing guide on the Aucilla, and for wild hog and deer hunts. He claimed to know more than anyone about the river basin. Joseph said that he probably did. Wingfield was born on the Aucilla and only left once, after being drafted into the Army and sent to Korea in the early 1950s.

We pulled into the parking lot next to a white ice machine and tin buckets hanging from the outside of it. A sign said, "Fill the Buckets and Pay Inside." There were a couple of gas pumps out front, two gray wooden picnic tables on the left side of the cinderblock building and a double-wide trailer behind the store with a fenced area full of hens and roosters in front of it. Probably where Wingfield lived, I thought.

We walked to the front door and saw a big brown hound dog sleeping next to it, his ears large enough to cover a newborn child. The dog didn't open his eyes as we went inside. The store was musty and smelled of cigarettes and dust and previous decades. There were a few big saltwater trout and redfish mounted on the walls and underneath them many photographs of people holding large fish they'd apparently caught.

A wild hog head was on the wall above a red metal Coca-Cola cooler full of bottled drinks and crushed ice. The white tusks on the hog were as long as an ink pen. The store sold food, bait, fishing tackle, and cold beer.

There were no customers inside that we could see. Behind the counter was a man of medium build, probably in his thirties. He wore a white Panama hat with a black band and a Led Zeppelin T-shirt that listed the U. S. tour dates from 1977. Abby picked up two bags of barbeque chips, and I pulled two bottles of Coke from the cooler. We set the drinks and chips on the counter, and Abby pulled money from her purse.

"What else for you?" the man said.

"That's all for now," she said and paid the man with a ten and put the change back in her purse. "We do have a question for you, if you don't mind."

"Yes, ma' am, the fish *are* bitin' on the flats," he said. "Been gettin' that question all week with this nice weather and all. Sure has been purty 'round here lately, and they breakin' lines out on the water." That was the second time I'd heard that line since we arrived on the Panhandle. The first time was from Deputy Leach last night at our cabin.

"We got a few nice ones yesterday," I said. "Some trout and a big redfish. Man, they tasted good last night."

"See what I mean," he said. *"They breakin' lines!"*

"We want to ask you about something else," Abby said.

"Go ahead." He put both hands on the counter and leaned toward Abby. I could smell his strong marijuana breath ten feet away. He had a regular cigarette burning in an ashtray next to a pack of Marlboros and a round glass jar of beef jerky sitting on the counter. He tipped his hat back slightly and smiled with light brown teeth, like the color of the sandbars on the Aucilla.

"Have you heard of any night scuba divers on the Aucilla lately?" Abby said. "Divers looking for old bones and tools?"

"Night divers?" He paused.

"That's right," I said. "Night divers."

"What's so important about old bones and tools? These woods are full of arrowheads the Injuns used. Big pieces of pottery, even. Why would somebody dive at night, anyway? You can find plenty during the day. Easier that way, ya know."

"These bones would be an important scientific discovery," Abby said. "They'd probably be much older than the arrowheads you find around here."

"So?"

"They'd be worth a lot of money, too," I said. "That's what a scientist at FSU just told us."

"Scientist? Whatta they know?" He pushed back from the counter and crossed his arms over his chest. "No, I reckon I never heard of that. Why, you gonna dive the Aucilla at night? That dang water's dark enough during the day."

"Good point," Abby said. "So, you haven't heard of any diving at night?"

"No ma'am. Sure haven't."

We waited several seconds.

"Does J. W. Wingfield own this store?" I said.

"Sure enough. He's my granddaddy. I'm Ivan Wingfield." We extended our hands and introduced ourselves as reporters with the *Chronicle*. Man, that pot was *strong*.

"Can we speak to him?" Abby said. "Your granddaddy."

"No ma'am. He ain't here right now."

"Please call me Abby."

"Okay . . . Abby." He smiled and swayed backwards. I thought he was going to lose his balance and fall.

"Where is he?" she said.

"Took a man fishin' on the river. Came all the way from Tennessee. That's what he said, anyway. Or maybe it was Thomasville. I get them mixed up sometimes."

"When will he be back?" I said.

"You two come in here to buy somethin' or ask questions? My momma ain't got that many questions. Never had."

"We can do both," I said.

"Yeah, but I don't get paid for answerin' questions. Not that kind anyway."

"We just heard that there were some divers pulling some interesting things out of the river, and your granddaddy might know something about it," Abby said. "We're just curious about it, that's all. We write stories."

"Heard? From who?"

"We can't say right now," I said.

"You want me to answer your questions but you won't answer mine? Now that's some real bullshit if you ask me. Bigtime bullshit." He took another pull from his cigarette and blew smoke toward us.

"When's he coming back?" Abby said. "Your granddaddy."

"Dang! I don't know. He'll be back sometime. Maybe tomorrow. When he's good and goddamn ready to come back. He does what he wants. Always has."

"Okay, just one other thing before we go," she said.

"No more questions about divers," he said. "Or my granddaddy."

But Abby kept asking. "We heard your store was robbed the other night. Was anybody hurt?"

"Robbed? Dang, you two got some wrong things inside your heads. We ain't never been robbed. No one 'round here goin' fuck with my granddaddy. He don't carry that forty-five on his hip for show."

Ivan put his hands again on the counter and leaned toward Abby. Closer this time. I was about to knock the stoned shithead in the nose but thought better. Abby took three steps back.

"Looky over yonder," Ivan said and nodded toward an area behind the counter near a storage rack that contained cigarettes and chewing tobacco and condoms. "See next to the Red Man? And the Trojans?" There were three shotguns leaning upright from the floor. "There's another one under here." He pointed underneath the counter next to where he was standing.

"You are well armed in here," I said.

"Anybody tryin' to rob this place, we'll fuck 'em up. Everybody 'round here knows that."

"No one robbed this place, then?" I said.

"Dang, you two can ask questions but you sure can't hear good. No, I said. *No!*"

"Do you know a Deputy Dwight Leach with the Jefferson County Sheriff's Office?" Abby said.

"Yep, what about 'im?"

"He told us this store had been robbed and they were looking for a man who lived around here," Abby said. "He said the man was Seminole."

"Was he drinkin'?"

"Who?" I said.

"Leach. He might've gotten his stories mixed up. He'll take a shot or two on the job. Likes to get stoned, too. No one robbed this store and there probably ain't been any night divers. That's all bullshit, too."

Then three men came into the store. All had straw hats on and looked dressed for a fishing trip. "See those men there? I bet they don't ask any questions. I bet they just pay for their shit and leave, like the rest of my customers."

"Okay, Ivan, thank you for your time and help," Abby said, as we picked up our drinks and chips and headed out the door.

"We'll be back to talk to your grandfather," I said.

"I hope not." He blew his cigarette smoke toward us again as we left the Bearded Clam.

CHAPTER 10

I wished Abby and I were on the water fishing or walking on a beach or making love back in our cabin and drinking wine and making love some more. That was our plan for the long weekend trip. We could've done all of that. Love-making in the morning, on the water in the afternoon. I had it all worked out. She did, too.

Instead, we were driving around the Panhandle trying to find out who shot Joseph "Quiet Bird" Threadgill and who was scuba diving in the Aucilla last night. They were probably the same.

"You hungry?" I said.

"Yes, the chips didn't last." She turned the bag upside down and a few crumbs fell out on my floorboard.

"You're messing up my car."

"Impossible. Have you seen the inside of your car lately? Those crumbs won't make it worse."

"Okay, whatever you say, but now I'm hungry, too. Talking to Ivan the Terrible at the Bearded Clam worked up a big appetite. It's one of the all-time great names, though. The Bearded Clam."

"If you say so." She finished her Coke and placed the empty bottle on the back floorboard.

"How about Whataburger? There's one a few miles away."

"That'll work."

A few minutes later we pulled into Whataburger, and I bought three hamburgers and three orders of fries. We got the food to go and drove back to Joseph's hut. That took another ten minutes or so. We looked for Jefferson County patrol cars but didn't see any.

I parked where I did the night before, and we walked along the same trail to the hut. I set the food on the table and noticed the single bed had been made, all smooth on top. The sleeping bags folded and placed in a corner. Joseph was gone.

"Well, what do you think?" I said.

"He's restless, he's pissed that somebody's trying to kill him, and he can't go to his house," Abby said. "He seems fearless. He's probably out searching for answers."

"Where?"

"The river. The Big Hole. Maybe he went to see his friend. The guy who owns this land."

"Maybe so."

We sat at the table, and I poured two cups of water from the same jug we used last night. I was about to take my second bite of the hamburger when the door opened and Joseph walked in.

"Are you looking to rent or buy?" he said. "Great location. Nice neighborhood. Zoned for good schools."

"It's a little too fancy for me," I said.

"Me too," Abby said. "I don't want to come across as uppity. Like some rich southern belle. I don't trust the Blue Bloods. Do you have something more modest you can show us?"

"Most of my clients feel the same way. Especially fox and racoons." Joseph sat down at the table, and Abby slid the bag to him that contained his hamburger and French fries.

"We thought of you," she said.

"I know that already. Thank you again."

"Where've you been?" I said.

"You talk first. What did the archaeologist say?"

"He said he wants you to show him where you found the bones," Abby said. "If it is mammoth, it would draw international attention and be worth a lot of money. He thinks it is. Museums and private collectors — the black market — would all be interested."

"Seems like a decent guy," I said. "Apparently good at what he does."

"I had heard of him before I went to his lab," Joseph said. "I'm aware of his work along the Panhandle. I have read a couple of newspaper stories about him recently. That's why I took the tusk to him. He seems to be well-respected."

"We didn't, of course, tell him someone tried to kill you and we pulled you out of the river," Abby said. "We said we ran into you at the fish camp. At the marina. We told him we were doing a series of stories on the Panhandle."

"You lied to him."

"We don't like to think about it in those terms," I said.

"A necessary lie," Joseph said.

"We thought so," Abby said.

"Did you go to J. W.'s store?" Joseph said. "The one Deputy Leach said I robbed. The Bearded Clam."

"We did," Abby said. "J. W. wasn't there, according to his grandson, Ivan."

"I know him. What did he say? Did you talk with him?"

"Said he didn't know anything about night divers at the Big Hole and that the Bearded Clam had not been robbed," I said. "Never would be robbed because people knew his granddaddy would shoot them. Even showed us a few guns."

"He got tired of our questions, too," Abby said. "We told him we'd be back to talk to his grandfather."

"He is of simple mind," Joseph said. "Ivan, not J. W."

"I'd probably agree with that," Abby said.

"Where'd you go this morning?" I said.

"I walked to my friend Walt Gosser's house. The man who owns this land we're on. I explained to him what has happened. Everything. What I've found in the river lately and where. Showed him where the bullet creased my head. He said we could use his truck. Leave your car at his house, John. Safer that way since Deputy Leach can likely identify your car."

"Okay, we'll do that," I said. "Anything else?"

"Yes, there is. Walt was netting mullet this morning and saw a man with J. W. in his airboat near the Big Hole."

"Who was the man?" Abby said.

"He couldn't recognize him. Maybe from here, maybe from somewhere else. J. W.'s airboat is easy to recognize, though. Big sign on the back that says 'Bearded Clam.'"

"No one was diving the hole?" I said.

"Walt said that he didn't see anyone in scuba gear."

"You walked to Walt's house?" Abby said.

"About a mile through the woods. The same way back. Doesn't take long. We need to go there and leave John's car. He wants to help. I trust Walt. Even got me out of jail a few times during my Dark Days. Drunk days."

We finished eating and before we drove to Walt's, we walked to my car and got our belongings and carried them into the hut. Our new home. Joseph directed me to Walt's house by way of a series of dirt roads. The ride took about five minutes before we came to a big maroon and gold mailbox with GOSSER painted in black on both sides.

The fifty-yard-long white gravel driveway led to a modest redbrick ranch-style house. A canopy of oak, pine, elm, and poplar kept the house mostly in shade throughout the day. A green Pontiac Bonneville and a gray Ford pickup were parked out front near a flat-bottom aluminum boat under a white metal shelter. Both vehicles looked well kept. Beyond the house were endless trees and ferns and palms. Then the river.

Joseph said Walt lived alone and in the middle of his two hundred acres he inherited from his father. Walt's family had lived along the Panhandle since the late-1800s. He had a couple of sisters, but they both married and moved out of state. Walt eventually bought out their share of the land. He stayed in the Army after World War II until the early 1960s. He trained new recruits at Ft. Benning in Columbus, Georgia. Since then he occasionally sold real estate but was financially secure from his parents' money. He was divorced and had no children.

From his house, we were only a couple of miles from the Aucilla. Closer by foot. We walked to the front door, and Joseph knocked on it, and we waited. He knocked again. We waited longer.

"Could he be back in the woods or on the river?" I said.

"Probably not. Both his car and truck are here. I talked to him when he was putting his boat up. Maybe he's in the shower. He had fish to clean, he told me. We finished talking, and I left and he went inside."

This was only about an hour ago. I told him we would be coming soon to get the truck. I know he is home, maybe taking a nap."

Joseph knocked again, harder this time. Then the door eased halfway open by itself. It hadn't been shut securely. He looked inside then hollered for Walt. No response. Then he pushed the door wide open and looked inside again.

Then he quickly entered the house.

"*Walt!*" he said.

We followed Joseph inside.

Walt was lying face-down over a large brown coffee table in the middle of the living room.

"Help me," Joseph said. "Help me turn him." It looked as if he'd been hit hard in the back of the head. Blood oozed from a swollen area. We gently slid Walt off the table and face-up on the carpet, legs fully extended. His eyes were closed. He hadn't moved on his own, but he was breathing.

Joseph placed a sofa pillow under his head. "There is a towel hanging in the kitchen near the sink. Get it and soak it. Please hurry." I did what Joseph asked and handed him the towel. He folded the towel and placed it between Walt's head and the pillow. Joseph knelt over him and Abby and I stood next to them.

"Walt! Walt!" Joseph said. "Talk to me Walt. You love talking, Walt. Don't stop now. Do not stop talking now."

Several seconds passed before Walt moved his head to the right, then back to the left. We waited and no one spoke. Several more seconds later, Walt's eyes opened. He stared at the lime-green turtle shell light fixture hanging from the ceiling.

Then he spoke. "My ex-wife always hated that thing."

"What'd he say?" I said.

"Something about that light fixture and his ex-wife," Abby said. "He's talking."

"Yes, he loves to talk," Joseph said. "You will find that out."

Walt looked at me, then Abby, and finally to Joseph before he spoke again. "Are you gonna scalp me now? Is that why you're here?"

"Walt, I told you I do not scalp live white men. Maybe John and Abby do. Besides, your hair is already gone." Walt seemed to have thick gray hair but had it cut tight, 1950s style.

"I guess you came here to steal my women and horses," he said. "I can't trust any of you people."

"You have no women here, Walt. Your wife divorced you five years ago after she caught you in bed with Wanda from the Rock Island Oyster Bar. Remember? Nor do you have any horses. Never had. We came here to help you."

"It's 'bout goddamn time," Walt said.

"Sometimes Indians move slow but purposeful," Joseph said.

"That's the goddamn truth," Walt said. He rubbed the back of his head with his right hand. "Help me up. Help me to the sofa." We eased Walt off the floor and onto the sofa. He kept the towel pressed against the back of his head. The bleeding seemed to have stopped. Abby got Walt a glass of water, and he drank half of it and set the glass on the end of the coffee table.

"Walt, I need to look at your head," Joseph said. "You may need stitches."

"Ain't goin' to no doctor. You fix it. You know where my medic's kit is."

Joseph went into the kitchen and came back with white metal box with a red cross on it. The kit, dented and rusty, looked to be a hundred years old. He took the towel and cleaned Walt's head and put a thick bandage over the wound. "Shit! That hurts."

"You told me to do it."

"You shouldn't do what white people tell you to do."

"Walt, if it doesn't heal in a few days, you must go see a doctor. All right?"

"Okay, okay. Least I know you and your renegade friends are not here to scalp me."

"Your side was pretty good at that, too," Joseph said. "Scalping, that is."

"Don't believe everything you hear," Walt said as he removed the towel from his head and felt the golf ball-sized lump. "I'll be a dirty sonofabitch. I fought my way through Belgium in '44 and never once had a German sneak up on me. America's going to shit."

Walt enlisted in the Army in 1942 and eventually became part of the highly-trained soldiers of the 101st Airborne Division, paratroopers who fought their way through Europe beginning with D-Day, June 1944. His reference to Belgium was the Battle of the Bulge, from December 1944 into the following January. About ninety thousand U. S. military personnel were killed, wounded, or missing. Walt was not wounded in the battle but had two toes amputated because of frostbite. All of this Joseph had told us. Sometimes Joseph referred to him as Eight Toes.

"Yes, I know how you feel, Eight Toes," Joseph said and rubbed the side of his head where he'd been shot yesterday.

"These are the two you told me about?" Walt said.

"That's right. John Maynard and Abby Sinclair. They pulled me out of the river." We introduced ourselves to Walt.

"Thank you for helping me," Walt said. "Looks like you got one helluva a story here, unless they kill us all."

"Our plan is to stay alive," Abby said.

"My plan was to have a quiet lunch, some Crown Royal and watch the afternoon news," Walt said. "That didn't work out worth a shit."

"Tell us what you remember," Joseph said. "What happened after I left you?"

Walt told it this way. After he returned from the river, he was cleaning mullet out front when Joseph arrived on foot. Joseph explained to him the events of the past twenty-four hours. Then Walt suggested we use his truck for the next few days or as long as we needed, safer that way. The conversation lasted a few minutes, Joseph left and fifteen minutes later Walt went in the front door to get some ice for his fish.

"I opened the door and someone knocked the shit out of me," Walt said. "Next thing I know you're here taking care of me."

"Did you lock your doors when you went to the river this morning?" Joseph said.

"Never do. You know that."

"Figures. Whoever did it, came through the woods on foot. Probably came by boat, got out and made their way to your house. They saw you on the river today. Saw you when you saw them."

"Sounds about right," Walt said. "Helluva thing, ain't it?"

For the first time since we entered Walt's house, I looked through the living room and toward the entrance to the kitchen and saw a piece of eight-by-ten white paper on one of the end tables next to the sofa opposite Walt. I saw writing on the paper and picked it up. The note was in crooked capital letters, but I could clearly read it.

"You guys need to see this," I said. "I think we got a message from whoever attacked Walt."

"Read it," Joseph said.

"IF YOU DON'T STAY AWAY FROM THE RIVER AND YOUR INJUN FRIENDS NEXT TIME I'LL USE THE BARREL END OF THE GUN. THIS IS A GODDAMN PROMISE."

CHAPTER 11

Walt had been knocked out and left a life-threatening note, but that didn't change his mind about letting us use his truck. Loyalty and toughness, he seemed to have. If he could find out who hit him over the head, he'd likely give much worse than he'd gotten.

Eight Toes. Helluva nickname.

I parked my car behind Walt's house near a tool shed at the edge of the woods that led to the Aucilla. I positioned it out of view from anyone coming up the driveway. Then I went back inside as Walt reached in his pocket and handed Joseph the keys to his pickup. Walt remained on the sofa drinking Crown Royal and water that Joseph had poured for him.

"This is better than anything a doctor can give you," Walt said as he sipped the drink from a thick, clear glass that read, 101st AIRBORNE: KILLERS FROM THE SKY.

"The liquor can't put stitches in your head. You may still need them."

"I don't need no goddamn stitches in my head. I know what I need."

"That's right. Walt knows everything. Walt always knows everything. Forever and ever, amen. And God bless America."

"Of course, I do." He took another sip of Crown.

"How about locking your doors when you leave your house or when you sleep at night?" Joseph said. "That could have prevented all of this."

"They could've got me while I was cleaning the mullet. Lockin' doors don't always keep you safe."

"Walt, you are a stubborn jackass."

"My ex-wife, Gladys, used to say that."

"She was right. You still have that forty-five?"

"I do. And the shotgun. And an old M1 I stole form the Army. I hope that sonofabitch that hit me does come back."

"We're leaving now," Joseph said. "We *will* be back to check on you."

"I got liquor, I got guns and ammo. Just like WW II. Before you go, hear this . . . thank you. To all of you." Walt lifted his glass high and drank. We said goodbye and left his house.

Joseph drove Walt's pickup, and I sat in the middle of the cab as we headed back to the hut. A small colorfully dressed doll hung from the truck's mirror in the cab. A Seminole man dressed in traditional clothing. Joseph saw us looking at it.

"I gave that to Walt a few years ago. My aunt on the reservation, down in South Florida, made it for him out of palmetto fiber and cotton. I took Walt down there once to meet my family, and they all fell in love with him. Just like I figured they would."

"He's one tough man," Abby said. "And a good friend, it looks like."

"A good man. We met several years ago on the river when I moved from Tallahassee. I was drunk and mad a lot back then. Mad at the whole world. Wanted to fight everybody. He helped me. He listened to me. I trusted him then, still do."

Joseph drove slowly on the dirt road but then stopped unexpectedly. He saw them before we did. An adult wild hog was leading five piglets across the road, and the whole family was midnight-black.

"Stikini must be after them," Joseph said. He looked across the cab and smiled.

The hogs crossed over, and we drove farther away from Walt's house and into the woods.

"I think we need to go back to the Bearded Clam," Abby said. "Maybe J. W. is there by now. We need to talk with him. What about it, John?"

"That is very dangerous," Joseph said. "What happened to Walt means that they are willing to hurt not just me. They are willing to hurt others."

"You think J. W. is involved in this?" I said.

"I don't know. I do know that places I thought were safe along the Aucilla are no longer that way."

"We're willing to take that chance," Abby said. "You can stay at the chickee, and we'll go try to talk to J. W. Maybe we can get something out of him. You okay with that?" She turned to me.

"We'll try. They may think twice before knocking us over the head at the store."

"You do what you must," Joseph said. "We all understand the danger. I'll wait for you."

"Then we'll figure out our next move," Abby said. "I want to talk with J. W. and see what we can get out of him."

"If he's had the chance, I bet Ivan the Terrible has told his grandfather about our visit this morning," I said.

"If you are not back in an hour, I'll come for you."

"How?" Abby said. "We're taking the truck, remember?"

"I'll walk."

"We'll be okay," I said. "We're a pretty good team. And we've got the doll. It will keep us safe."

"It did not keep Walt safe," he said.

"They won't do anything to us at his store," Abby said. "I don't think so, anyway."

*

Joseph stopped, got out of Walt's pickup, and walked toward his hut. I drove to the Bearded Clam. We arrived around two and saw a few other vehicles parked there. Busier now than it had been that morning.

Something caught my eye when we pulled into the parking lot. After I parked, we looked toward the double-wide trailer.

"You see what I see?" I pointed toward the trailer.

"I do. Hard to miss an airboat with a big sign that says 'Bearded Clam.'"

"Maybe he's inside the store."

"Let's go."

The airboat was still hitched to a green pickup. We didn't see anyone outside of the trailer or near the boat. We walked into the Bearded Clam.

Behind the counter this time was a young woman, maybe late twenties. She wore a red, white, and blue bikini, a patriotic motif with tiny stars. There wasn't much fabric. She seemed to be wearing three eye patches. She had blond hair, a golden tan, grapefruit bosoms, and a slender, athletic waist. A contender for a *Playboy* cover.

She sat on a black-cushioned stool but had her right foot on top of the counter and was painting her toenails red. As red as Mrs. Shank's lips. The smell of nail polish had replaced that of marijuana. We didn't see Ivan anywhere in the store.

"Excuse me," I said. "We'd like to talk to J. W."

"That don't matter. He ain't here." She didn't stop with the nail painting, didn't even look up. "I ain't seen him all day. He's like that sometimes. Comes and goes. No one knows when J. W. comes and goes . . . see, I'm just like a poet."

"We just want to ask him a few questions," Abby said. "I'm Abby Sinclair and this is John Maynard. We're reporters for the *Albany Chronicle*."

"Hey, y'all." Still didn't look up. The smell of nail polish caused me to breathe through my mouth. "Everybody wants to talk to J. W. He comes and goes. He comes and goes . . . like the wind, just like the wind."

"What's your name?" Abby said.

She took her foot off the counter, put the cap back on the nail polish, and stood straight and looked at us. I thought both of her breasts might fall onto the counter. "I'm Inverness. Last name Cousins. *Inverness Cousins*. I go with Ivan. You know Ivan? He's J. W.'s grandson."

"We met Ivan earlier today," I said. "We were looking for J. W. then."

"Ivan's granddaddy is J. W.," Inverness said. "But I already said that, didn't I?"

"You did," Abby said.

"Wanna be sure, that's all. One day Ivan will own this store. We been goin' together almost six months now. I'm from Sopchoppy, ever been there?"

"We've been through it several times," I said. "Never stopped."

"Ain't nothin' there," she said. "No reason to stop. Just an itty-bitty place. Ain't bigger than a gnat. That's why my momma named me after a whole country. *Inverness*. It's a lot bigger than Sopchoppy. "

"I believe Inverness is a city in Scotland," I said. "Not a country. Scotland is the country."

The bikini woman stared at me as if I had wronged her in some life-changing manner. "That's not what my momma told me. Ivan is gonna take me there one day. Take me to see Inverness. He done told me that already. *Dang,* I can't wait to go. We gonna get outta here one day."

Questions about the geographical significance of Inverness seemed to bother her, and Abby shifted the conversation back to why we'd come to the Bearded Clam the second time that day. "Do you expect J. W. back today?"

"I expect J. W. when I see him. Ivan'll be back sometime. We're gonna close up at ten."

"Is that J. W.'s airboat by the trailer?" Abby said.

"Don't belong to nobody else. Everyone on the river knows that boat. I can tell you two ain't from 'round here. Right?" She grinned as if what she said made her feel superior to us. "He went fishin' this morning, came back and left with Ivan and some others. That's all I know. Comes and goes. He comes and goes."

"What others?" I said. "Ivan's father?"

"No, that sorry ass ran away ten years ago after Ivan's momma died. Ivan don't even know where he is. Maybe California, maybe dead. Can't y'all just stop with the questions? My brain's startin' to hurt."

"Okay, Inverness," Abby said. "We understand."

Two customers came to the counter with a case of Budweiser, two large bags of pork rinds, a block of hoop cheese, and a box of Ritz crackers. Inverness quickly punched the cash register and made a final statement to us. "J. W. opens at five tomorrow. You can see 'im then. Bye now. He comes and goes."

"Thanks for talking with us," Abby said. "Goodbye."

Once outside, instead of getting in Walt's truck, Abby stopped and looked toward J. W.'s airboat and double-wide. "Let's walk back there just in case he's home. It won't hurt."

"It could hurt. Ask Joseph. Ask Walt."

"Inverness might not know what she's talking about."

"What was your first clue?"

"Be nice, John."

"Always. Just like one of those scientists. Remember what Ivan said, 'What do they know'?"

We walked to the back of the Bearded Clam, next to J. W.'s airboat and pickup. We stopped and looked at both. The gray trailer needed painting, two out of the four screened windows in the front were ripped. Next to the concrete steps that led to the front door were four empty cardboard boxes, the kind that a case of beer fit in. Next to the boxes was an empty half-gallon of Canadian Lord Calvert, or as a friend of mine back in Albany who owned a liquor store often said: "Cry Lady Cry."

"Does he live alone?" Abby said.

"We didn't ask. We don't know."

"It's not like us not to ask."

"My mind was fogged by the nail polish."

I knocked on the screen door that led to a white metal door that led to the inside of the trailer. We waited several seconds with no reply. I knocked again and still nothing.

"Miss Inverness may be telling us the truth," Abby said. "He doesn't seem to be home."

"She doesn't come across as the lying type. If she thinks it, she says it."

"Let's get back to Joseph."

Back in the parking lot we saw a Jefferson County patrol car parked a couple of spaces from Walt's pickup. "Deputy Leach, you think?" Abby said. We saw no one in the car or standing next to it.

"Whoever it is must be inside. Let's go. Let's get the hell outta here."

As I was backing out of the parking lot, a sheriff's deputy wearing a Stetson came out of the Bearded Clam followed by another man.

"We didn't get a good look at Leach that night at the cabin, but that could be him," Abby said. "But the other guy looks familiar, doesn't he?"

"Sure does. Looks like Dr. Growdy from FSU."

"I think it is."

CHAPTER 12

We spent the rest of the afternoon at the chickee with Joseph and decided to return to the Big Hole after dark to see if the scuba divers were working again. We needed to identify who was taking the mammoth bones from the Aucilla, if we were to learn who wanted Joseph dead.

Before dark we drove a few miles to Shield's Marina to use the public showers and change clothes. Joseph took one of the revolvers he'd taken from the men he'd dispatched on the trail and put the gun in the pickup's glove compartment. An hour later we were back at the hut, clean but hungry.

He opened a green portable propane Coleman stove, lit it, and poured two cans of Van Camp's pork and beans in a pan and found a big wooden spoon for stirring. Then he opened three cans of StarKist tuna fish, put paper plates, paper towels, and plastic forks on the table. A feast in front of us.

"This is the best restaurant in the Panhandle," he said. "I'm sure you've heard about us."

"It's all part of the reason we came down here," Abby said. She smiled and dipped her fork into her can of tuna. "An exclusive resort."

"Reminds me of my college days," I said.

"It's our best dish," he said.

We ate and talked for the next few minutes. "Who else knows about this hut?" I said.

"If anyone does besides Walt, I am not aware of it."

"How long have you had it?" Abby said.

"A couple of years. Walt suggested I build it. A place to come and think. I don't hunt out of it, but it is a good place to come think. I don't like the sound of guns. Heard enough of them."

"How often you come?"

"Rarely in the spring and summer. Several different times when the weather is cool."

"We're the first ones to come inside besides Walt?" Abby said.

"Yes, that I know of."

"I like it here," she said. "It's close to the earth."

Around eight Joseph drove us to a spot along the Aucilla about a half-mile from where we were the night before, when we saw the divers. He parked next to two large trash bins the county maintained for residents along that stretch of the river. There were no other vehicles there. He stuck the revolver in his pants, and we followed him toward the tree line.

A familiar pattern.

The night was like the last one. Clear with a sky full of stars. The aroma of saltwater crisp, the breeze lifting it to the shoreline and beyond. Joseph stopped at the entrance of the woods and turned to us. "This trail runs about a quarter of a mile before intersecting the one we were on last night. From there, just a minute or two to the Big Hole." Joseph pointed the flashlight's beam along the trail.

"We're right behind you," Abby said.

"Stay close," he said.

We entered the woods and remained silent and walked single file, Abby in the middle this time. At the intersection of the trails, Joseph turned to us again. "The river is near. We will walk to a big plant. It's called yaupon holly. It is where I go to gather leaves for the black drink. From there we can see the river again."

"Black drink?" I said.

"I will explain it to you later. Follow me." He turned the flashlight off, but my eyes adjusted easily, and I could see several feet all around me. Just like last night.

A minute later we came to the big plant but close enough to see the Aucilla.

"Let us stay behind the yaupon," he whispered.

There were three flat-bottom boats again on the river, but this time in two of the boats there were men with long guns. "Probably one of those guns they used on me," Joseph said.

Divers emerged from the river and put large objects in the boats, same as was done the night before. "More old bones," I whispered. "Who are they and where are they taking them?"

"We'll find out," Joseph said. "We will find who is trying to kill me."

We watched for a couple of minutes before Abby pointed to a boat slowly coming from the south along the east bank. *"Look!* It's an airboat. Isn't it?"

A few seconds passed with the boat still coming. "Looks like one," I said. "J. W.'s?"

"That does look like J. W.," Joseph said. "The man with him, I can't tell who he is."

The boat got closer and we kept watching. "Is that Professor Growdy?" I said. "It looks like him, but I can't tell for sure."

"I don't think so," Abby said. "He looks to be younger and smaller than Growdy. What about you, Joseph?"

"I can't say for certain. I'm not fully certain of the driver, either. He has the look of J. W. If we were closer, I could tell for sure. We could be wrong. We're all just guessing."

The airboat eased up to the nearest flat-bottom boat, one with a man in it holding a long gun. There was another man in that boat, but he didn't appear to be armed.

More objects, big and small, were brought up by divers and placed in the other two boats. I counted three divers and four men sitting in boats. Plus J. W., maybe, and his passenger. Growdy — maybe. We just couldn't tell for certain.

The driver of the airboat threw a rope to the unarmed man in the boat nearest him. He held onto the rope to keep the airboat from drifting away. It looked as if a conversation began between the two men. Divers continued working.

"What are they doing?" I said.

"Nothing," Joseph said. "Just talking it seems."

"They know each other," Abby said. "We can identify one person involved. J. W. Wingfield. Can't we?"

"Owner of the Bearded Clam and now part of an attempted murder scheme?" I said.

"We can't be certain," Joseph said. "The other man I still cannot tell, either."

The conversation was becoming more animated. The man we believed to be J. W. pointed his right hand toward the Gulf. The unarmed man in the flat-bottom boat pointed his right hand at the men in the airboat. *"Goddamn you!"* We clearly heard that.

"They may be talking about us," Abby said.

"It's possible," I said.

We kept watching and a minute later the talking ended this way. The unarmed man in the flat-bottom boat reached down under his seat for a revolver and shot the two men in the airboat. Both bodies tumbled into the river. The man who shot them, stood up in the boat and apparently fired two more shots into each body.

"Sonofabitch!" I said.

"God, we've got to do something!" Abby said. "We've got to do *something.*"

"Do what?" I said. "Go down there and get shot?"

"That's right. They will shoot us if we go down there," Joseph said. "Look what just happened. They already once tried to kill me. Now it looks like two men are dead. For certain."

We kept watching.

*

The two bodies floated face down and slowly drifted south toward the mouth of the Aucilla. Then the man who did the shooting motioned to the three divers to come to the airboat, still secured to the flat-bottom boat by the rope.

The divers arrived and pulled the bodies out of the water and stacked them on top of one another at the back of the airboat.

"Joseph, where you think they're taking those bodies?" I said.

"A good guess would be out to open water with a few cement blocks. The sharks would get to them quickly. Other animals, too. Strip off their clothes before you dump them and there will likely not be much left by daylight."

Now the other two flat-bottom boats were next to the airboat and the shooter. There seemed to be a conversation, probably on what to do with the bodies, with the shooter doing most of the talking. He appeared to be in charge of the operation.

"They could take them up river," Abby said. "They could put the bodies in a truck and take them somewhere else. Far away from here."

"I doubt they do that," Joseph said. "There are plenty of places along this river to dispose of them. You have seen enough of it to know that by now."

"I don't expect they'll be taking them to the Jefferson County Sheriff's Office," I said. "Or the state game and fish folks."

"We have to call the police *now*," Abby said.

"No, we should not. We should wait," Joseph said.

About thirty seconds later, one question was answered. They were not going to the Gulf. The airboat, with one bright front light, sped upriver and away from open water, with the three flat-bottom boats following it. A few seconds later, they all disappeared into the darkness.

Abby turned to Joseph and spoke without whispering. "How many houses are there along the river?"

"They will pass mine in just a few minutes. Then for the next several miles, just a few and after that fewer still."

"How about public boat ramps?" I said.

"The best one is south of here, near where you found me. Going north like they are, there are a couple of old ones that are rarely used. They're small but big enough to handle those boats."

"What about the shoreline farther north?" I said. "Is it like it is here?"

"Yes. The Aucilla is less than a hundred miles long. Its origin is Thomas County, Georgia. Where it runs into the Panhandle, the forest is thick on both sides. For miles."

"You think they'll get rid of the bodies along the river?" Abby said.

"I do. Plenty of hideaway places to dispose of them," he said.

"They *could* put them into a pickup and take them somewhere else," Abby said. "That's possible."

"They could, but I doubt it," Joseph said. "Why do that? There are few people up and down the Aucilla. Safer here for them, I think. We're all still guessing."

"Let's go, then," Abby said. "Maybe we can find out where they're going."

"That may not be wise," he said. "We are out gunned, out manned, and out to get ourselves killed. Almost happened to me." Joseph rubbed his head where he'd been shot. "Remember?"

"We can play it safe — safe as we can," Abby said. "If we find out what they do with those bodies, it might lead us to who's behind all of this."

Joseph looked north up the river, then south toward the Gulf. He waited several seconds and said, "What say you, John?"

"I'm with her."

"I knew it but asked anyway." He grinned and shook his head. "You two remind me of stubborn Indians."

"I'll take that as a compliment," Abby said.

"That is how I meant it."

We followed Joseph away from the big yaupon holly plant that had concealed us from the violent men on the river. Day two of my getaway with Abby. One attempted murder, two successful ones.

Maybe we should've stayed in Albany.

CHAPTER 13

We drove slowly for a few minutes and came to an old cement boat ramp, cracks in the middle, and saw a half dozen big and small raccoons eating mussels along the bank. No signs of flat-bottom boats or an airboat or scuba divers.

Or two dead men.

"There is one more of these ramps not far from here," Joseph said. "After that, the next one on this side is several more miles upriver."

Another few minutes and we stopped next to the second old boat ramp, in worse condition than the first one, and saw no indication of what we were looking for.

"Are there houses nearby with docks?" Abby said.

"A few on this side, but they are several miles north. Mine is on the other side not far from here."

"What should we do?" I said.

"We have to go back and cross the bridge to get to the chickee, and then we can take a look on the other side of the river," he said. "Somewhere they are getting off the Aucilla. It will be easy to miss them."

Joseph's home, hut, and Walt's home were all on the east side of the Aucilla along about a three-mile stretch. There were just a few other houses and trailers in that area and no public boat ramps, he said. Most of the homeowners had small docks and boat ramps.

"They could run several miles upriver past Highway 98 before getting out," he said. "Or someone along the river here allows them to use their property. Somebody living along here might be involved. We are simply guessing where they might have put in. But we have been doing a lot of guessing lately."

"All right," Abby said. "Maybe we should get back to the hut and talk this through. That might be the safest move for us. For now."

"We will do that," Joseph said. "Before we get there, I want to go to my house and get some clothes and other things. It will take me no longer than three minutes to get what I need."

"You think it's safe?" Abby said.

"No, none of this is."

Twenty minutes after we saw two men murdered, Joseph pulled into his driveway along the river. A security light on a tall pole shone in the front yard several feet from the log-cabin-style house.

He parked a few feet from the front door and to our left near the river was another security light on a pole, casting a reflection on the water. There were no neighbors within sight. Trees were thick along the north-south run of the river. Dark and secluded. It was what we had come to expect along the Aucilla.

"Stay in the truck," he said.

Joseph picked up one of the bricks that marked his front door walkway and lifted what seemed to be a house key he'd hidden underneath. He unlocked the door and went inside.

I looked around his property and saw a shed, about a third the size of his house, in the backyard toward the river. "That's probably where he kept the bones and old tools he found in the Big Hole," I said and pointed to the structure. "That's the one they broke into. See it? Do you see it?"

"I see it."

Then I saw something near the shed I couldn't identify.

"What's that?" I pointed again.

"What's what?"

"That. Can't you see it?"

"I'm looking. I see the shed. I see the river and lots of trees. It's kinda dark out there, John."

"Look where I'm pointing."

She looked and I waited. "Okay, what is it? Looks like a pile of something to me. Maybe dirt. Maybe Joseph was building something or putting in a garden."

"Are you sure?"

"Sure? The last time I was sure of something was yesterday morning before we found Joseph. Remember? We were fishing and having fun. I was sure of that."

"It just looks odd to me. Not like a pile of dirt. Maybe a pile of old clothes."

"Old clothes?"

"Shit, I don't know, Abby."

We both focused on the pile of something in Joseph's backyard while sitting in Walt's truck. A few seconds later, Joseph emerged from the house with a green Army duffel bag and what appeared to be a long gun in a canvass case. He placed both of them in the bed of the truck.

"Not even three minutes," he said as he slid back into the driver's seat. "See anything out here?"

"Lots of things," Abby said.

"I love this place. It's a shame we can't stay. I would cook a fine meal for you two, if we could."

"Are you building something in your backyard?" I said. "A garden maybe. Or . . . something else?"

"No, the shed was the last thing I built. That was a few years back. Not enough sun for a garden out here. I would have to take down several trees, and I don't want to do that. Bad karma taking down trees. The universe does not approve."

"Then what is that in your backyard?" I said and pointed in the direction of the pile.

Joseph looked and waited a few seconds, and said, "I don't know. It was not there when I left yesterday morning."

"Somebody has been digging in your yard?" Abby said. "You don't know anything about it?"

"Somebody is trying to kill me. Why not dig in my yard? Burn my house down?"

"Don't we need to see what's back there?" I said.

"Why?" Abby said.

"I got a bad feeling," I said.

"I know what you're thinking, John," she said. "I'm not even going to say it."

"Don't then. We still need to look."

"We have sat here long enough, let's check it out," Joseph said. "Quickly, now. I do not feel safe at my own house."

The three of us jogged toward the backyard and toward the Aucilla as Joseph again pointed my flashlight to guide us. Half way to where we were headed, I realized I'd been right in my thinking.

"Oh, shit!" I said.

Joseph stopped walking and aimed the beam directly on the pile we could now identify. "I do not leave dead men in my backyard. I know that for certain."

"It has to be the men from the river," Abby said. "The two men who were shot and put in the airboat. Who are they? Do you know?"

"We are about to find out," he said. Both bodies lay face down with one on top of the other, stacked liked two big dominoes. They were wet and their chests and heads bloody. "Hold the flashlight, John, I will turn the top one over and we will see up close."

Joseph gave me the flashlight and moved closer to the bodies.

Then we heard the piercing sound of a siren, and another and another and another. The police were coming.

"Joseph! Joseph!" Abby said. "We don't have time. Let's get out of here."

He was ten yards from the bodies when he turned to us. We raced to the truck, got in and sped away in the opposite direction of the oncoming sirens.

I looked behind us and saw four, maybe five, law enforcement vehicles pulling into Joseph's driveway, with their blue lights flashing.

"Any idea about the bodies?" Abby said.

"No. I still can't say for certain who they are," Joseph said.

"You think one of those was J. W.?" I said.

"Still guessing. Not the man on top. J. W. is over six feet. The top man looked to be a few inches under six. And looked younger than J. W. Both had holes in their heads. I did see that. Seen a lot of that in-country."

"We do know something for certain now," Abby said.

"What's that?" I said.

"We know where they dumped the bodies."

"Why Joseph's?"

"He robbed J. W.'s store and now murdered two men. One may even be J. W.," she said. "Now police all over the state — the Southeast — will be looking for him. This is their way of trying to get him away from here."

"One big lie and one bigger lie," Joseph said.

"Now where do we go?" I said. "Your chickee is not safe. The police will be all over this river looking for you."

"You are right," he said. "I have another plan."

"Okay," I said. "I hope it's a good one."

CHAPTER 14

Joseph drove west on Highway 98, and we passed a Florida State trooper with the siren blaring and the emergency light flashing, headed toward the Aucilla. "They should not be looking for Walt's truck," Joseph said. "Maybe your car, but not this truck. My truck is still at the dock where I put my boat in yesterday. They will find it, if they have not already."

"They'll get to Walt eventually and one of those deputies that knows him might start asking questions about his truck," Abby said.

"Maybe," I said. "Probably before the night's over."

"We have time," he said. "Not much but we have some."

"Where we going?" Abby said.

"Panacea. It's about one hour away. We'll get a couple of rooms there and think this through. Do you know of it? Panacea?"

"I've heard of it," Abby said, "but never been there."

"I know where it is," I said. "Fished there quite a bit. Usually put in at Alligator Point near Panacea. I caught a two-foot-long trout there a few years back. Gator trout."

"We won't be fishing," she said.

"That's where we're going," Joseph said. "There is a motel there for fishermen mainly."

"The Oaks?" I said.

"That's right."

"I've stayed there," I said.

"One step above my chickee."

"That's about right. They do have showers and a toilet."

Home to a few hundred permanent souls and in Wakulla County, the population of Panacea increased some during spring and early summer as fishermen came in for the trout, redfish, red snapper, and grouper. Originally the settlement was called Smith Springs, but the name was changed to Panacea in the late 1800s, when land was bought by some Bostonians.

"That name is out of Greek mythology, isn't it?" Abby said.

"Could be," Joseph said.

"Abby would know," I said. "She loves those old gods and goddesses."

"She's the goddess of universal remedy, I believe," Abby said. "Panacea is."

"Universal remedy?" I said. "We could use some of that about now."

"It'll be a new place for me," Abby said.

"You're seeing lots of new things on this trip," I said.

"Some I want to forget."

The parking lot at the Oaks Motel was about half full with pickups and boats on trailers in front of the single-floor units, fifteen on one side and fifteen on the other. Joseph parked in the back next to an empty space in front of unit sixteen and a massive oak tree hung with Spanish moss.

He got out of the truck, removed something from his duffel bag and got back into the cab. "Here. Get us two rooms." He handed Abby four twenties.

"We can get ours," she said.

"I know you can but you will not. You saved my life, let me do this."

"All right, thank you," she said.

Abby and I went into the office and rented rooms six and sixteen and returned to the truck and gave Joseph the key for room sixteen. "We'll check our room out and come see you in a few minutes," I said. Joseph nodded as he got his rifle and duffel bag from the pickup.

Inside, room six was exactly how I remembered the Oaks when I'd stayed there about a year or so ago. It was built in the early 1950s and nothing had changed since then. There was no telephone or television. One double bed, a window air-conditioning unit, a small brown wooden table and two chairs, a small sink and a white and black-tiled shower without a tub, tight for an average size adult.

Shower sex would require great determination and imagination.

"A little better than Joseph's hut, don't you think?" I said.

"A little, but there was a certain charm to the chickee. I kinda miss it."

We looked around for a few seconds and realized that was too long. Then we walked across the street to a store, Crum's Mini Mart, that sold food, drinks, household supplies, and bait. It was the only such store in Panacea.

Abby picked up two toothbrushes, tooth paste, and deodorant. I got a six pack of Budweiser, a six pack of Coke, and a big bag of salted pretzels. I paid the woman behind the counter, probably in her forties, with long bleached blond hair and a T-shirt that said, "You Shuck 'Em, I'll Suck 'Em." She had a lit cigarette in her mouth that somehow remained motionless when she talked. It must've been glued to her lower lip. "Thanks, hun. Y'all come back, ya hear." Her smile was big and her teeth were slightly brown and reminded me of Ivan Wingfield's at the Bearded Clam.

We returned to the motel, and Abby knocked on the door at room sixteen. Joseph pulled the curtain back slightly, saw us and let us in. He popped the cap from a bottle of Coke with the opener attached to the wall next to the shower. I popped two beers and gave one to Abby. Joseph and I sat at the table identical to the one in our room, and Abby sat on the edge of the bed. I opened the pretzels and laid the bag on the table. We all got a handful.

We drank and ate and remained silent for the next several seconds. We were tired. Tired of running from people out to hurt us.

"We may be safe here tonight," Abby said, "but they're looking for us. By tomorrow we might not be safe here or anywhere around here."

"We're screwed," I said. "We're fucked. Especially Joseph. They want to charge him with a double murder and us as accessories to murder."

"We don't know that for certain," she said. "It is a good guess, though."

"Yes, they do," I said. "That's why the bodies were dumped at his house."

"They would rather kill me than arrest me," he said.

"This is turning out to be quite a weekend," Abby said. "It's just how we planned it. Right, John?"

"We could've stayed in Albany had pizza at Gargano's and gone to a movie."

"That's not near as much fun as this," she said. "Gargano's is a good restaurant, but I prefer beans and tuna fish at Joseph's chickee."

"See, everyone loves my cooking," he said.

"What do we do tomorrow?" Abby said.

I took a drink of my beer, grabbed another handful of pretzels, and waited for Joseph to answer. He didn't say anything but kept looking at his bottle of Coke as if what was in there could help us get out of this mess. I didn't know what to do next, neither did Abby.

"Come on, guys," she said. "Talk to me. What do we do tomorrow? Go to the police and tell them the truth? What's the right move for us?"

"No, we can't do that," Joseph said. "If you must go home, then go. I will not stop until I know who tried to kill me, who is taking the bones from the Aucilla, and who killed those men in my yard. If I turn myself in now, I will likely die in prison. Or worse."

"We need sleep," I said. "We're just too tired to think clearly. I don't know what the hell to do next."

"*Sleep?* If we don't figure something out, you won't be sleeping next to me much longer. You'll be sleeping next to Bubba in a Florida state prison."

"See what I mean? I'm too tired to laugh at that."

"What did you say, Abby?" he said.

"Which time?"

"John will be sleeping next to *who?*"

"Next to Bubba. It's a joke and it's used a lot."

"Yes, I have heard it before, but I'm glad you said it now," Joseph said. "The man lying on top of the other man in my yard tonight. The smallest of the two dead men. That could be him."

"Could be who?" I said.

"Bubba. That could be Bubba Fanning. His name is Frederick or Freddy Fanning. He has been called Bubba since he was a little boy."

"Why do you think it's him?" Abby said.

"The dead man is about the same size as Bubba. Five ten, kind of thick in the shoulders. Bubba, Freddy Fanning, is probably in his late twenties. If he is still alive. J. W. is a father figure to him. Bubba's own father went to jail several years back for almost beating Bubba's mother to death. Bubba fishes with J. W., sometimes works in the store for him. Hunts with him, too. Makes Bubba feel important. J. W. looks after him."

"Where's Bubba live?" I said.

"About five miles east of the Bearded Clam off 98. Just him and his mother in a double-wide. She waits tables at a Waffle House outside of Tallahassee. She had Bubba when she was fifteen. Ruby Belle is her name. She got her maiden name back after the divorce. Ruby Belle Stalls. I know all of this because Walt told me. Nothing happens on the Aucilla without Walt knowing it."

"What about Bubba's father?" Abby said.

"A few years back, he was working as a diesel engine mechanic in Tampa. Damn good mechanic when he was not drinking. When he lived here with his family, J. W. hired him sometimes to work on trucks and boats. He could fix any kind of engine but drank his money up quick. With a belly full of whiskey, he was looking for somebody to fight. Always. We had that in common."

"What's his name?" I said.

"Uriah. Uriah Fanning."

"You know how to get to Bubba's house?" Abby said.

"I do."

"Do we have to take 98 or are there back roads?" she said.

"This is the Panhandle. There are always back roads. Why do you ask?"

"Those two men killed tonight on the Aucilla, the press will eventually identify their bodies," Abby said. "It may not be in the morning papers, but by noon the television stations will have it. By the end of the day, it'll be all over the Southeast. The AP will pick it up."

"Depends on how quick they confirm the ID's and notify their families," I said.

"That's right," she said. "If the two victims are not from around here, it could take longer for the ID's."

"You want to see if we can find Bubba?" I said. "Is that what you're getting at?"

"I think we need to," Abby said. "We need to leave here first thing in the morning and drive to his house. What do you think, Joseph?"

"What if the *Tallahassee Democrat* tomorrow morning says it was somebody else, not Bubba Fanning?" he said.

"We still go looking for him," Abby said. "He knows J. W. Maybe we can get him to talk about what's happening at the Big Hole. If he's alive. If he's dead, we can try to interview his mother."

"That comes across as heartless," I said.

"I don't mean it that way. Look, here's the problem. We've talked to Growdy at FSU, Ivan and Inverness at the Bearded Clam, we've seen two men murdered on the river, been chased by Deputy Leach and two guys who wanted to hurt us, Joseph took a bullet . . ."

"Okay, I get it," I said. "You're right."

"What I'm saying is, if we want to find out what's happening, we've got to interview more people around here," she said. "Somebody knows something that can help us, and we got to get them to talk. Whoever it is."

"What's the mother's name again?" I said.

"Ruby Belle Stalls," Joseph said.

"Maybe she can help," Abby said.

I popped another beer for myself and one for Abby and looked at the small black alarm clock on the nightstand that read ten-fifteen. Shit, I was tired.

"Let's finish these and go to bed," I said. "We need sleep. I got a whipped ass." I took a drink of beer and got more pretzels.

"Joseph, maybe you ought to stay here tomorrow morning if we go see Bubba's mother," Abby said. "I think if his name doesn't show up in the morning papers, we need to go. We don't need to wait. It may be safer here for you."

"You're right about going but wrong about me staying," he said. "We will go together. It is dangerous for all of us now."

"Okay, that's the way it's going to be, then," she said.

"I hope you don't have to use that rifle," I said and nodded to the corner near the nightstand where he'd placed the gun standing upright near his duffel bag. "Or any other gun. What kind of gun is that?" He'd removed the gun from its case.

"It's a Springfield thirty-aught-six. I used to shoot wild hogs and deer with it when I was a teenager, but I don't hunt anymore. My Seminole grandfather taught me how to shoot it when I was twelve living on the reservation. It was his once, then it became mine when he died."

I looked closely at the gun's shiny wooden stock and thought for a moment about the difference between his upbringing and mine, then remembered something he'd said earlier on the Aucilla.

"On the river tonight, after we walked to that big plant, you talked about the *black drink* before those men were killed. What did you mean by that? *The black drink.*"

"The leaves from the yaupon holly are used to make it. It is a sacred drink for my people. It induces vomiting."

"A sacred drink that makes you vomit?" I said. "Is that something you do? Drink the black drink?"

"I do. A few times a year. It signifies purification. Afterwards you are stronger, more courageous. Seminole warriors sometimes drank it before battle. Indian cultures all over the Southeast used the black drink."

"Sounds like we need to be drinking that instead of beer and Coke," Abby said.

"I didn't bring any leaves, but you're right. In our predicament, we will take help from anywhere we can."

CHAPTER 15

I awoke with my right arm around Abby, the same way I went to sleep, and tried not to wake her when I got out of bed to the low humming of the window air-conditioning unit. The alarm clock read seven-fifteen, a solid night's sleep. I felt rested.

She looked lovely in sleep, the same way she looked awake. I thought that a few years ago the first time I saw her walk into the *Chronicle's* newsroom. Dark hair, olive skin, coal-like eyes, and a shape that the Greek goddess Panacea would've envied. She was hired just a short time after I was, and we've been together since. Fishin' buddies.

Her beauty struck me first, but then I came to understand what a thoroughly decent and caring person she was. Plus, a damn good reporter and writer. As Bob Dylan says in a song called Idiot Wind: "*I can't help it if I'm lucky.*"

I eased out of bed, dressed, and went to the motel office and bought two cups of coffee in thick blue paper cups that said, "Oaks Motel: A Family Tradition" and a copy of the *Tallahassee Democrat,* the most widely read paper in the Panhandle. There was nothing on the front page about the murders last night on the Aucilla.

Back in room six, Abby was still asleep, and I sat at the table, drank coffee, and read the paper, quietly turning the pages. I went through the front section and the state and metro sections three times and didn't read anything about the killings. By noon the local television stations would report it, and by the end of the day, it'd be all over the state, as Abby had said. The *Democrat* would likely run it on the frontpage tomorrow.

I read a couple of stories about President Reagan's predicted re-election victory next month against Michael Dukakis and a story on increased fall tourism in Panama City and other parts of the Panhandle. The headline said, "Fall Fun for the Whole Family." Maybe not, I thought.

Fifteen minutes later, Abby began to stir. "I smell coffee. I need coffee. You know I need coffee."

"Yeah, that's why I got you some." I set her cup on the nightstand next to her.

She sat up in the bed and took a drink. "Ah, well done, Johnny Boy."

"Sleep well?"

"I had a terrible dream."

"Wanna talk about it?"

"No, but I will. We were on a trip to the Gulf and got caught up in the middle of a violent gang war."

"Drugs?"

"No, animal bones."

I walked over and kissed her and said, "That could never happen."

"If I had dreams last night, I don't remember them. I slept the sleep of a lifetime. Isn't that what the poets say?"

"If you say so. You're my favorite poet. The only one I know."

"Sometimes you *do* say the right thing." She smiled and drank more coffee and turned to the predicament we were in, not a dream. "Have you talked to Joseph?"

"Not yet. Just went to the office for the coffee and the morning paper and back here."

"Is it on the front page?"

"No, it's not anywhere in there. I've checked three times. Their police reporters would've gotten the story after deadline."

"By the end of the day, the AP will've picked it up. Papers all over Florida will have it."

"That's right," I said. "Papers in South Georgia, too."

"What's our plan?"

"You said it last night. Go find Bubba Fanning. It's a new lead, so let's play it out. Our only new lead. If he's still alive. Even if he's not."

She drank more coffee naked under the brown bed spread and looked around the tiny room a couple of times. "Give me a few minutes to finish this, and I'll get ready."

I showered, brushed my teeth, and dressed, taking all of about seven minutes. Then Abby showered, taking just a little longer. We went to Joseph's room. He was ready to leave. We got more coffee from the office and were back in Walt's truck headed to Highway 98, east toward the Aucilla. Saturday morning. Our third day of the Gulf of Mexico getaway.

Joseph kept us on Highway 98 for only a few miles then turned onto a paved county road, and a few minutes later we went from Wakulla County back into Jefferson County, home of J. W. Wingfield and the Bearded Clam.

"Bubba's place is not much farther," he said. "It's with a few other trailers, coming up in a few minutes." He took a dirt road northeast, and we were probably fifteen miles or so from the Bearded Clam when the trailers came into full view.

"He lives in one of these, but I'm not certain which one." There were about fifteen trailers on small lots carved out of the piney woods. There was a playground with a swing set, sandbox, and an asphalt basketball court without a net on the crocked hoop. A few dogs crisscrossed the neighborhood, but we didn't see anyone outside.

Joseph drove slowly through the neighborhood as we looked at each trailer and finally, I said, "Stop here. I can see some folks moving around inside that one. I'll go up and ask about Bubba. Fanning, right?"

"Correct," Joseph said.

I talked to a woman, probably early twenties, wearing a white bathrobe and bottle-feeding the baby she was holding. "Ruby Belle lives over yonder. Her and Bubba." She nodded her head to the right. The baby was sucking hard. "Third trailer from mine, but I don't see her car. Sometimes she works a double at the Waffle House, sometimes just midnight to eight." I thanked the woman for her time and got back into the truck.

I directed Joseph to the dark gray double-wide that the woman had indicated. There was no grass out front but a few potted red geraniums, and the outside seemed to be well cared for. The trailer itself looked in good condition with a black welcome mat on the wooden front porch.

By the time Joseph parked, a gray Volkswagen Beetle, that seemed to match the color of the trailer, pulled into the parking space next to the front steps. There was a large dent on the back of the Beetle and a smaller one on top. A woman got out wearing a Waffle House uniform and stood by the car and looked at us.

"That is some good timing," Joseph said. "You two go. You're good at asking questions." Abby took her notepad and pen, and we walked toward the woman in the uniform.

"Good morning," I said. "I'm John Maynard and this Abby Sinclair. We're reporters for the *Albany Chronicle*. Can we ask you a question?"

"You just did," she said. The woman looked tired and irritated. Ruby Belle was just a few inches over five feet tall, slender, auburn hair, and aspirin-white skin. Her haggard appearance was of someone whose hard, physical work was likely making her look older than she actually was.

Joseph said that she had Bubba when she was a teenager, he was around thirty now, that placed Ruby Belle in her early-or-mid-forties. If someone had told me she was sixty, I would've believed it.

"I just spent more than eight hours on my feet servin' mostly drunk men, some grabbin' my ass," she said. "Their tips were awful. I hate that fuckin' job, but that's all I've had for the last couple of years. Now you want me to talk nice? Is that what you want?"

"You are Ruby Belle Stalls?" Abby said, flipping open her notepad as if we were about to get a newsworthy quote.

"No, I'm Nancy-goddamn-Reagan, welcome to the White House." She pointed at her nametag that read "Ruby."

"We just wanted to be sure," Abby said. "We want to speak with your son, Bubba. Is he here?"

"You see his big dang truck? The one with the two big lights for deer shinnin'?" She put both hands on her hips and leaned toward us.

"No, ma'am, we don't," Abby said.

"My bones are tired and here's the deal. He's been stayin' with J. W. Wingfield, sleepin' in the back of his store he says, anyway. Says he's doin' some work for 'im. J. W. takes care of 'im. His daddy never did. Wasn't worth a goddamn . . . why a couple reporters from Albany snoopin' 'round for my Bubba? You did say Albany, didn't you?"

"Yes, ma'am, we did," I said. "We're here doing a story for our travel section. Our paper goes all the way to the Florida line. We heard Bubba works as a fishin' guide with J. W."

"Fishin' guide?" she said. "Bubba can't even guide his own pecker straight. Gets him in trouble all 'round here. Three girls in this trailer park would like to cut it off. That ain't the kind of work he does for J. W. Usually he washes his boats or waits on customers or stocks his shelves. At least his daddy taught him how to fix an engine and he does that sometimes. That was the only goddamn decent thing his daddy ever did."

"You think he's repairing J. W.'s truck or boat?" Abby said.

"Could be, but he said he and J.W. are going to Panama City to see J. W.'s brother. He's got a charter business near Captain Anderson's. You know, that fancy restaurant? I ain't got enough money to eat there. Never will."

"We know it," I said.

"Why drive a truck there?" Abby said.

"He didn't say, I didn't ask. Now I'm tired, done said it once. Tired of your questions, too. If you see Bubba, tell 'im to call me. I ain't heard from 'im since Wednesday. Or maybe Tuesday. I'm goin' inside to have my Captain Morgan and juice and goin' to bed. Fuckin' Waffle House. Whatta a fuckin' job."

Ruby Belle turned from us and disappeared inside her trailer. We returned to the truck and Joseph drove away, but before we got out of the trailer park, a Jefferson County patrol vehicle slowly rolled toward us.

"*Shit!*" I said. "They followed us here?"

"No, they are not here for us," Joseph said as the vehicle with two lawmen in it passed us and stopped in front of Ruby's home. "She is about to learn that her only child has been murdered and his body was found in my yard."

CHAPTER 16

Now it appeared that one of the men we'd seen murdered last night was Freddy "Bubba" Fanning. The two Jefferson County Sheriff's deputies arrived at Ruby Belle Stalls' to take her to the county morgue to identify him. It was a reasonable conclusion to make but difficult to accept after just speaking with the mother of the dead son.

"Maybe one of those deputies dates Ruby Belle," Abby said. "Maybe Bubba's still alive. It's possible."

"We haven't seen or heard proof that it was him," I said. "The evidence is mounting, though." I turned to look back at the patrol car that stopped next to Ruby's trailer.

"Yes, it's possible," Joseph said. "It's possible that it wasn't him that we saw last night. He may still be alive. We'll know soon enough. What did his mother say? Did she give us anything that will help?"

Abby summarized what we learned, including what Ruby told us about Bubba's plan to drive to Panama City with J.W. to visit J. W.'s brother.

"I didn't know J. W. had a brother," Joseph said. "What does the brother do? Did she say?"

"He owns a fishing charter," I said.

"What is the name of the business?" he said.

"She didn't say," Abby said. "She was tired from work and tired of our questions. Pissed off you might say. But she did say it was next to Captain Anderson's, the restaurant on the bay."

"So, we go there next?" Joseph said.

"What about it, John?" she said.

"I think so," I said. "But first let's drive by the Bearded Clam and see what we can see. Then we can go to PC. I'm good with that. Besides, that's where you wanted to go all along instead of the fish camp.

Right? White sandy beaches. Pretty blue water." She was sitting in the middle of the cab, and I used my left knee to bump her leg.

"If we'd gone there, we would've never met Joseph." She bumped me back. "I do love that beach, though."

"I will drive by J. W.'s then we will head north to Blountstown and on to Panama City. It will be a little more than a hundred miles from the Bearded Clam. Not a bad drive."

"We need to slip in and get our clothes out of the chickee, if we can," she said. "We're going need a change of clothes. Sometime."

"We will take a look there after the Bearded Clam. If it looks safe, we will stop and get what you need. I can always make us some more pork and beans and tuna fish."

No comment.

*

A few minutes later we pulled into the Bearded Clam, but it was closed. Nine-fifteen in the morning on a beautiful fall day? Something was wrong. We didn't see J. W.'s truck or airboat or any other vehicle near the store or next to his trailer. We sat in the truck and Joseph kept the engine running.

"He's dead, too," I said. "They're both dead. Bubba and J. W. I just bet they are."

"Could be," Abby said. "There may be another explanation for this."

"What would it be?" Joseph said.

"I'm thinking," she said.

"Joseph, does J. W. have any other family around here other than his grandson, Ivan?" I said.

"If he does, I'm not aware of it. I did not know about the brother. J. W. had a wife, Dora Mae, but she died of cancer about three or four years ago. J. W.'s only child and Ivan's father, Tom Crocket, ran away to California with a girl from Crawfordville several years ago. Left a note taped to a whiskey bottle."

"Crocket his middle name?" I said.

"It was the last time he lived here. People called him 'Tom Crocket' because that is what he wanted. Said he wanted two names."

"Ivan's mother?" I said.

"Left a month later. No one knows where she went. Her name was Jolene. The couple was drunk a lot. Fought a lot. Both of them left here."

"People do a lot of leavin' around here, don't they?" I said.

"I suppose they do."

"If the big body last night was J. W., the police would either contact Ivan or his brother — if they know about his brother — to identify the body," Abby said. "Don't you think?"

"I do," Joseph said. "Sounds logical."

"Ivan lives with J. W., is that what you said, Joseph?" I said.

"He has since his mother left him several years ago."

"There is nothing for us to do here," Abby said. "Will you go by your chickee now and maybe we can get our clothes?"

"Let's go take a look," he said. A few minutes later, he stopped at the trail that led to his hut. We didn't see any vehicles along the dirt road that sliced through the woods. "You two stay here, and I will get your belongings."

Joseph stuck the revolver in the back of his pants and jogged toward the chickee. Five minutes later he returned with our two small suitcases and the other revolver he'd left in the hut. He put both guns in the glove compartment and our suitcases in the back of the truck with his belongings and the encased thirty-aught-six. "Now we will go find J. W.'s brother," he said. "If he has one."

He took Florida State Highway 267 north toward Blountstown and said we'd be in Panama City before noon. On the way we cut through Apalachicola National Forest and tried to figure out some things, but this had gotten a lot more complicated and dangerous than catching redfish and trout.

"Let's assume they're both dead," I said. "The two bodies we saw last night at Joseph's were J. W. and Bubba, let's assume that. We're not certain, but now there's a lot of evidence to indicate it was them. Cops at Bubba's house talking to his mother and the Bearded Clam being closed."

"We'll know by noon for sure, like I said," Abby said. "The local televisions stations will have it. Radio news, too."

"It's clear, Joseph, they want to frame you," I said. "Remember, you robbed J. W.'s store, too, according to Deputy Leach."

"Yes, but Leach was lying. Then they dumped the bodies in my yard hoping to connect me to the killings. I understand their plan, but why were J. W. and Bubba killed in the first place? Answer that correctly, you win the prize."

"Here's how I see it," Abby said. "It can be only one of two things. J. W. and Bubba were both involved in the scheme of taking and selling the bones but got into an argument with their partners. Or they just happened to be on the river that night, saw the divers and stopped to talk. The man in charge of the operation wanted no witnesses. Same as with Joseph. Then they shot them."

"I don't know," I said. "That sure is a lot of killing over old animal bones. And if they were just passing through on the river, why not just let them go?"

"Old animal bones that are worth a lot of money," Abby said. "Don't forget what Dr. Growdy said."

"Did they think J. W. and Bubba were going to find out about the bones?" I said.

"I am thinking about that and something else," Joseph said.

"What else?" I said.

"How much I want to stay alive and out of prison."

*

We pulled into the parking lot at Captain Anderson's a little before noon and parked near the water that led to St. Andrews Bay. A yellow neon sign said, "Margarita Special: Two for One."

I had been on that bay several times on deep-sea fishing trips with friends from Albany. Twenty miles offshore fishing for red snapper in a hundred feet of water with the sun bright overhead, the water calm and blue. A long dock ran adjacent to the restaurant and many of the slots had boats with names such as Lucky Day, My Girl, and Reel Therapy. I knew there were usually a handful of boats for hire along the dock. Guides would take you inland fishing for trout and redfish or for grouper and snapper in deep water. Joseph decided to wait in the truck and we got out and started walking toward the dock.

"Let's go take a look," I said, as we walked away from Captain Anderson's and toward the bay. "I know there are some charters down here. Maybe J. W.'s brother is one of them."

Walking along the dock, it took us about a minute to find what we were looking for. "There's your answer," Abby said, as she pointed to a big white wooden sign with black lettering that said, "Wingfield Charters." Three large brown pelicans were sitting on top of the sign and stared at us when we stopped. Necks extended, big brown eyes rolling toward us.

The business had a blue wooden front and there were two boats slotted next to it, Wingfield I and Wingfield II. They were white and looked identical in size with large enclosed cabins and enough room to comfortably fit eight adults. We saw no one on the boats or on the dock next to them.

We walked inside the small building and three bells attached to the thick glass door rang loudly to announce our presence. To the right was a counter with a cash register and on the wall behind it a mounted three-foot-long red snapper. A table near the counter had several magazines, including copies of the *Florida Sportsman*, a couple of ashtrays, and four black vinyl chairs. Two vending machines sold drinks and candy. Sparse but functional.

A few seconds later, the swinging doors to the back of the business opened and a man wearing a long white apron appeared. From the smell in the back, he may've been cleaning fish or shucking oysters. He had thick dark hair parted on the right, a slender build and was around five nine or ten and appeared to be of Asian heritage. His English was fluent but with a slight foreign accent.

"You looking to charter for snapper and grouper?" he said. "This is one of the best times of the year. It's not hot out there. Not like summertime. When do you want to leave? How many will be going?"

"Not today," I said. "We're just checking prices. We're going to be in town for a few days and would love to catch some fish before we leave."

"There's our chart on the wall with the prices." He pointed to the information behind the counter. "We have full-day and half-day rates.

We can take you today, leave at one and back at six. We've got the best captains on the beach. We provide the tackle and bait, and we clean and ice what you catch. It's all included. It's all on the wall. You will catch big fish."

"That sounds good, we may take you up on that while we're here," I said. "What's your name? I'm John, good to meet you. This is Abby."

"I'm Harry Tran." He nodded toward us. "Thank you for coming."

"You own the place?" Abby said.

"No, see the name?" he pointed to the sign out front. "Gene Wingfield. Some people call him Big Gene. He owns it, he's a big guy." He stretched his right arm over his head to indicate Wingfield's height. "He hired me a few years ago, and I'm here every day."

"Can we meet him?" Abby said. "We'd like to ask him a few questions about the boats."

"No, he's not here and probably won't be back until tomorrow. I can answer all your questions about the boats. Any questions you have, I can answer them. That's why I'm here. It's my job."

"What time tomorrow?" I said. "What time will Mr. Wingfield be in?"

"I'm not sure," Harry said. "He may not be back until the day after that. It's up to him when he comes in, not me. I have the keys. I open and close most of the time."

"Does he own any other businesses around here?" Abby said.

Harry Tran's expression turned to irritation. "That's not important. Do you want to hire a boat, or not? Mr. Wingfield likes his privacy."

"Does he live here at the beach?" I said.

"What does that have to do with renting a boat?" Harry said. "You want to fish or not?"

"Like we said, we're just shopping prices and trying to learn everything we can," Abby said. "We just want to make the right decision."

"Then please make it," he said.

I knew I might piss him off further, but I asked anyway. "Does he have a brother over on the Aucilla? Is his brother J. W. Wingfield?"

"I don't talk about Mr. Wingfield's personal life, and he doesn't talk about mine. I have work to do in the back, if you're not going to rent a boat." He nodded toward the front door.

"Okay, thank you Mr. Tran," Abby said. "We may come back later."

"It's a free country," he said. "You come back, and we'll take you fishing." He disappeared beyond the swinging doors and into the back room with the fish smell.

We returned to Joseph and told him about our conversation with Harry Tran and that he was of Asian descent, maybe China.

"The name was *Tran?"* Joseph said.

"That's right," Abby said.

"He is likely Vietnamese. The name is more common in Vietnam than China. Since '75 and the fall of Saigon, we have had thousands of Vietnamese settle along the Gulf. Had they stayed in Vietnam the communists would have killed many of them. They helped our side."

"Vietnamese, not Chinese?" Abby said.

"That's my guess."

"Wherever he's from, we pissed him off a little with our questions," I said. "I got a bad vibe around him before we left, didn't you Abby?"

"I did. I bet he had some big knives in the back he was cleaning fish with. He probably wanted to use them on us."

"Sonofabitch," I said. "That gives us something else to worry about."

CHAPTER 17

I was hungry and sure as hell didn't want to think about Harry Tran carving us up with a fillet knife like walking red snappers. With a thirty-minute wait for a table at Captain Anderson's, I suggested Billy's Oyster Bar just a few blocks away. I'd been there before and liked it. Billy's served fresh raw oysters, decent food, and had an old-time jukebox. It reminded me of Jim's Oyster Bar back in Albany off Pine Avenue, a place Abby and I loved. And Billy's was half the price of Captain Anderson's. We parked and Joseph locked our belongings in the cab of the pickup.

We found a table away from the bar and next to a big Jimmy Buffett poster. Buffett had his trademark smile and an orange and yellow parrot sitting on his right shoulder. At the bottom of the poster it read, "Parrott Heads Do it in the Sand!" The jukebox played "Margaritaville" as we took our seats and a waitress walked toward us.

We ordered two dozen raw oysters, a large order of onion rings, a basket of fried grouper, and three glasses of iced tea. The food came in under ten minutes and we talked and ate.

"I think we need to go back and see Mr. Tran," Abby said as she dipped an onion ring in a mound of ketchup. Sometimes I thought she loved ketchup more than me.

"So he can cut us up with a fillet knife?" I said. "Then deep fry us in hot grease? I bet we'll taste good."

She ignored what I said. "Maybe not see him but just hang around the dock and see who comes and goes for a few hours," she said. "It may be worth it. What do you think, Joseph?"

"We are here and looking for something that can help us," he said. "It is the only new lead we have right now, as you two enjoy saying."

"You sound more and more like a reporter," I said.

"Maybe Gene Wingfield shows up and we can talk with him," Abby said. "Maybe Harry Tran lied about that. It could be he's coming back this afternoon. He sure got pissed when we asked about him."

"Or it could be he was notified that his brother was murdered, and he's at the Jefferson County morgue," I said, then I placed an oyster on a saltine, added horseradish and Tabasco sauce before eating it. It was delicious and remined me of Jim's Oyster Bar back in Albany.

"I just got the feeling Harry Tran was keeping something from us," Abby said.

"Lying you mean," I said.

"Yeah. That's what I mean."

"About what, then?" I said.

"The thing we're after," Abby said. "The truth. The reason a group of people are willing to kill in order to take what Joseph found. Take old bones from the river and sell them." She dipped another onion ring in ketchup, ate it, and took a drink of tea.

Joseph was sitting at the back of our table facing the bar and the other tables and patrons. Every couple of minutes he scanned the bar methodically as if to prepare himself for something that was about to happen. Intense dark eyes. He'd eaten a couple of oysters and a few pieces of fried grouper. "I learned a few things about the Vietnamese when I was in-country. They do want old animal bones."

"What do you mean?" Abby said.

"One time my unit, in '68 after Tet, was at a little village near Da Nang along the South China Sea. One of the most beautiful places I have ever seen. Lush green rice fields . . . the coast, the land. Just beautiful. Beautiful people, too.

"I saw an old woman in tears and our interpreter spoke with her. She was holding her four-year-old grandson who had just died, dysentery maybe, because the war had prevented medicine from getting to the village. She told our interpreter these things. The medicine she wanted was ground-up bones of elephant tusk."

"Elephant tusk?" I said.

"The Vietnamese, Chinese, and other Asians still use traditional medicines they've used for centuries," he said. "They use it to treat fevers, diarrhea, malaria, stomach-ache, dysentery, even cancer."

"What else is used besides elephant tusk?" Abby said.

"Rhinoceros, tigers, bears, and elephants are all popular. Many body parts are used in these medicines. They are ground up. Everything from eyeballs to gallbladders. Poachers kill these animals all over the world."

"How widespread was it when you were in Vietnam?" I said.

"Everywhere. Small villages and big cities like Saigon. Like I said, this is an old, old culture we are talking about . . . like mine." He picked up an oyster shell and slid the oyster down his mouth without anything on it. His eyes still scanned the bar.

"These traditional medicines still popular in Vietnam?" Abby said.

"Yes, they are. Bigger markets now since the war ended. Now it is safer for sellers to get their products to their customers. American bombs are not blowing up the countryside. Vietnam's economy is being rebuilt. Money is flowing in. Legal and illegal. These traditional medicines are still used all over Asia."

"Elephant tusks represent a lot of money in the black market?" I said. "That's what you're saying?"

"Absolutely. How much per pound exactly, I don't know for sure. But our interpreter in-country said one average adult elephant tusk could be sold for a few thousand dollars. Probably much more today."

"Would they want tusks and bones from a mammoth?" Abby said.

"Cannot say for certain," Joseph said. "But if you can grind up ivory from an Asian elephant, you can do the same with a mammoth."

"The ivory itself," Abby said. "Not being used for medicine, what's the market for that?"

"It is very profitable," Joseph said. "Was then, is now. Lots of products are made from ivory. Musical instruments, decorative objects, knife handles. Many things."

The conversation stalled for a few moments, the three us paying attention again to our food. Joseph still on watch for signs of trouble. Then a couple of new customers walked in, a man in tan slacks and a green Izod who seemed high from pot or drunk or both, probably in his early forties, and a woman about half his age in beige shorts, wearing a white Panama City T-shirt and brown sandals. She had both hands on him and guided him to an empty table.

"They start early around here," I said.

We watched the couple for a few moments until they sat down and a waitress approached them.

"Are you two thinking what I'm thinking?" Abby said.

"Yeah," I said. "He's drunk."

"Not about those two," Abby said.

"We should all be thinking alike," Joseph said.

"Joseph, how many tusks and big bones did you see at the Big Hole?" Abby said.

"I can't say for sure, but probably enough to fill up my truck a few times. There may be more I did not see. There may be many more."

"They could be worth a lot on the black market," Abby said. "For traditional medicine and other things."

"Enough for some greedy bastards to kill for."

"Tens of thousands of dollars?" I asked.

"At least," he said. "Maybe hundreds of thousands. We can't make that kind of precise judgment. We would need more information."

I ate an onion ring and a piece of grouper and leaned over the table. "Abby, you are right. We've got to go back to the dock. Keep an eye on Wingfield's charter business for a while and see who comes and goes."

"You know how much I love the beach," she said, and smiled and took a drink of tea.

It was settled that we'd return to the dock, and a few minutes later we finished our meal and left Billy's. Abby and Joseph headed to the truck as I went to the bar to pay our tab.

That being done, I was about to leave, when I saw Joseph's face appear on the television screen behind the bar. The TV was angled high near a row of liquor bottles, and the volume was off.

"Could you please turn that up?" I said to a bartender. She did and I listened to the thirty second story about two bodies on the Aucilla River, and the man wanted for murder. Joseph "Quiet Bird" Threadgill.

I got into the truck and before we left the parking lot said, "Well, it's out there now. Joseph, you are wanted for murdering J. W. Wingfield and Bubba Fanning."

"Local news?" Joseph said.

"Yeah, they had your picture on the screen and you looked like shit."

"I was probably drunk when it was taken a few years ago."

"You looked that way. Drunk. The story said you have a long criminal record in Jefferson County. Two cases of public drunkenness, two of disorderly conduct, and an assault, and let's see . . ."

"Driving under the influence of alcohol," he said. "A couple of those. Anything about robbing the Bearded Clam?"

"No, that wasn't included in the report," I said.

"I told you about my past but not in every detail. I have been sober and well-behaved for some time now. I told you that."

"Said you spent a few weeks in the Jefferson County Jail on separate occasions," I said.

"Everything you heard is true, except the part about murdering J. W. Wingfield and Bubba Fanning. Did they say it was Walt who got me out of jail? Both times." Joseph's stare was through the window of Walt's pickup and toward Billy's Oyster Bar.

"The story didn't mention his name, but it did call you a war hero and said you earned the Army's Distinguished Service Cross for Bravery and the Purple Heart in Vietnam." Joseph nodded his head and tapped his right hand on the staring wheel.

"That is not a lie," he said. "Remember the old woman I told you about? The one holding her dead grandson?"

"Yes, what about her?" Abby said.

"The day after we saw her, a VC sniper shot me right there." Joseph pointed to a scar on his neck we'd not noticed until then. "Clean entrance. Clean exit. Didn't even bleed much."

"Lucky man you were," I said.

"I was that day, but things have changed here in America." He started the truck, and we headed back to the dock and Wingfield's charter business.

CHAPTER 18

When we returned to the parking lot near Captain Anderson's and the dock, the afternoon crowd had grown, the margarita two-for-one special was bringing in the snowbirds, I thought. Joseph parked next to a thirty-foot-long RV with a Michigan license plate. A white-haired couple, who had just gotten out of the vehicle, held hands on the way to the restaurant.

"The snowbirds have arrived," I said.

"They heard about the margaritas," Abby said. "That kind of news travels fast."

Joseph pulled an Army cap from his duffel bag, put it on, and pushed it over his eyes as if to keep the sun out. "Maybe this will hide me a bit. If anyone around here was paying attention to the afternoon news." The cap matched his green Army jacket he wore, the sleeves cut off above the elbows.

"You'll probably be okay," I said. "You're not near as important as happy hour at Captain Anderson's."

"Good idea though, the cap that is," Abby said. "Maybe we should play the part. There's a giftshop in there." She nodded toward the entrance to the restaurant.

"I can handle that. Be right back."

I went into the giftshop and bought two Captain Anderson's T-shirts and two caps with the same logo. We put the T-shirts and caps on. Joseph walked between us as we headed for the dock and St. Andrews Bay for the second time that day.

"Stay in the middle and we'll be okay," she said to Joseph.

"I can be good at following orders," he said and tapped the Army symbol on his cap.

We passed the restaurant and several other people heading there.

No one paid attention to us. Along the dock about fifty yards from Wingfield's business, there was a long black metal bench occupied by a couple of white and black seagulls. Abby pointed to the bench.

"Maybe they'll let us join them," she said. When we were about twenty feet from the bench, the birds flew away and landed on a nearby boat called "Tequila Sunrise."

Joseph sat in the middle, and we were all in a good position to see who entered and left Wingfield's charter business. I wondered if Mr. Harry Tran was in the back sharpening his knives for some evil deed. The man had that kind of look about him.

"Let's just see what happens," Abby said. "It is a beautiful day at the beach. Let's enjoy it. No one will pay any attention to us."

Three men and three boys, all wearing caps with long blue bills, passed us carrying two red and white ice chests and boarded one of the boats. A few minutes later, another boat docked and two men and two women, all probably in their forties, got off, and the men carried a large ice chest to a water hose and gray wooden platform, where they cleaned red snapper and grouper. The fish got the attention of two brown pelicans on the water below the men.

The men filleted the fish and threw the remains toward the pelicans. The birds caught each piece the men threw, like Willie Mays playing centerfield for the San Francisco Giants. Another easy meal on the Gulf. We watched this show for a few minutes, then something else got our attention.

"See, Joseph, that's Harry Tran," Abby said. "The guy we told you about. He just came out of Wingfield's. There he is." She pointed up the dock, as Harry walked to one of the boats, Wingfield II. He stood next to it and pulled a pack of cigarettes from his front shirt pocket. He was not wearing a white apron as he did earlier. He had no long, sharp knife.

Tran lit a cigarette and looked toward the boat's cabin. He said something we couldn't understand, and I thought whoever he's talking with must be inside the cabin, out of our view. Or he's talking to himself. Or to the nearby pelicans.

"You see him, don't you?" I said. "Right next to that boat."

"Yes, I do. Vietnamese probably."

A few moments later two people emerged from the boat's cabin. A man and a woman, and they both looked familiar. The man was wearing a Panama hat.

"Do you see what I see?" Abby said. "Is that them? The two from the Bearded Clam?"

"Led Zeppelin and bikini momma with red lipstick," I said. "I'd say yes, that's them."

"Ivan Wingfield and Inverness Cousins," Joseph said. "That is them. I have seen them enough to know. I have seen them at J. W.'s and on the river."

"That's right," I said. "Her mother named her after a whole country. That's what she told us."

"The family seems to be a little weak on geography," Abby said.

"You are so kind," Joseph said. "So very kind."

We watched Tran, Ivan, and Inverness talk for a few moments, then they went inside the charter business.

"It doesn't appear Ivan's mourning the death of his grandfather," Abby said.

"I'd say not," I said. "It appears that he was enjoying a little personal time with the Queen of Scotland on the boat."

Joseph pushed his cap on top of his head a bit, looked around the dock and back over his shoulder toward Captain Anderson's. "When I was waiting on you two earlier, I noticed a back entrance to the storefronts. There are cars parked around there. Probably for employees like Harry Tran. We can go there and get closer to them, if you want."

"When we talked to Tran earlier, he was in the back of the business and came out through double doors," Abby said. "There's probably a backdoor." She looked at me, then at Joseph. "Let's go."

We walked back toward Captain Anderson's, veered through the parking lot and weaved through cars and trucks parked behind the charter businesses and other shops along the dock. There were a few more charter services, a couple of giftshops, a bait and tackle store, and a small oyster bar called "One-Eyed Pirates."

We saw a sign over one backdoor that read "Wingfield Charters." There was a screen door, then a solid white door that led inside. Next to the building was a large brown and rusty-metal trash bin and on both sides of the door were glass windows, both raised allowing the cool fall air to filter inside.

Joseph pointed to the trash bin and said, "Over here. Get behind this. Maybe we can hear what is being said inside." We were concealed from view from anyone walking to or out of the backdoor, and only a few feet from an open window. It was a good spot. Then we heard voices from inside.

"I don't like this shit," Ivan said. "I'm ready to get rid of it and get my money. This shit is startin' to worry me now. I think you've really fucked up, Tran."

"Do not worry," Tran said. "Follow our plan and everything will be all right. When you worry, bad things happen."

"Who said that, goddamn Buddha? Jimmy Buffet?"

"Maybe both of them," Tran said.

"Listen to what Harry says," Inverness said. "If it wasn't for your granddaddy's will, we wouldn't be here. Ivan . . . baby . . . everything's goin' be okay. Everything. Right?"

"He fucked me on that, that's for sure," Ivan said. "Never thought he'd do that to me."

"Well, babe, when we get our money, we're gettin' out of here and never comin' back, right?" Inverness said. "That's our plan."

"That's right," Ivan said. "That's right, babe."

"Inverness — I want to go see Inverness. I've seen pictures and it's a beautiful country," she said.

"City. Inverness is a city in Scotland," Tran said. "Not a whole country."

"Well . . . whatever," she said.

"The hell with goin' to Scotland," Ivan said. "I just don't want to go to prison. This goddamn thing has done gotten out of control, Harry. It's all your fuckin' fault."

"I did what I had to do. Your grandfather was going to ruin the plan." Tran said. "Now we all must be calm and see this through. Soon we'll have what we want. Lots of money. But we've got to stay calm."

"Calm? Is that what you said?" Ivan said. "First you tried to kill that Injun. Then you shot my granddaddy and Bubba. Now you want us to be calm? Fuck you and your fuckin' Buddha."

"Yes, that's what I said. Stay calm," Tran said. "Follow the plan. I had to do what needed to be done. And telling the cops that the Indian killed them will get him out of the way for good."

"I don't give a shit about the Injun. Or my granddaddy after he told me 'bout his will. But Bubba Fanning? We grew up together. Chased a lot of pussy . . ."

"I heard that, Ivan," Inverness said. "You better watch your mouth."

"Enough of this senseless talk," Tran said. "All we have to do is get the load to Mobile and it's over. Take your money and go. You can go to Scotland. You'll have enough money to go anywhere and stay as long as you want."

"I know what needs to be done," Ivan said. "That doesn't worry me. I can get the boat to Mobile. It's what has already happened that worries me. Two dead men, Tran. They get you for murder, they get us, too."

"Nobody's getting anybody for anything," Tran said. "What we're going to do is get the money. A lot of it."

"That's right, Ivan, you listen to Harry," Inverness said. "We get our share, we'll make a good life. Won't we?"

"If you say so," Ivan said. "I just want to stay alive and out of prison. Not be a fuck-up like my daddy."

"I dang sure do say so," she said. "We get the money and we're never comin' back to Jefferson County. No more Redneck Riviera. Right, Ivan?"

"Yeah, I reckon."

For a few moments the conversation among the three stopped. We heard some walking and metal clanging, like furniture being moved.

"You can use this extra space we have when the other loads come in," Tran said. "I spend the nights here now since the bones are here. Everything we've brought in from the river so far is here and safe. Tomorrow we load and head to Mobile. We make the delivery Monday morning. Now, are we all clear on what has to happen?"

"What about what I stole from the Injun?" Ivan said.

"It's all right here," Tran said. "Everything is here. No worries. Just follow our plans."

"Yeah, we know," Ivan said. "We'll make one more dive tonight and we'll be back here tomorrow. Inverness likes your boat and she wants to ride with us to Mobile."

"That's right, Harry," Inverness said. "Ivan promised me I could go."

"Fine. You can come," Tran said. "Let's just finish the work tonight and keep calm."

"Calm my ass," Ivan said.

"Mine, too," Inverness said.

CHAPTER 19

The last sentence we heard while hiding behind the trash bin and underneath the window at Wingfield Charters was from Inverness. "Mine, too." In reference to her ass and staying calm.

A few seconds after that, we heard what sounded like the double doors that led to the front of the business swinging open. Ivan and Inverness were heading back to the dock and to their vehicle, I thought. Or maybe back to the boat.

We'd learned enough to know who killed J. W. and Bubba and how all of this was supposed to play out. There were others we knew who were likely involved with the scheme to sell wooly mammoth bones. Deputy Leach, the men who were with him at our cabin and on the river, maybe J. W. and Bubba and maybe Gene Wingfield were, I believed, all part of this criminal enterprise. And maybe Dr. Growdy, too.

We couldn't prove it yet, but that's what I believed. And there was the Mobile connection, whoever that was. The buyers, based on what we heard, were to meet Tran, Ivan, and Inverness in Mobile in two days, Monday. They planned to take the bones by boat. We needed a plan to stop them and prove to the police that Joseph was innocent of murder.

Sounds so easy, doesn't it?

"Let's get out of here," Abby whispered about thirty seconds after we heard the double doors. "We don't need to be seen by them."

We quickly walked back to the truck and got into the cab. Then we looked back toward the dock to see if Ivan and Inverness were leaving.

"Let's wait a few minutes to see if they come out to the parking lot," Abby said. "To see what kind of car they get in."

"What do you want to do if we see them?" I said. "Follow them? For what?"

"No, I don't want to follow them. I want to see if anybody else joins them. I want to know what they're driving. Joseph, any idea what they drive?"

"No, never paid any attention to that. Never a reason to do so before today."

"Okay, let's find out," I said. "You good with that, Joseph? You're the one the cops are after. We've taken chances already being out in public like this."

"We will wait inside the truck," he said, as he gripped the steering wheel with both hands. "We will wait as long as you want." He turned to Abby when he said it. "I need answers. I need proof."

Five minutes later we realized Abby had made the right call. A blue Camaro passed us and stopped in a parking slot only a few feet from the dock. The driver wore a cowboy hat that looked like a Stetson and was alone.

"I do know that car," Joseph said. "It belongs to Deputy Leach, and that looks like him driving. It's a '69 Camaro. See the two white stripes on the hood and the Confederate flag decal on the back bumper? That's him. He is in love with that car."

"You sure it's him?" Abby said. "The same Deputy Leach that came to our cabin and followed us to the river?"

"There's only one around here," he said. "Deputy Dwight Leach of the Jefferson County Sheriff's Office. I know that car. His father-in-law bought it for him after he got married. Leach did not tell me that, but he told everybody else in the county."

"If Leach is in on all of this, what about the sheriff? His boss," I said. "What did you say is name was?"

"I didn't, but it's Roy Lee Askew."

"Do you trust him?" Abby said. "Could he be caught up in this, too?"

"Trust him? No, I do not. How can you trust someone who told the public you're wanted for murder and you didn't kill anybody?"

"Did Sheriff Askew ever give you reason to believe he's capable of being involved with something like this?" I said.

"No, he has not. But never underestimate the corruption of the Great White Fathers. Leach does not have a strong enough mind to lead anyone, even himself. Someone is giving him orders."

"Leach's father-in-law?" I said. "What about him?"

"Jefferson County Superior Court Judge Josiah Clark Stripling. Twenty years on the court. Respected and fair in my judgement. Yes, he could be involved."

"Why do you say that if he *is* 'fair and respected?'" Abby said.

"Never be surprised by people. It will dilute your thinking. I will say it again — never underestimate the Great White Fathers."

"You sound like our editor, Mickey Burke," I said.

"That's the same advice we got from him when we started working for the *Chronicle,*" she said.

"Great White Fathers?"

"No, the part about never being surprised by how people behave," Abby said. "That part. 'Surprises are for children's birthday parties,' he'd often say."

A minute later, Ivan and Inverness got into the Camaro with Leach. They drove by us and out of the parking lot toward Thomas Drive and the Gulf. We watched them closely, but they didn't look toward us.

"Should we follow them?" I said.

"For what?" Abby said. "We don't need to play cat and mouse with them right now. I just wanted to see what else we could see from here. We've got some decisions to make. We know enough to act on."

"What about the cops?" I said. "Should we contact the state police, maybe the FBI . . ."

"We can't do that now," Joseph said. "No cops until we can prove to them that I did not kill J. W. and Bubba. Remember Sheriff Askew and Judge Stripling? We don't know how powerful the forces against me are."

"John, he's right. We'd be taking too big of a chance to go to the police now. We're going to have to find a way to catch these men ourselves."

"Don't forget Inverness," I said. "She's part of this gang, too. She's got blood on her hands."

"I couldn't ever forget the girl named after an entire country." Abby then spoke directly to Joseph. "Do you know anybody that works at the Jefferson County Courthouse?"

"Not personally. Why?"

"I want to find out what's in J. W.'s will."

"Something that pissed Ivan off," I said. "That's pretty certain. We heard him say it."

"We know that. We need specifics," Abby said. "We know whatever is in there likely drove him into all of this. He hooked up with a murderer to compensate for what his grandfather didn't leave him. That's my guess. Bubba Fanning could've inherited something, we don't know. It may be information we can use, maybe not."

"Fair enough," I said.

"What about it, Joseph?"

"I don't know anyone personally at the courthouse who might help us. The people I met there were the ones who arrested me. I was usually drunk. Not on my best behavior. But my friend Walt knows a woman there he sometimes spends time with. Alice Dennison. She works in probate."

"Perfect!" Abby said. "You think Walt would contact her and see if she can find out the details of the will?"

He pointed to a pay phone next to the giftshop at Captain Anderson's. "I'll call him and ask that question. If he can, he will help. I won't be long. We need to leave here soon. We've been here too long already."

He scanned the parking lot for anyone who might be looking for us, then left the truck. We still seemed to be inconspicuous to the snowbirds at margarita-happy-hour.

At the pay phone, Joseph pulled his cap low over his eyes again, made a quick call, hung the receiver up and sat at the bench next to the phone. Just a few minutes later, he answered the phone and spent a couple of minutes talking before he returned to the truck.

"What did you find out?" Abby said. "Anything to help us?"

"He got Alice on the phone and she said the will was on file. She had not read it herself, but one of her coworkers had. That woman said J. W. had a hundred and twenty-five acres of land. He left the land and the store to the state of Florida. No land or money for Ivan. Nothing for anyone else. Nothing for Bubba Fanning."

"State of Florida?" I said. "To do what with? Did he say?"

"He did. The state is to create a nature preserve with hiking trails and an interpretive center to be open to the public. It is to be named after his wife."

"Nothing at *all* for Ivan?" Abby said. "The hateful grandson. Are you certain?"

"It does include something for Ivan. The will states that Ivan must be employed by the state to help manage the preserve. But he receives no cash from J. W.'s personal estate, the land, or the selling of the Bearded Clam."

"Anything else we need to know?" Abby said.

"Not as important as the first part, but Walt told me he had to agree to take Alice fishing and cook fresh mullet for her before he got the information."

"Everything has its price," I said.

"Ivan gets no land, no cash, and no ownership in the Bearded Clam," Abby said. "Everything to the state of Florida. That pissed him off and he gets involved with Harry Tran to sell mammoth bones . . . is that the story?"

"That's a good summary," Joseph said. "So far."

"Walt have any idea how much the land and the business are worth?" I said.

"I did ask him. He guessed close to a million and placed the land around five thousand an acre. Then a couple hundred thousand for the store. He's probably close. Walt would know. J. W. had several thousand dollars in savings and stocks."

"Grandson could've been a millionaire," I said.

"J. W.'s got a son, remember?" Abby said. "What's his name again?"

"Tom Crocket Wingfield," he said.

"Nothing for him, either?" I said.

"Nothing. Not even a job at the preserve."

"He's got a brother, too," I said.

"Nothing for him."

"Poor family," I said.

"Poor J. W.," Abby said. "He's the one dead."

*

We sat in the truck a few more minutes after Joseph shared with us what he'd learned from Walt about J. W.'s will. We figured Ivan had been left out of the will and then became involved in the scheme to sell the mammoth bones. We all agreed with that premise. It didn't start out as murder, but Tran ended it that way for J. W. and Bubba Fanning. That had angered Ivan, based on what we'd overheard earlier at Wingfield Charters.

If what we overheard was true, there'd likely be another dive tonight at the Big Hole before the boat left the next day or the day after for Mobile. Exchanging bones for cash.

"Should we go back to the river tonight?" I said. "Maybe we'll be able to identify others involved in this. Whatta you guys think?"

"I think we should," Abby said. "We just need somehow to get closer to the divers and the boats. Maybe we'll be able to figure out who else is involved."

"I say no," Joseph said. "We get any closer, they may see us. We know they are willing to kill. They will kill again."

"All right, then what's our plan?" I said.

"I think it has to end here on the docks before that boat leaves for Mobile," Joseph said.

"How do we do it?" Abby said.

"I'm working on it," he said.

CHAPTER 20

For the second time that afternoon, Joseph used the pay phone at Captain Anderson's to call Walt Gosser, the only person along the Panhandle that he trusted. We needed his help again.

The conversation with Walt was quick, and three hours later he met us at the Lagoon Motel, just a couple of blocks from Captain Anderson's, where we rented two rooms. Walt drove his '78 four-door Pontiac Bonneville and said he pushed it near a hundred miles-an-hour on one stretch of the highway, then thought better and slowed to around seventy.

"I wasn't gonna be worth a shit to you if one of those trooper boys pulled me over and took my license," Walt said as the four of us were in the room where Abby and I planned to stay. Walt and Joseph sat at a small table, and we sat at the end of the bed. "That Bonneville has been good to me. I can outrun any cop, anytime, on the Panhandle."

"No, Walt, you would be no help to us if they pulled you over and put you in jail," Joseph said. "I know how you get angry when someone tells you what to do. Anyone. Anything. Anytime. And, no, you cannot outrun the police."

"Well, goddamnit, I'm here now. What do you want me to do?" Walt said. "Whup somebody's ass? I'm good at that. I hope I find the asshole that put the knot on my head." Walt wore a cap that read "101st Airborne," took it off and rubbed the back of his head where he had been hit yesterday inside his house and knocked unconscious.

"We're glad you're better," Abby said. "We need your help."

"Crown Royal did it," Walt said. "All the doctors prescribe it. I call it *traditional* medicine. My Crown made me better."

"I always said you would make an excellent Seminole," Joseph said. "We believe in traditional medicine, too. You have got the perfect name — Eight Toes."

"Thank you, Mingo," Walt said referring to the Indian character from the television series *Daniel Boone*. I loved watching it when I was a boy. "Now, tell me what we need to do to see this thing through."

"We overheard Ivan Wingfield and his girlfriend Inverness talking to a man who runs Wingfield Charters," Joseph said. "They're going to take a load of mammoth bones by boat to Mobile tomorrow to sell them."

"Who's the man?" Walt said. "What's his name?"

"Harry Tran," Joseph said. "We heard him say he killed J. W. and Bubba. Then they dumped the bodies at my house. Last night we saw the bodies in my backyard. Like I told you on the phone."

"J. W. and Bubba were involved in all this?" Walt said.

"We don't think so," Joseph said. "They were killed by Harry Tran after they saw divers pulling up bones from the river. As I told you, we saw the killings."

"He's in charge of all this," Abby said. "Harry Tran is. That's what we believe at this point."

"What about J. W.'s brother, Gene?" Walt said.

"We don't know," Joseph said. "I didn't know he had a brother until now."

"I did," Walt said. "I think I even met him once at the Bearded Clam. Quiet guy. Tall guy. Not a big talker like J. W."

"What do you know about him?" Abby said. "Could he be involved in this? Does he have a criminal past?"

"I don't know enough to know about Gene, you know what I mean?" Walt said. "This all is just FUBAR to me. A bunch of FUBAR."

"What?" I said. "What did you say?"

"FUBAR," Walt said. "We said it during the war. Said it a lot. 'Fucked Up Beyond All Recognition.'"

"We feel the same way," I said.

"Tran is Vietnamese?" Walt said.

"Probably," Joseph said. "That's my guess. Our guess."

"I bet Vietnamese," Walt said.

"Why's that?" I said.

"There have been some well-armed and well-organized gangs work-ing the Gulf the last few years. Some of them are refugees who came here after Saigon fell. Drugs. Mostly marijuana and cocaine. Even kid-napping and prostitution. They're living the American Dream."

"How do you know?" Joseph said.

"I read the papers," Walt said. "Just like these two." He pointed at Abby and me. "You should do it more often, Joseph. I do have another source, though."

"That would be who?" Joseph said.

"An old Army buddy named Chet Collinsworth," he said. "Met him at Ft. Benning before we both got shipped out to Europe. He's with the PC police force and been a detective last several years. Prob-ably going to retire this year or next. Me and Chet get together every now and then for beers and talk about what it was like killin' Germans. It's an exclusive club."

"If the Vietnamese gangs sell drugs, would they sell animal bones?" Abby said. "Joseph told us there's a big market for that in Asia. What do you think, Walt?"

"They'd sell anything to make money — has to be a lot of money," Walt said. "Makes sense to me. They'll kill you over it, too. Right, Jo-seph?"

"Yeah, they've already proven that," I said.

No response from Joseph.

"This may not be the first rodeo for your Mr. Tran," Walt said. "Ivan and Inverness, they probably don't know what a rodeo is. Some-body has to tell them when it's time to breathe and shit. A dozen oys-ters is smarter than those two."

"Walt, can you do something for us?" Abby said.

"I already have, and I'll do whatever I need to for Joseph. He knows that. What is it?"

"Can you call your detective friend and find out if he knows any-thing about Harry Tran? Maybe he's got some information that might help us."

"I sure as hell will. Maybe I can get him at home. He doesn't work Saturdays unless the bodies are stackin' up 'round here. Sometimes that shit happens."

Walt looked at the black rotary telephone for a few seconds and said, "Shit, I don't know Chet's home number. I usually call him at the office." He found the Panama City phone book in the nightstand drawer underneath the Gideon Bible. He flipped through the pages quickly, found the number and dialed.

Walt gave his detective friend a description of Harry Tran and where he worked, but he didn't mention Joseph or Abby and me, or why he wanted the information. The conversation was short, then Walt hung up and turned to us. "Chet doesn't know anything about your Harry Tran. Said there have been Vietnamese gangs working the area recently. I figured that. Two cops were shot over in Ft. Walton Beach last week, both survived. Big cocaine bust. I remember the story in the papers. Several pounds and a street-value of three-quarters of a million. That's big-time shit. Five arrested, all born in South Vietnam."

"When you say *area*, you mean all of the Panhandle?" Abby said.

"Yep, Chet said all over the Gulf. Just like I said. Remember? It's been in the papers, too. You should read 'em sometime. You can learn a lot that way."

"Maybe Harry Tran's been into drugs and now he's into animal bones," I said. "He goes where the money is, right?"

"We don't know about the drugs, but we know about the mammoth," Abby said.

"We still don't know about Gene Wingfield," I said. "Could Tran be using his boats and Wingfield not know about it?"

"He could be," Walt said. "If Wingfield trusts him enough to let him run the business, he's got access to the boats anytime."

"What about him?" I said. "Shouldn't we try to get to him? Maybe he could help us get to Tran."

"I don't think that's the right move," Abby said. "Gene Wingfield's probably back in Jefferson County dealing with his brother's death. If he's not, we may see him on the docks before this is over. Whether he's guilty or not."

"Abby is right," Joseph said. "Let's keep our focus on who shows up at the charter business and those two boats. What do you say, Walt?"

"I say I'm ready to knock the hell out of somebody. Remember my head?" Walt pointed to the back of his head. "I'm thinking a lot better since the swelling went down. May need some more Crown, though."

"You've already mentioned your head and how you would like to beat the shit out of someone," Joseph said. "But no Crown Royal. Not now."

"What kind of beach trip is this?" Walt said.

"We need you clear-headed," Joseph said. "Let us figure out how we're going to approach this thing without getting ourselves hurt. Killed even. What do you think?"

Walt said we should return to the dock and disable both boats by cutting the fuel lines on the twin outboard motors. He kept the necessary tools in the back of his Bonneville. If Harry Tran was still at work, it'd be up to Abby and me to create a diversion in the parking lot to get his attention. Then Walt and Joseph would slip onboard, cut the lines, and quickly return to their car. It sounded simple and safe. That's what worried me.

"What kind of diversion?" Abby said.

"I don't know," Walt said. "Can't you think of one? Throw a rock at the window. Honk your horn. Play loud music. Hell, it's Panama City. Shit happens."

"Firecrackers," Abby said. "We can get some on Thomas Drive. We'll set off some firecrackers out back, he'll come out, and that will give you two time to do what needs to be done. I hope."

"Maybe Tran won't be there," I said. "That'd make it a helluva lot easier."

"He'll be there," Abby said. "He's not leaving those bones in that store. They're worth a lot of money."

"Yeah, I forgot about that," I said.

"Walkie-talkies," Joseph said. "I have a couple from my Army days in my duffel bag. We'll need them later. We can communicate that way."

"Very good," Abby said. "We have a plan."

"What comes next?" I said. "You two disable the boats, then what?"

"We wait," Walt said. "We wait until Ivan and Inverness come back. Let them get on the boat, then we take them."

"They're not going to let us just take them without putting up a fight," Abby said.

"What are they going to do, jump in the bay and swim away?" Walt said.

"Tran has killed two people and tried to kill Joseph," I said. "He'll be armed. Whether Ivan and Inverness, and whoever else might show up, will be armed, we don't know."

"The hell with them," Walt said. "I'll do to them what I did to the goddamn Germans in Belgium."

"No more killing," Abby said. "We've got to be able to help Joseph without anyone else dying. Including you two."

"Listen here, Abby. I ain't aimin' to kill anyone. I know what that feels like. But I do aim to help my friend here." He put his right hand on Joseph's left shoulder. "Right, Mingo?"

"That is right, Daniel," Joseph said.

"Okay," Abby said. "Let's play this out. You and Joseph disable the boats, Tran and his crew get on one or both of them. What comes next?"

"We're going to need a team effort to keep them on the water until the cops come," Walt said. "You heard me tell Chet he be may getting another call from me. He'll bring help as soon as we call."

"Team effort?" I said. "What do Abby and I do besides the firecrackers? Where do you want us?"

"That's right. We're gonna have to keep them on the boat at gunpoint," Walt said. "All of us. Can you two use a gun or do you just use typewriters and a notepad?"

"No," Joseph said. "They will stay away from the dock. I will not do this unless they stay away from the dock. Both of them. I am not going to put them in any more danger. They have done a lot for me. They kept me alive, and now I will do the same by them."

"Okay, you two are gonna miss all the fun," Walt said. "Let's follow what Joseph says . . . I'm hungry. Anybody else?"

Walt drove alone to Captain Anderson's and got four fried shrimp platters and iced tea for everyone. We ate in the hotel room. The sun was setting over the Gulf, and another clear night was beginning, full of stars. For a few moments my mind relaxed, and I forgot about what was ahead of us until after we finished eating and Joseph reached into his duffel bag.

He handed me a walkie-talkie and gave one to Walt. "Go outside and see if these are still working right," Joseph said. A couple of minutes later, with Walt standing near his car, we confirmed that they were.

"What time should we leave?" Abby said.

"What do you think, Walt?" Joseph said.

"We don't need to wait," Walt said. "We need to be on the lookout all night and until the sun comes up, if we have to."

"Here's what we'll do," Abby said. "John and I will get the firecrackers and go to the parking lot. We'll use the walkie-talkie to contact you when we get back. Then we'll work the plan."

Walt looked at Joseph and then us and said, "Well, by God, let's get this beach party started."

CHAPTER 21

Around eight o'clock Joseph and Walt left the Lagoon Motel for Wingfield Charters, and I drove Walt's truck with Abby toward Thomas Drive to buy firecrackers. We knew from our trips together there were several places in the area that sold them.

We crossed the bridge next to Captain Anderson's, and I rolled my window down to feel and breathe the salty air. White and yellow lights shone everywhere along the waterfront, in restaurants, condos, and boats on the water. Everything looked peaceful. Happy people at the beach.

"We had some fun around here last spring, didn't we?" I said.

"You talking to me?"

"No, I'm talking to Ferdinand Magellan out there on the water."

"Oh, Johnny Boy, just kidding. We had a great time at that little cottage on Thomas Drive. Wish we were there now, don't you?"

"Yeah, I do. Remember making love in that hammock — tryin' to make love — and falling off on the back porch? My butt was sore after that for the rest of the trip. Remember that?"

"No, I don't. You must've been with someone else." She looked away from me and out the window as we passed Mrs. Newby's Lounge, a place where men drank liquor and watched naked women dance. One of several "titty-bars" at the beach.

"I think I'm going to put you on Magellan's ship anyway," I said. "Send you around the world."

"Just kidding. I loved trying to make love with you in that hammock. Too many margaritas that night."

"Or just enough."

"We both had bad heads that next day when we went snorkeling at St. Andrews Park. I remember that, too."

"I had a bad head and a bad butt."

"What a great memory," she said. "We'll have to tell our children all about it one day."

After a couple of minutes on Thomas Drive, I pulled over to Big Daddy's Fireworks and parked near a large painted sign that had a woman in a bikini holding long sparklers in both hands. The picture reminded me of Inverness Cousins. We walked in, and I picked up five strings of firecrackers with twenty-five on each string.

"Do you think this'll be enough?" I held them up so Abby could see them.

"Looks like enough to me, but I'm no expert on how much noise it'll take to get Harry Tran to come out his backdoor."

"Imagine that. I thought you knew everything."

"Almost everything."

I paid for the firecrackers, and we drove back to Captain Anderson's, where the parking lot was full. We looked for Walt and Joseph but didn't see them. Then we drove through the parking lot, stopped about fifty yards behind Wingfield Charters, and saw a few cars and trucks in that area.

I turned the engine off. At Wingfield's the two back windows were still raised, as they were earlier in the day. From the light inside, we saw movement.

"Harry Tran?" Abby said. "What do you think?"

"Probably. It looks like him, but I can't tell for certain."

"Where's the walkie-talkie?"

"I put it in the glove compartment."

Abby removed it and made a clear connection with Walt. He told her they were parked between two big RV's next to the dock and a hundred yards or so from Wingfield's. He instructed us to call back before we lit the firecrackers. Then tell him Tran's response after they ignite.

"I'll let you know when we're through," Walt said. "When we've cut the fuel lines. Then you may need to light some more and get his attention again so we can get back to our car without him seeing us. But you'll have to stay in touch so we know what's going on at all times."

"All right," Abby said. "Let me be sure I got this. Right before we light them, we let you know. Then we tell you Tran's reaction. Then you'll contact us telling us to light some more so you can get off the boats without Tran seeing you. What happens if you're on the boats and he comes out on the dock?"

"Then we wait," Walt said.

"For how long?"

"I don't know," he said. "We'll figure it out as we go."

"Whatever you say. We're following your lead on this."

"Roger," he said, ending the conversation with Abby.

She laid the walkie-talkie on the seat between us and said, "We need to figure this out. Where should we set them off?"

We discussed a few possibilities, and Abby suggested the best place was near the trash bin just outside Wingfield's backdoor, where we'd overheard the conversation earlier that day. With the windows still raised, the sound should easily carry inside and bring Tran outside. Hopefully it would all work out. But a lot of things could go wrong.

"What if he thinks somebody's shooting at him and he doesn't come out?" I said. "Or he shoots back?"

"Good point. That'll be a problem. If we at least see him come to the back of the building, we'll give Walt the go-ahead. We'll know he's away from the docks and the boats."

"What if he comes out, sees us and shoots at us?"

"Anything could happen. We know that by now. Shit, John, we just can't worry about it."

I said nothing but shook my head and kept looking toward the trash bin. Then I remembered something I didn't have. "Matches. We don't have any."

"Drive me to Captain Anderson's," Abby said. I dropped her off near the front door and she went inside and bought two boxes of matches. "Now we got some."

We drove back to the same spot, and I turned the engine off. "All right, this is simple," I said. "Let's keep it simple and it'll all work out. I'll take one of these strings."

"Twenty-five on a string?"

"That's right. That's what the package says."

"You bought five?"

"Right again."

"Good. Very good."

"No more talking," I said. Then I told Abby to radio Walt as soon as she saw me behind the trash bin. "I'll light the package and hustle back to the car."

"It sounds so easy," Abby said.

"It's been that kind of trip." I wrapped my right arm around her neck and kissed her on the lips.

"Be careful out there," she said.

"I won't be long." Abby clutched the walkie-talkie with both hands as I got out of the truck and jogged toward the trash bin.

Here we go.

The light inside the charter business remained on, but I didn't see Tran or anyone else inside. Between me and the trash dumpster was open space. A white van was parked next to the backdoor. It looked like the same one that was there earlier in the day. Must be Tran's, I thought.

I ran hard to the trash bin and crouched behind it and out of view from anyone inside. Exact same spot when we heard Tran admit to two murders and an attempted one.

I had the matches in my left hand, the firecrackers in my right. I never did like the sound of firecrackers up close. My uncle in Indiana used to light them when I was a boy, and I'd run the other way. But Uncle Kevin was always fun to be around. I pulled a match out of the box and lit it on the first strike. I put the match to the firecrackers and when they were lit, I laid the string on the asphalt next to the trash bin. My part was done.

I ran back to the truck and a few feet before getting there, the popping began.

Abby had Walt on the walkie-talkie and said, "They're going off. You hear them?"

"Damn sure do. Reminds me of German Beretta submachine guns. I hated that sound. What do you see? Talk to me."

"Just sparks for now . . . there he is. Tran just opened the backdoor. *Go! Go now.*"

"Roger."

Abby laid the walkie-talkie back on the seat between us, and we watched Tran walk around the trash bin near where the last of the firecrackers were igniting. He stood there for a few moments, then silence. They'd stopped igniting. He looked across the parking lot toward us and the few vehicles we were near.

"Is he coming out here?" I said. "He looks like he might walk this way." Tran took a few steps in our direction and stopped. "Should I get us the hell out of here?" I had my right hand on the keys to the ignition.

"No, wait. Let's see what he does. If we have to, we'll leave."

We waited.

Tran walked back toward the building, stopped again and looked around before he went back inside. "Firecrackers in PC," Abby said. "He hears them all the time. He probably thinks some teenagers are out roaming around."

"I hope so."

"They should've had time to cut those lines, don't you think? It shouldn't take too long. Should I call him?"

"Wait a little longer," I said.

"Okay."

"Everything's gonna be okay."

A few seconds later, a car raced past us and stopped next to Wingfield's backdoor. We saw three people inside but no one immediately got out. An animated conversation seemed to be happening among the three inside the vehicle. Arms waving about. The group looked familiar.

"Is that Deputy Leach and his Camaro?" Abby said.

"I think so. Who's with him?"

"I can't tell."

A few moments later, we knew. The driver got out wearing a cowboy hat. Deputy Dwight Leach and his Stetson. Then the two passengers, one wearing a Panama hat, got out of the car. Ivan Wingfield and

Inverness Cousins. We were sure of it. They stood near the car and trash bin.

"No diving tonight on the Aucilla?" I said. "Something has changed. Maybe they're leaving tonight for Mobile."

"They won't be leaving by boat."

"They'll be pissed when it won't start."

"I hope so."

Then Walt's voice came over the walkie-talkie. "Abby, come in. Where's Tran now? Do you see 'im?"

"He went back inside," Abby said. "But we got company."

"Company? Already?"

"Leach, Ivan, and Inverness."

"I'll be a dirty sonofabitch," Walt said. "We didn't expect them this early. What are they doin'? Can you tell?"

"The three of them are out back . . . wait, here comes Tran. Now they're all out here together."

"Okay, we're getting off these boats. I'll stay in touch. Keep watching 'em."

"We will." Abby ended the conversation with Walt but kept hold of the walkie-talkie.

"You think they went all the way back to the Aucilla and dove the Big Hole?" I said.

"It's possible. We'll see if they pull anything out of that car. More bones."

The four of them continued talking for the next couple of minutes. We rolled down our windows but were too far away to clearly hear what they said. Then Inverness returned to the Camaro, opened the front passenger door and removed something from the car.

"Is that a gun?" Abby said. "Does she have a gun?"

"I can't tell for sure. Could be."

She approached Tran and pointed the object — it was a gun — a couple feet from his head. "Shit! She's gonna shoot him," I said. "She's gonna kill Tran!"

Then she turned away from Tran and shot Leach in his chest. He crumpled to the asphalt. The gunshot reminded me of the firecrackers.

She quickly turned to Ivan and shot him in the chest, too. Ivan staggered a few feet to the trash bin, grabbed it as if to steady himself, then lost his grip and fell to the asphalt.

"Oh my God, she's killed them both!" Abby said.

The two men lay motionless, both the Panama hat and Stetson lying nearby. Inverness then shot Ivan and Leach again. She opened the Camaro's trunk and she and Tran removed a long object, but we couldn't tell what it was. They put that in the back of the van, and Tran drove them out of the parking lot. It all happened in just a minute or two. They didn't see us.

Abby called Walt and explained what we'd seen. Then we ran to Ivan and Leach.

I went to Leach and his eyes were closed, blood covering the front of his shirt and oozing out of his forehead. I checked for a pulse, but he was dead.

"Dead. Leach is dead," I said.

Abby kneeled over Ivan and a few moments later said, "He's still alive! Ivan is breathing. Barely. But he's breathing. Go inside and call an ambulance. Hurry!"

The door was unlocked, I made the call and when I returned, Walt and Joseph were standing over Abby. "Jesus Roosevelt H. Christ!" Walt said. "Inverness did this? You gotta be shittin' me."

"That's right," I said.

"Have you called an ambulance?" Joseph said.

"They're on the way," I said.

Abby had Ivan's head propped on her right hand and said, "They better hurry."

"Take this," Joseph said, he gave her a red bandana from his pants pocket. "Press that against his chest."

The second bullet into Ivan entered the right side of his head, but little blood appeared from that shot.

Abby did what Joseph said and leaned over Ivan. His eyes were open and his lips slowly moved as if he wanted to say something. She stayed in that position for several seconds and then Joseph approached them.

Ivan's eyes were now closed and Joseph checked his wrist and neck for a pulse. "Nothing. He is gone."

CHAPTER 22

We heard the ambulance approaching and Walt said, "We gotta get out of here. We can't do nothin' for these two now, anyway. We gotta protect Joseph. Let's move!"

"We'll meet you guys back at the Lagoon," I said. "Abby, let's go." We ran to the truck and drove out of the parking lot about thirty seconds before the ambulance turned into it. By the time the ambulance stopped next to the bodies, Walt and Joseph were gone, too.

About ten minutes after Ivan died, we were back at the motel. Walt and Joseph were again sitting at the table, with Abby and me on the edge of the bed.

"Now can I have my Crown and water?" Walt said. "Mercenaries have to be paid somehow. I don't even want money anymore."

"You have earned some compensation," Joseph said.

"Thank you, Mingo." Walt went to his car and brought back a fifth of Crown in the purple sack and six bottles of Coca-Cola packed in a white Styrofoam cooler full of ice. He opened a bottle of Coke and gave it to Joseph. "You two wanna have some Crown or are you drinkin' what Mingo is?"

"A Crown and water sure would be good," I said. "Maybe it will help me wrap my head around what just happened."

"It might help a little. Abby?" Walt said.

"Same as Joseph. Maybe something stronger later. I'm sick. Sick all over."

"We all are," Joseph said.

Walt popped the top off a Coke for Abby, gave it to her and made two drinks using the white paper cups wrapped in plastic next to the bathroom sink. He put ice in the cups first, then Crown and water. He gave me one of the cups and sat back down at the table and said, "Now,

I'm ready to think this thing through." He took a drink of the Crown.

"Anybody here see that coming from Inverness?' Abby said. "I completely misjudged her. The girl that says she's named after a country."

"People can surprise you, can't they?" Walt said. "You think you know 'em, but they can shock the shit out of you." He took another drink, another one like that and there'd be nothing but ice left in his cup.

"Does she have any kind of criminal record?" I said. "Hasn't she lived around the Aucilla her whole life?"

"If she's got a record, I don't know about it," Walt said. "Yes, is the answer to your second question, as far as I know. You know any different, Joseph?"

"No criminal record that I know of. We already know about her father running off. Nothing but odd jobs for her since her high school days. Lives with her mother. Very little money, and she appeared to hang on tight to Ivan. Until she killed him tonight. That's about all I know."

"When you say it like that, it does sound like some crazy shit," Walt said. "FUBAR."

"She and Harry Tran are partners," Abby said. "They planned this whole thing tonight. How could they have gotten together?"

"Can't help you there," Walt said. "Never heard anything about her being with anyone like Harry. Remember, I spend most of my time on the water. Don't talk to a lot of people. Don't want to. I like people, I just don't want to be around them."

"Same as Walt on that. Every time I've seen Inverness, she's been glued to Ivan. Either in the store or on the water."

"She told us she'd been with Ivan several months," I said. "She could've met Harry Tran before Joseph made his first dive in the Big Hole. Before he found the mammoth bones. It's possible."

"Could've," Abby said. "Maybe Gene Wingfield brought Harry to J. W.'s store. Maybe Ivan and Inverness chartered a boat and met Harry that way. We don't know how or when they met. And we don't know how Deputy Leach was mixed up in all this. We only know what our eyes saw tonight." She sipped her Coke.

"What's the attraction between Inverness and Tran?" I said. "Money?"

"Probably a pretty good guess," Abby said. "She killed Ivan. It had to be about money, one form or another. Decided to take Ivan's cut, whatever that's supposed to be. And Leach was just in the way."

"Is she in love with Harry Tran?" I said. "Sex and money. You can count on 'em to screw things up."

"Big-ass maybe," Walt said. "The love part, that is. Talk about your odd couple."

"We saw what we saw," I said. "The big question is, how are we going to find those two? Doesn't matter how Inverness and Tran hooked up or what Leach was doing with them all. What matters is Joseph and getting to the truth."

There was silence in the small motel room for several seconds. Joseph took a drink of Coke, and I sipped my Crown and we looked at each other as if we were hoping to hear from the person next to us a plan that would take us to Tran and Inverness and end all of this.

We were stuck in a maze of murder and lies.

"Will they go back to the boats?" Abby said. "They talked about taking those bones to Mobile by boat. Will they try to do that?"

"They'll have to get new fuel lines," Walt said. "They can't use either one of those boats until they do. That's for goddamn sure." He finished his drink and set the cup in the middle of the table. "Shit-almighty that was good."

"They will not go back to the dock," Joseph said. "The place will be covered with cops. No, they will not try that. Too risky."

"Cops are all over that place by now," Walt said. "I agree with Mingo. Too risky for 'em to go back to the boats. They'll do it some other way."

"What do they do next?" Abby said. "Drive to Mobile? If that's where they're supposed to make the sale. We don't know where exactly to go, even if the final destination is Mobile."

"We don't know for certain if those bones are in the back of that van, either," I said. "We saw two men killed tonight, but we didn't see anybody load bones in that van."

"John, they didn't leave them inside. They are worth thousands and thousands of dollars," Abby said. "That was the plan, I bet. Tran had them loaded, Inverness kills Ivan and Leach and they take off. But where?"

"We did see Tran and Inverness take something out of the Camaro and put it in the van," I said. "Looked like something rolled up in a blanket or a piece of carpet. Big enough to be bones. Big bones."

"If the bones they stole from my shed and others they got from the river are in the van," Joseph said, "then we have to find the van before the exchange is made."

More silence in the room. Walt poured himself another drink. I was still on the first one and drinking slowly. I knew we'd be leaving that room soon to try to find that van, I just didn't know in what direction. One drink was plenty for me.

"Mingo is right," Walt said. "We find the van. We find the bones. Then we prove he's innocent of killing J. W. and Bubba. Sounds easy as shit, right?"

"That would be the best part," Joseph said. "Proving that I did not kill anyone."

"Walt, we need your help again," Abby said. "Can you call your detective friend one more time?"

"Yeah, I can call Chet anytime, Blood Brothers and all that. Whatta you want me to ask 'im this time? Send in the infantry? Air cover?" He took another sip with eyes focused on Abby.

"Not yet. Find out about any place around here — bars, motels, houses — any place that might be connected with Vietnamese gangs. Places where the cops suspect criminal activity."

"You got it." Walt finished his second Crown and water and picked up the phone book still open to PC Detective Chet Collingsworth's home number. He hesitated a moment and said, "Anybody got pen and paper? Bet you two don't go anywhere without 'em."

Abby removed a pen and notepad from her purse and gave it to Walt. "Here, join the team."

"Thought I was already on it," Walt said, as he grinned and placed the pen and notepad by the phone and dialed Chet's number for the second time. The conversation lasted about five minutes, and Walt wrote on the first two pages of Abby's notepad.

We could tell that the detective was pressuring Walt to tell him in full what was happening. Why Walt needed the information he was seeking. Walt again didn't mention Joseph or the mammoth bones from the Aucilla River and twice said, "Now, Chet, I can't tell you all that right now, good buddy. I'm just helpin' a friend here. You'll know the whole deal soon enough. I promise you."

After Walt finished the call, he picked up the notepad and looked at us, then at the paper. "Ever hear of a place called the 'Lucky Seven?' It's several miles west of here."

"Not me," I said.

"Me neither," Abby said.

"Joseph?" Walt said.

"I been there a few times. Do not remember exactly how many, but I was drunk each time." Joseph took another drink of his Coke. "Very drunk."

"Your answer is yes?" Walt said.

"Yes, but I have no clear memory of it."

"It's a titty-bar . . . excuse me, Abby," Walt said. "I need . . ."

"Walt, I know what titties are," she said. "What about the Lucky Seven?"

"It's like Mrs. Newby's just across the bridge from here. The Lucky Seven has got dancin' girls, sometimes live music. Motorcycle riders stop in a lot, according to Chet. Drugs, prostitution, gambling, the full-course meal, he said. Just gotta know the right people there."

"If it has all of that, why hasn't it been shut down by the police?" Abby said.

"Here's the thing, Chet said they've been watchin' the place for the last couple of months. Even had some undercover folks workin' it. Men and women. So far, not enough hard evidence. He says they're gettin' close . . ."

"What about the Vietnamese connection?" I said. "Did he give you any details?"

"Shit, I'm gettin' there. Is this how you treat everybody? You two are beatin' me up with questions."

"People tell us that a lot," Abby said.

"Sorry, Walt," I said. "We're listening. Please finish."

"Chet said on paper the owner is a guy by the name of Parks Falwell, but, and here's the *big* but, actually it's Jerry Dao. Here's the part of the story you're gonna like — I think. Our buddy Jerry is Vietnamese, got criminal records in New Orleans and Mobile. Drugs, small amounts, pimping, some other minor charges. Served a few months in Pascagoula jail. Chet thinks Jerry's gone big-time here in PC. They've been watchin' him the last few months, like I said."

"Big-time?" Abby said. "Explain that."

"That big cocaine bust in Ft. Walton recently, the one where two cops were shot," Walt said. "Chet says that this Jerry Dao dude may have been involved but there's just not enough evidence so far to arrest him. He may be moving large amounts of drugs into the PC area."

"Are you saying Jerry Dao is the one who put up the money for the Lucky Seven, but used this Parks Falwell guy as a front?" Abby said.

"Yep, that's what my Blood Brother said. He said this Falwell character wouldn't have enough money to start a sidewalk lemonade business. Said he's a forty-year-old PC beach bum that two years ago was living out of a broken-down Volkswagen van drinkin' warm quarts of Schlitz and tryin' to pick up teenage girls."

"Went to the top in a hurry, didn't he?" I said.

"You could say it that way," Walt said.

"How do we get to the Lucky Seven?" Abby said.

"We'll cross the bridge onto Thomas Drive, hit Front Beach Road, and stay on it for several miles. It's on the opposite side of the road from the beach. Chet said we'll see a big, lighted dancing girl on a marquee. Strings over her nipples."

"Shouldn't be hard to miss," I said.

"That's right, any and everything goes on along that part of the Strip," Walt said.

"We need to go visit the Lucky Seven," Abby said. "We don't need to wait."

Joseph opened two bottles of Coke and gave one to Walt and the other to me. "No more Crown," he said. "You drink these before we visit the Lucky Seven."

"Mingo, you know how to spoil a good time," Walt said, as he took a long drink from the Coke.

"Do what I say, Daniel."

CHAPTER 23

We drank the Cokes and left the Lagoon Motel in Walt's Pontiac, headed for the Lucky Seven. Joseph rode in the front with Walt, Abby, and me in the back. We were with Daniel Boone and Mingo, I thought. Or Mingo and Eight Toes.

Maybe what we needed was a little of that frontier magic to make things come out right. To vindicate Joseph and bring some bad people to justice along the Panhandle.

We passed Mrs. Newby's, the titty-bar I'd visited a couple of times with my college roommates, then we'd stop by Spinnakers, one of the biggest bars in PC. Along Front Beach Road, traffic was light. Had it been during the spring or summer, when the white-sandy beaches are packed, it'd be bumper-to-bumper along Front Beach, with lots of loud music and plenty of drunken drivers, motorcyclists, and marijuana smoke curling through the air. Redneck Rivera.

We drove for about twenty minutes and around eight-thirty Walt pulled into the Lucky Seven parking lot. About a dozen black Harleys were parked in front of the club, some were two-seaters and a couple had Confederate flag decals on the back and front. Around fifteen cars and trucks were parked on the right side. On the left of the building there was an access road without any parking spots, likely used for unloading delivery trucks. We didn't see a white van like the one Tran and Inverness drove off in from behind Wingfield Charters, after she murdered Ivan and Leach. We were all looking for it.

Neon yellow lights indicated that the club was open until four in the morning. A flashing red Budweiser sign was next to the entrance, plus another sign that read, THE LUCKY SEVEN: PC'S MOST EXCLUSIVE GENTLEMEN'S CLUB.

Walt eased into a parking spot facing the building and turned off the engine, then he faced us. "How you wanna play this out?"

"I'm thinking," Abby said. "I've been thinking."

"Don't overthink it, that's how things get confused," Walt said. "People get all mixed up by thinkin' too much. I've seen it all my life."

"I'm thinking we probably don't want to mess with a motorcycle gang," I said. "That's not overthinking things, is it?"

A few moments of silence, then Joseph said, "John and I will walk inside, order a drink and look around for a few minutes."

A longer period of silence, then Walt said, "Okay, take that walkie-talkie just in case. We'll keep this one on." Walt had laid both walkie-talkies in the front seat. Joseph picked up one and stuck it in his Army jacket. "You packin' heat?"

"I am not. I will leave it in the car." Joseph took his revolver and placed it in the glove compartment.

"Suit yourself," Walt said. "'Fraid one of those bikers gonna take your gun from you?" He smiled and leaned into Joseph. "Maybe slap you 'round a little bit?"

"That's unlikely to happen. We're just going in to look. You and Abby stay here and do the same. You okay with this, Abby?"

"I'm good, as long as John is."

"Fine by me," I said.

"Okay, Mingo. Everybody's in. Check with us in about thirty minutes," Walt said. "Or were comin' in with guns blazin' . . . just kiddin'."

"Let's go Joseph," I said. "Maybe one of the nice bikers will buy us a drink." We headed for the front entrance of the Lucky Seven.

There was a dancing stage in the middle with two women, naked except for G-strings, big-big-breasted and tassels covering their nipples. Men in black leather jackets were sitting around the stage, some cheering and throwing one-dollar bills on it as the women performed. Thick cigarette smoke engulfed the place. It smelled of liquor and smoke and dirt and sweat. Plenty of neon beer signs, a jukebox in one corner played *D'yer Maker* by Led Zeppelin, and there was a long bar with several stools and a big Captain Morgan mirror behind it. The only women I saw were the ones dancing for the exclusive gentlemen.

Joseph found an empty table near the front entrance and took a seat facing the stage and bar. I walked to the bar and ordered two Cokes. The white bartender wore a light-blue T-shirt that read, I GOT LUCKY AT THE LUCKY SEVEN. He was over six feet and muscle-bound, as if he spent part of each day lifting weights. He had sandy-brown hair, tanned skin and a beard with flecks of red that he kept neatly-trimmed.

I was looking for anyone behind the bar or anywhere else in the club who looked Vietnamese. The crowd was all white and rowdy. I paid for the Cokes and returned to Joseph.

"See anything back here that might help us?" I said.

"Nothing. You?"

"Nothing. Nobody here looks like Harry Tran or Inverness Cousins. So far, anyway."

We sipped our Cokes for the next few minutes but neither one of us were interested in drinking the whole bottle. We kept steady eyes on the crowd and saw someone join the bartender behind the bar.

"That man behind the bar," I said. "I don't think it's Tran, but it looks like him. Vietnamese?" I nodded toward the man.

Joseph focused on the bar and after a few seconds said, "Yes, I would say so. Looks that way from here. Could be Chinese, though."

"Could be Jerry Dao. The guy who actually owns the place."

"We will find out before the night . . ."

"Hey, Injun! What the fuck you doin' in here? You didn't see the sign out front that said no Injuns allowed? This place is for gentlemen, like me. You probably can't even read. You dumbass Injun."

The man who spoke to Joseph had just walked into the club and was standing directly over him as if he was counting hairs on the top of his head. Joseph didn't respond, didn't look up, didn't move.

The man wore a black leather jacket with a rattlesnake design stitched into it and a couple of silver chains hanging from his neck. The snake's mouth was open, fangs long and ready to strike. Around his head was a Confederate flag bandana. His black beard looked to contain spittle. He was six three or four and well over two hundred pounds. About the size of an NFL lineman. He smelled awful. A putrid combination of liquor, body odor, marijuana, and other things I couldn't identify. This was not a good situation.

He waited ten seconds and spoke again. "I'm talkin' to you motherfucker. You better get out of here right now. Your kind don't belong here. Never will . . . fuckin' Injun."

"We're not causing any problems," I said, looking up at the man's blood-shot eyes. "Just watching the show like everyone else, that's all."

"Did I say somethin' to you, little white boy? I don't think so. Keep your goddamn mouth shut or you won't have one."

I looked at Joseph and his eyes were closed as if he'd fallen asleep or was in a meditative trance. Zen like. We're going to have to get out of here before this man and his friends beat the shit out of both of us, I thought. But how?

I was hoping Walt would walk in with guns blazing.

"Listen here, Injun," the biker said. "You need to get your Geronimo-ass up and get out of here like I said. Take your little white boy with you." He put both hands on the table and leaned into Joseph, six inches from his face.

Joseph waited a few seconds and said, "We will go if just you — not any of your friends — walk me outside. Then only you and I will talk on the side of the building. We can settle this there and talk over our disagreement. Like gentlemen."

"Now that's what I wanna hear. I ain't kicked someone's ass in a week. Ain't beat an Injun since last summer when we rode up to South Dakota. 'Bout kilt that Sioux-boy . . . let's go. You can bring your sissy-ass boy, so he can see what happens to an Injun 'round here."

We walked outside with the nasty-smelling biker behind us. Then to the left side of the club, the one without a parking area but an access road for deliveries. We stopped next to a pile of empty liquor boxes near a side-door entrance. A security light on a long pole provided enough light that I could read the boxes. Jim Beam, Jack Daniels, Crown Royal, Smirnoff, and others. And I saw clearly the faces of both Joseph and the big man in the black-leather jacket with chains.

Joseph approached the man and stood about a foot from his face, looking up at him. "You stink, my friend. You need to bathe and brush your teeth and learn some manners. You have terrible social skills. Terrible hygienic habits. You will never get a girlfriend smelling like you do. You are a disgrace to the white race. To the entire human race."

"Fuck you Injun . . ." with his clinched right fist, the man swung down hard, but Joseph quickly slid back to avoid the blow. The hate-filled man charged Joseph and swung again. Missed again as Joseph's quickness prevailed. Then the man stood straight but shouldn't have done so.

Joseph used his right foot and kicked him hard in the crotch, and the man cried out and grabbed his balls with both hands. With his right fist, Joseph lifted him off his feet with an uppercut to his chin, Muhammad Ali style. Then he moved in close, pummeling the biker's midsection with his left and right fists. The powerful blows rattled his head, and his bandana flew off and landed near an empty case of Jack Daniels.

Finally, as the man was bent over at the waist and moaning, with two hands Joseph drove down hard on the back of his neck. It was over. The big biker lay face down in the middle of the road.

Don't fuck with Mingo. Don't fuck with Panther.

Joseph flipped him over on his back and said, "My friend and I are going back inside to finish our Cokes. We have talked all this out like gentlemen. No more problems. Right?"

More moans from the big man. Joseph waited a few seconds for an answer and finally the man said with a quivering voice, "Yeah . . . I reckon we have. It's all worked out. Just like gentlemen."

"Good. Now maybe you ought to go somewhere, take a shower, and brush your teeth. Learn some manners."

"Maybe I will."

We walked away from the bearded bigot as he lay on the ground. I followed Joseph to the front door, but as we were about to re-enter the Lucky Seven, a white van pulled in off Front Beach Road.

"Look, is that the same one you saw at Wingfield Charters? The one Tran and Inverness were in?" Joseph nodded as the van entered the parking lot.

"Looks just like it," I said.

The van drove to the right side of the building, past the Harleys and Walt and Abby waiting in the Pontiac. It then disappeared behind the nightclub. We walked back to the car and got inside.

"Did you see that, Abby?" I said. "That van. It looked like Harry Tran and Inverness."

"It was them, wasn't it? I told Walt it was."

"I think so. Not certain."

"You see anybody else with them?" Walt said.

"No, we didn't, but it doesn't have any side or back windows," I said. "It's possible they picked up some help before they got here. We wouldn't be able to see them."

"Will they park in the back and go inside?" Abby said.

"Probably," Joseph said. "We will know that answer soon."

"If they pull all the way around the club and leave, we'll see them come out," Abby said. "I bet they're here to stay for a few minutes, anyway. Jerry Dao may be involved in all of this. The guy Detective Collingsworth told Walt about. What did you guys see inside?"

"We saw a lot of dancing . . ."

"I don't mean naked girls."

"I know what you mean. We saw a man behind the bar that could be Jerry Dao. Looked Vietnamese. Joseph thought so, too."

"Anything else? Anybody talking to this Dao character?"

"Yeah, the bartender. White guy, probably in his thirties. Beach-lookin' guy. Look, we only stayed in there a minute or so. Things came up."

"Minute or so?" she said. "You've been gone longer than that. What do you mean, *things came up?*"

"We spent some time outside on the other side of the building," I said. "We made a new friend. A redneck asshole biker. He told us to leave, then he and Joseph had a short conversation outside."

"Joseph, you were nice and polite, weren't you?" Walt said. I could see him grinning.

"It was a quick conversation. He didn't need an ambulance, but he does need to shower and brush his teeth and learn some manners."

"What did you do, John?" Abby said.

"Watched, but it happened quick. Kinda like those two men that followed us on the Aucilla the other night." I patted Joseph on the shoulder. "I was his back-up man. But that big biker would've whipped my ass."

"Okay boys and girls, back to the problem at hand," Walt said. "We think Tran and Inverness might be inside, but we need to know for certain. Who's going back in there?"

Before anyone spoke, Walt started the Pontiac and pulled out of the parking spot. "Hang on. We're gonna cruise 'round back to see what we can see."

At the back of the Lucky Seven, the van was parked next to the back door. There was a large trash bin near the door similar to the one at Wingfield Charters where I'd lit the firecrackers and where we overheard the conversation among Ivan, Inverness, and Tran. No one appeared to be inside the van.

Walt parked about a hundred feet away from the van and not far from a four-door BMW Sudan and a jeep. There was a single light bulb over the backdoor and in the darkness of the parking lot, I couldn't tell for certain the colors of the vehicles, but they both appeared dark-colored. From where Walt parked, it'd be difficult to clearly identify who came in and out the backdoor.

"We need a little distance from those assholes," Walt said. "From here, at least we can keep some eyes on the van."

"John, what about you and Walt going back inside?" Abby said. "Take a look around again. Then maybe we can figure out how to handle all of this. Stay away from the bikers."

"That's good with . . ."

"No, that ain't gonna happen," Walt said. "That biker that Joseph whipped may see John. I'll go alone. Just keep your walkie-talkie on. They won't mess with an old white man. I'll kick their asses if they do."

Walt walked toward the side of the building where Joseph had dispatched the biker and in a few seconds was out of sight. Five minutes later his voice came through the walkie-talkie.

"I got somethin' here," Walt said. "You listenin'?"

"We got you," Joseph said. "Go ahead."

"Looks like our man Tran is talking with Jerry Dao, the guy Chet told me about. They're at a table in a corner next to the bar. Two Vietnamese-lookin' dudes, anyway. Gotta be them."

"What about Inverness?" Joseph said.

"Don't see her. Looks like there's an office in the back. There's a door with a sign that says EMPLOYEES ONLY. Maybe she's in there."

"Anything else?"

"Just those two talkin' and a few naked dancers. Damn sure are a lot of bikers in here. Saw one guy with an ice-pack on his face."

"My new friend."

"Everywhere you go people love you, Joseph."

"It has always been that way."

"I'm comin' out. We gotta figure out what's next."

"Roger, that. We have got to make a move before they slip away."

"That's a big ten-four, good buddy."

CHAPTER 24

After his walkie-talkie message to us, Walt returned to the car and we talked for a few minutes and agreed on what to do next. The white van remained parked by the club's backdoor. We needed to act before Tran and Inverness returned and drove away. That was the consensus.

The first part of the plan was simple. Walt got out of the car and from his trunk took a ten-inch fillet knife and used it to puncture all four tires on the van. As he walked away from the van, he stopped and returned to it, grabbed the backdoor handle and pulled.

The door was unlocked, and it swung open. Walt looked inside for several moments, then returned to us.

"Are they in there?" Joseph said. "Are the bones in there?"

"Empty, Mingo. Nothing inside that van except a couple of old, goat-ass-smelling blankets. Nothing. I mean nothing. Surprised as shit it was unlocked."

"You sure?" Joseph said. "Nothing at all?"

"I did have a couple of Crowns, but I can still see straight. It's *empty*. Had I known . . . I never would've cut the tires. They could've led us to what we're looking for."

"They dropped the bones off somewhere between the dock and here," Abby said. "Remember we heard them say they were going to Mobile by boat? Maybe they're already on a boat. I bet Tran made other arrangements all along."

"They never intended to take one of the boats for the charter business?" I said. "That's what you're saying?"

"That's right," Abby said. "That was just something they told Ivan so he could tell Leach. Or whoever else they're trying to screw over. Makes sense, doesn't it? They'd planned to kill Ivan and Leach all along, I bet."

"You could be wrong," I said. "You don't think they carried the load in the backdoor before we came around? Maybe the van was full when they pulled up."

"Could have," Abby said. "They would've had to been quick. We came back here right after we saw them."

"It's possible they had help and moved everything inside in just a minute or two," I said.

"We don't even know how much — how big a load they have," Abby said. "I think that van was empty when they got here. Can't prove it, though."

"I'm with Abby on this," Walt said. "They dropped the load somewhere else. It was empty when they pulled in here."

"We don't know that is what happened," Joseph said. "We waited a minute or so before we drove back here after seeing the van. That would have given them enough time to unload."

"I'm tellin' you my gut says they dropped the load before coming here," Walt said. "I think they came here for something else."

"What?" Abby said. "Why would they come here? To make a deal with Jerry Dao?"

"That's exactly right," Walt said. "He's in on it somehow. Maybe make a deal or pick someone up. Both. Maybe get some money. We'll find out why soon enough. You'd think Inverness might want to leave the country after killing two people."

"She's staying for the money," I said. "What now? We don't have the bones. We can't prove that Joseph is innocent."

Then the Lucky Seven's backdoor opened and three people walked out. It looked like Tran, Inverness, and the man Walt said might be Jerry Dao, a leader in the Vietnamese crime syndicate along the Gulf. They passed the van and headed toward the four-door BMW not far from us. Now we clearly identified Tran and Inverness. The other man looked Vietnamese, just like Walt had said.

"That's the two guys I saw sitting together," Walt said. "That's our Tran and Dao. And that damn silly-ass girl, Inverness. That's a helluva team, right there."

"That *silly-ass* girl murdered two men tonight," Abby said.

We watched the three come within about twenty-five yards of our car and then get into the BMW. Tran drove, Inverness sat up front, and the other man rode in the backseat. They backed out of the parking spot and slowly eased around the club on the access road, away from the cars and the Harleys.

Our eyes were on them and Abby said, "We've got to follow them. We can't lose them."

"Will do," Walt said, as he started the Bonneville and headed for the access road.

We saw the red taillights of the BMW several car-lengths in front of us as it stopped, waiting to turn onto Front Beach Road. Five seconds later, they turned east and back toward St. Andrews Bay and where that "silly" girl shot dead her boyfriend Ivan Wingfield and Jefferson County Sheriff's deputy Dwight Leach.

"It's possible those bones are inside the Lucky Seven," I said. "We're taking a chance leaving here, aren't we? They could be back at that club."

"Been doin' that all night," Walt said. "Takin' chances. I'm stickin' to these bastards right now. They ain't getting outta my sight." Walt then turned east, and now we were about twenty yards or so behind the BMW on Front Beach Road.

With light traffic, we had no difficulty staying close to them. For the next couple of miles, we passed a few motels and a liquor store, an amusement park with go-carts and goofy golf, another titty-bar, and two businesses selling fireworks.

"You think they suspect something?" I said. "That we're following them?"

"We're just cruisin' the Strip, like everybody else," Walt said. "They ain't payin' no attention to us. Don't matter anyway, I ain't losin' 'em. Already told you that."

"Hope you're right," I said.

"Of course, they are suspecting something," Joseph said. "They're suspecting the cops to be looking for them, if not tonight, soon. If you murder two men, you must expect the police to be after you. They have mirrors in that vehicle. They can watch behind them."

"They'll figure it out eventually that we're following them," Abby said. "They may know already."

"Depends on how far they go," Walt said. "If they stop somewhere on the Strip, somewhere soon, they may not know we're following. We probably can't follow 'em to Mobile without them knowing."

A few minutes later, the BMW turned into the parking lot at the Fiesta Motel on the beach-side of the Strip. The Fiesta was a three-story, brown-brick structure with red aluminum roofing and concrete arches. A sign and blinking light announced "Vacancy," and the parking lot was about a third full. We made the turn into the Fiesta, still several yards behind the BMW. They weren't going to Mobile, not yet anyway.

Tran drove toward the office, then veered right and parked in front of the last room on the first floor. Walt kept us in the front of the parking lot near Front Beach Road and close to a couple of tall, bent palm trees and a big yellow sign that read FIESTA MOTEL. We got out and stood by Walt's car and were refreshed by the cool, fall breeze.

We were probably more than a hundred yards from the BMW, but the security lights allowed us to clearly see the three of them walk to a door, knock, and wait. A few moments later the door opened and they went inside.

"Mingo, I'm tired of followin' these people all over PC," Walt said. "Whatta you say we go knock on that door and end this thing? Me and you have a little fun."

"Bad idea. Let's be patient a little longer," Joseph said. "We don't know who's in that room and how many guns they have."

"I'm still wantin' to kick somebody's ass for puttin' that knot on my head," Walt said, referring to the visitor he'd had in his house who'd knocked him out. He gently tapped his head three times with his right hand.

"Blind revenge destroys the soul," Joseph said. "A man blinded by such revenge digs two graves. Patience is the mother of all virtues."

"Well thank you, Socrates. You're always full of witty sayings that I don't pay attention to, especially when someone's tryin' to kill us," Walt said. "How 'bout this: If someone knocks you on your head in your own house, find 'em and beat the shit out of 'em."

"Walt, what we need is Tran and Inverness and the mammoth bones," Abby said. "We have to be certain. Then we can call your detective friend, get some help and clear Joseph's name."

"Now you're tellin' me we need to wait?" Walt said. "We can't go in with guns blazin'? Shit, I hate waitin'."

"You watch too much television," Joseph said. "Let's all be as reasonable as we can."

"It worked during WW II," Walt said. "Guns blazin', that is."

"Let's see how this plays out," Abby said. "We know where they are. Let's just watch for a few minutes."

"Maybe those bones are in that room," Walt said. "They damn sure weren't in the van." He'd accepted our idea to wait.

A gust of wind blew the big palms, and the sound of them startled me as if there was danger overhead. I looked up and saw them gently swaying and looked long enough at the sky to see the Big Dipper over the Gulf. I heard the surf on the other side of the Fiesta lapping against the white sand. The smell of saltwater had suddenly gotten stronger.

Then I heard the roar of a truck and turned to look at the same motel-entrance we'd used. A U-Haul was slowly entering the Fiesta's parking lot. Once inside the parking lot, it turned right and headed to the same place Tran had parked his BMW. The last motel room on the right wing.

"Everybody watchin' this?" Walt said.

"Yeah, I believe we are," I said. "Things are pickin' up at the Fiesta."

"Y'all thought fall was the slow time of the year down here, didn't you?" Walt said.

The U-Haul backed up close to the same door that Tran, Inverness, and the man we assumed was Jerry Dao had entered. No one came out of the motel room. Three men got out of the cab of the truck and walked to the back of it. One man lifted up the truck's sliding door and the other two pulled out the metal walkway that was attached underneath the truck's body. The same thing that's done when a family hires a company to move their furniture cross-country.

Then the three men from the truck walked to the motel door, knocked and waited, same as the others had done. A few seconds later, the door opened and they went inside.

"Getting crowded in there, don't you think?" I said. "Probably got a bathtub full of beer. That's what happens in most of these places on the Strip."

"Probably not tonight," Abby said. "They're talking money and crime. We've been to some of those beer parties. I wish that's what we were doing tonight."

"They will not stay in there long," Joseph said. "They're ready to load something into the U-Haul and get out of here."

"They're either stealing the furniture or the old bones we're lookin' for are in there and about to be moved," Walt said.

"They aren't after the furniture in the Fiesta," I said. "I stayed there a couple of times with some college buddies. Everything was brittle and cheap, but there's a great view of the beach."

We were silent a few seconds, then Abby said, "There were no bones in the van because they're in that room and are going to be loaded on that truck. The question is, how do we stop them? There could be ten people in there. We don't know."

"I just don't give a shit how many are in there," Walt said. "I'm ready to get this over now. I'm tired of chasing these assholes."

"Abby is probably right," Joseph said, ignoring Walt. "There is a room full of men in there and all of them probably armed. We know what Inverness and Tran are capable of."

For the next few minutes, we kept straight eyes on the U-Haul and the motel room. We saw no movement in or out of the room. The Gulf breeze was cool on my face, but we still had no plan.

"If they do load that truck, we will just have to follow it," Joseph said. "I don't like our odds here. There are too many of them, not enough of us."

"Hell, it may get worse," Walt said. "We don't know where they're goin' and who they're goin' to meet. This may be our best shot. They don't know we're out here."

"Too many of them, Walt. We must wait," Joseph said.

"We need to wait," Abby said.

"Two against one," Walt said.

"Three against one," I said.

"Well, damnit-to-hell, you win."

Several seconds later, the door to the motel room opened and two men walked out carrying what appeared to be a wooden box, maybe six feet long. They took the box up the metal walkway, placed it inside the bed of the truck and returned to the room. Then two more men did the same thing with a box of equal size. We watched and counted at least a dozen boxes loaded onto the U-Haul.

Then the men closed the truck's big door, appeared to lock it, and went back inside the motel room.

"When these folks leave, who we gonna follow?" Walt said. "There's going to be that U-Haul and probably two, maybe even three other vehicles leavin' here. Ain't but one of us."

"We must stay behind the U-Haul," Joseph said. "The bones are in the back of that truck. They are to be sold to someone, somewhere."

"That certainly narrows it down, Mingo," Walt said.

"How do you know they haven't already been sold?" I said. "That truck goes one way, and Tran and Inverness go another direction with a shit-pot full of money."

"We don't," Walt said. "We don't know shit. Joseph's just guessin', like I did earlier about the bones not being at the Lucky Seven."

"That's right, it is a guess but a logical one," Joseph said. "Let us assume that they have been moving the bones from the Aucilla to the Fiesta and were planning all along to move them by truck to the buyer. The next stop is the buyer. Maybe it is Mobile. We just don't know."

"Why do you think the buyer is not in that U-Haul right now and Tran and Inverness and maybe Jerry Dao are gonna ride away with the money?" I said.

"It's possible Jerry Dao is the buyer," Joseph said. "If he is — and Tran and Inverness do have the money — why haven't they left? The bones have been loaded."

"Good point," Abby said.

"Just a logical guess," Joseph said.

"Not a reasonable one?" Walt said.

"I will not answer you, Walt."

"I think Joseph is right," Abby said. "We have to follow that truck and hope our chances improve. We have to be there when the exchange is made."

"If Joseph is right, then Tran and Inverness will follow the truck, too," I said. "They'll get their money on delivery . . . this sure is a helluva lot of speculation. Isn't it?"

"Rational thinking," Joseph said.

"The question is, where are they going?" Abby said.

The door to the motel room opened and out walked Tran, Inverness, Jerry Dao and six other men. All of them stood at the back of the U-Haul for a few minutes and appeared to be talking. It looked as if Tran was doing most of it. The men we couldn't identify got into what looked to be an LTD Ford. And it appeared as if Jerry Dao got into the U-Haul's cab alone. Tran and Inverness returned to the BMW.

The three vehicles headed for the parking lot exit near us, and we hustled back into Walt's Pontiac. The LTD led the convoy's way and turned east on Front Beach Road, next came the truck and the BMW. They both turned west with the U-Haul in the lead.

Walt pulled out of the parking lot about thirty yards behind the truck and the BMW and said, "We're gonna follow that U-Haul, and I don't give a damn if it's all the way to Mobile."

CHAPTER 25

The U-Haul and BMW stopped long before Mobile. A couple of miles from the Fiesta Motel the two vehicles pulled into a deep-sea fishing service called Tight-Line Charters. Walt wheeled the Bonneville into the driveway next to the charter service. We parked behind a souvenir shop that was closed, well-lit with security lights and a bright yellow metal roof.

The BMW and the truck carrying the bones from the Aucilla, we believed, parked next to the charter office, a small wooden building with a big CLOSED sign hanging on the door. Tran, Inverness, and Jerry Dao got out of the vehicles and walked to the end of the dock as if they were waiting for a boat to arrive.

We saw clearly all of this.

There were three boats secured along the dock, all at least thirty-footers and probably owned by the charter service. We saw no other vehicles or anyone else in the area, the whole area well-lit by security lights. The closest motel, restaurant, and bar were about a quarter-mile away.

If Tran, Inverness, and their team of outlaws wanted to unload the U-Haul onto an incoming boat, or one already docked, there was plenty of room to do so. This would be a good place for the exchange, money for the bones, with so few people in the area. That must be their plan, I thought.

After the three people we were following walked to the end of the dock, we moved behind the fishing charter's office. They had their backs turned to us. Now we were not far from their truck and BMW, but concealed by the office.

"This is it," Walt said. "What else would they be doin' other than waitin' for someone to pick up those bones? Waitin' on the money."

"Walt, this may be the time to call your detective friend," Abby said. "They need to get here in a hurry. It's going to happen right here. I saw a phone booth on the other side of Front Beach Road, next to the gas station. What do you think?"

"I'm on my . . ." Walt didn't finish his sentence as the four of us saw a set of lights heading for the three people at the end of the dock. Lights coming in from the Gulf.

"That is the boat they're waiting on," Joseph said. "It must be. They're going to unload the U-Haul onto that boat. We now have to stop them from leaving. Now is the time."

"I'm not callin' now," Walt said. "We don't have enough time to get Chet and his boys out here. We got to handle this situation ourselves. We'll make it end here."

The lights from the Gulf were getting closer.

"Handle it ourselves?" I said. "Tell us your plan, Walt. That boat's coming in."

Walt had his right hand on top of his forty-five holstered to his hip. He looked at me then at Joseph and said, "You carryin' any heat, Mingo?"

"I have this thirty-eight I took off those two on the river the other night. It's behind my jacket."

"Good, you may be using it."

"We have got to do this without hurting anyone," Joseph said. "I did enough of that in Vietnam. We got to protect each other, but let's be smart and careful here, Walt."

"I did the same goddamn thing in Europe, killin' that is. I don't plan to shoot anyone tonight, either. If we can get the drop on those sonofabitches while they're loadin' those boxes on that boat, we won't have to shoot anyone."

"I am with you."

"Abby, I'm going to give you Detective Collingsworth's number, and you can call him on that pay phone," Walt said. "How 'bout it?"

"Give me the number."

Walt reached into his pants pocket for Chet's number written on a piece of paper but kept his eyes on the three people we were watching.

He gave the paper to Abby, still watching the activity on the dock. The boat now looked to be about a few hundred feet from the three who were waiting on it.

"What are they doin' now?" Walt said. "Look, what are they doin' that for?"

Tran and Inverness both took a few steps away from the man they were with. The man we believed to be Jerry Dao. Now the boat, similar in size to the ones that were docked, was only a few feet from the dock. Then a man wearing wide-brim hat appeared on the boat's bow and looked to be holding a pistol.

"Sonofabitch, they're goin' shoot 'im!" Walt said and as soon as he said it, three pistol shots were fired from the man on the boat and the middle man fell where he stood. "They shot him. *Sonofabitch!*"

The shooter threw Tran a rope, and he guided the boat next to the dock. The man who did the shooting, helped Tran and Inverness into the boat, then the boat turned and headed away from the dock, with a big wake churning behind it.

"Jesus, God Almighty!" Walt said.

"Now I'll go call an ambulance," Abby said. "Go see if y'all can help him." Abby ran toward Front Beach Road and the phone booth on the other side of it. I hustled down to the dock with Walt and Joseph to where the man we thought was Jerry Dao, was lying.

Joseph got to him first and checked his pulse but there wasn't one. He was the third man tonight to be murdered over old animal bones. Five in all. He had a large hole in the left side of his chest where all three shots had entered. His eyes were closed, blood pooling around him and a stream of it inched its way down the dock toward saltwater.

"It looks like the guy I saw at the Lucky Seven," I said. "That must be Jerry Dao."

"Same one I saw talking to our man Harry Tran at the table in the back of the club," Walt said. "It's probably that Dao fellow. This gang cannibalizes each other. Soon won't be anyone left for the cops to arrest."

Then Walt kneeled next to the dead man and from his back pants pocket removed a black leather wallet. The Florida driver's license said

Jerry Dao, and the picture matched the man with bullet holes in his chest. There were four one hundred-dollar bills in the wallet and when Walt counted them, a small piece of white paper fell to the dock. Walt put the bills back in the wallet and handed it to Joseph. Then Walt picked up the piece of paper.

"It says Lu Doc — NO — 504-555-4561," Walt said. "What the hell does that mean?"

"Lu Doc is a Vietnamese name," Joseph said. "That number is probably a phone number. It has enough numerals to be one."

"You recognize the name?" I said.

"Only that it's Vietnamese. I know no one personally by that name."

"N-O, what does that mean?" Walt said.

"Opposite of yes?" Joseph said.

"We'll figure it out, but we've got to get Abby and get out of here," I said. "We can't help this guy. Like we couldn't help Ivan and Leach or J. W. and Bubba."

"Let's move," Walt said. "On the quick step." He got the wallet from Joseph and stuffed it back in Dao's pants and kept the piece of paper with the name and number on it. He slid the paper in his front pocket, next to his holstered forty-five.

We turned to walk away, and Abby came running toward us. "The ambulance is on the way. Is he alive?" Walt shook his head. "Oh, God, this just gets worse," she said.

"Yep, 'fraid so," Walt said. "We gotta get outta here. FUBAR."

"Who was it?" she said. "Do you know?"

"His driver's license said Jerry Dao," Walt said. "Looks like we were right all along about that."

"We were all wrong about the bones," Joseph said.

"What do you mean?" I said.

"They are not in that U-Haul," Joseph said. "There are no mammoth bones in those boxes. People who murder other people would not leave behind something worth a lot of money. We have been tricked. Others, too."

"He's right," Abby said. "The fact that they killed Dao and left tells us what Joseph said is true. Nothing of value is in the truck or car."

"Why are they leaving them here?" I said. "The vehicles?"

"I don't have a good answer for that," Abby said. "Maybe somebody's on the way to get them. Maybe there *are* bones in those boxes. We won't know for sure unless we can get inside the truck."

"Comin' here was just about killin' that man," Walt said. "Is that what you're sayin', Joseph? Just a setup."

"That's what I'm saying, right now," Joseph said. "Just a setup."

"We still got to get out of here," I said. "Cops will be coming."

"We've got to take a look," Walt said. "It'll just take a quick New York minute. Got to be sure Joseph's right. There could be somebody else on the way to get the truck and the BMW, like Abby said. I'll meet you at the truck. Let's see if we can get in."

Walt hustled to his car, took a flashlight from the trunk and met us at the U-Haul. It wasn't padlocked and Joseph easily pushed up the sliding door. All four of us jumped in. The long boxes were not locked, either. We lifted all thirteen lids.

Nothing but driftwood and a few red bricks in each box.

"I'll be a dirty sonofabitch. Again," Walt said. "Those bastards went to a lot of trouble to fool somebody. Probably Jerry Dao."

"Us, too," I said.

"That's right," Abby said. "Now we need to get out of here and try to figure out what all this means."

Then we heard sirens.

We got into Walt's car, turned east back on Front Beach Road and in a quarter-mile passed the ambulance as we headed back to the Lagoon Motel.

CHAPTER 26

About thirty minutes after Jerry Dao was murdered at Tight-Line Charters by a man in a boat wearing a big-brimmed hat, and after we learned that the wooden boxes in the back of the U-Haul were full of driftwood and bricks and not mammoth bones, Walt drove us back to the Lagoon Motel, not far from the dock where Ivan Wingfield and Deputy Dwight Leach were murdered earlier in the day by Inverness Cousins.

The bodies were piling up.

But where the ancient bones from the Aucilla were, that was still a mystery. What wasn't a mystery was the fact that Joseph "Quiet Bird" Threadgill was wanted for a double-murder he didn't commit. I saw that on television.

It seemed like a year since we pulled him out of the Aucilla after, we now believed, he was shot by Harry Tran, the man who worked for Gene Wingfield's charter service, brother of the dead J. W., who owned the Bearded Clam near the Aucilla. It'd only been two-and-a-half days.

What about Inverness killing her boyfriend and Deputy Leach? That surprised all of us, even though our editor Mickey Burke at the *Chronicle* often repeated this phrase, "If you're surprised by anything in this business, Maynard, you don't belong in it."

Back in our motel room, Walt removed the piece of paper he'd taken off the dead Jerry Dao and placed it on the table. All of us hovered over the paper, staring at it for a few moments in silence as if the black ink and white paper was a sacred document.

Abby spoke first. "Anybody know the area code for New Orleans?"

"I know how to use the phonebook," I said and opened the one on the nightstand Walt had used earlier. I found the U. S. map in the front of the book that listed area codes for each state. I tapped my right index finger on Louisiana.

"Do you see 5-0-4?" Abby said. "What does it say?"

"Yeah, you called it. Looks like it covers most of New Orleans. The first three numbers on the paper match that area code. This is somebody's phone number in Louisiana."

"We're getting somewhere," Abby said. "I want to think we are, anyway."

"What does that prove?" I said. "That name and number could be connected to something else, not all these killings and the bones."

"Could be, but I bet not," Abby said. "Jerry Dao has — *had* — a contact in New Orleans involved in this. I bet he did. It makes sense. Why else is he carrying that paper and phone number in his wallet?"

"Maybe the number belongs to a friend or a relative and he's planning a visit to New Orleans soon," I said. "That's possible. Isn't it? A Dao family reunion."

"It is possible," Joseph said. "Many things are possible."

"The other thing possible is that Lu Doc is involved in organized crime," Walt said. "Maybe he's the Vietnamese Godfather. That's possible, too. A lot of that shit's going on around the Big Easy. I told you, I been readin' the papers."

"Apparently here, too," Joseph said.

"That's right, the good folks on the Florida Panhandle don't want to be left behind," Walt said. "Harry Tran may be the godfather 'round here. Who knows?"

"Walt, do you think . . ." Abby said.

"I know what you're gonna ask me. The answer is yes. I'll call Chet again and see if he has anything on this Lu Doc dude. If he is a dude. And if he doesn't, he may know someone who does. He knows a lot of cops between here and Galveston. Feds, too."

"Thanks, again," she said.

"I want to see this through just like you. More so even." Walt looked at Joseph who was now sitting at the table tapping his fingers and still looking at the piece of paper. "Nothin' I hate more than a liar. Sometimes a man has got to kill when it's needed, to save himself or his family or his country. These men, and Inverness, they're killers and liars. Greedy sonofabitches, all of 'em. Let me have that phone."

Walt dialed Detective Collingsworth's number, and they spoke for a few minutes about Lu Doc and the number we thought to be his in New Orleans. He still didn't give the detective any details about what we were up against and he even left out the fact that we'd just seen Jerry Dao murdered. Walt hung up and turned to us.

"Here's the deal. Chet wasn't certain but said there may be a file on this Doc fellow at the PC police station. He said the name sounded familiar, maybe heard it from the FBI. Said he'd go downtown to see if he could take a look at the file, if there is one. Then call us back."

"He's going to the station right now?" Abby said.

"Yep. Sure enough."

"That's a good friend," she said. "He still doesn't know why you keep asking all these questions?"

"I said it earlier — Blood Brothers. I'll tell 'em eventually. He knows it. I'd do the same for him."

Forty-five minutes later the phone rang and Walt picked up. Chet found the file on Lu Doc. Walt spent about five minutes talking to him as he wrote on Abby's notepad. Chet told Walt a couple of detectives had been sent to Tight-Line Charters after Dao's body was found by the EMT's. Chet asked Walt if he knew anything about Dao's murder and said it must be connected with the information Walt was after. "No comment," he said. "I'll tell you everything as soon as I can."

Walt hung up and summarized to us what Chet told him about Lu Doc, referring to his notes a couple of times.

"All right, here's the skinny on this Doc dude. He's one bad hombre. Chet says he's been working out of New Orleans for the past five or six years. DEA and FBI would both like to see him handcuffed and headed to a federal pen . . ."

"What are the details?" Abby said. "What kinds of crimes?"

"I'm gettin' there. I was just stoppin' to catch my breath. Pushy, ain't she?"

"I prefer to think of it as being thorough," Abby said. "Sorry, Walt."

Walt tilted his head toward Abby and said, "Here's the story. Co-caine, marijuana — big amounts — coming out of Central and South America. He distributes all over the Gulf. Gambling. Girls, too. Young girls sold into prostitution to rich men. Chet says Lu Doc may've or-dered a hit last month."

"Did he give you details on that?" Abby said.

"Yeah, five dead in Biloxi. Three Vietnamese and two white guys."

"The reason?" I said.

"Seems that Lu Doc doesn't want any competition along the Gulf. Wants to control everything from Galveston to PC. Came to America but apparently doesn't give a shit about the free enterprise system we all say we're so proud of. Wants it all for himself. Imagine that."

"Drugs, prostitution, gambling, murder," Abby said. "Anything else?"

"That's not enough?" I said. "That should keep anyone busy."

"That's a big ten-four," Walt said. "Here's the best part — if there is a best part in all of this — it seems our good buddy Lu Doc has a pipe-line to the West Coast for traditional medicines. Chet called it 'stuff made from animals.' He didn't have a lot of details but says the feds have been watching Doc for some time and believe he's selling this stuff to Asians in California, Oregon, and Washington. Same as they'd get in their home countries. He says there's a helluva black market out there."

"Are the animals — body parts — coming from here or overseas?" Abby said.

"He didn't say, I didn't ask. Just said it was all illegal activity. Killing animals and grinding them up. Even said they suspect some have been stolen from zoos on the West Coast."

Joseph stood up from the chair and walked slowly toward the door, turned and looked at us. "The dead Jerry Dao had contacted Lu Doc about the mammoth bones. Before that, Harry Tran contacted Dao. It was Inverness and Ivan who told Tran about the bones. That is what I think. Is anybody else thinking this?"

"We all should be," Abby said. "Then Dao is killed because Lu Doc, using Walt's words, 'doesn't give a shit about the free enterprise system.' It was all a setup to get Dao? You think so?"

"Maybe us, too," I said.

"What do you mean?" Abby said.

"Tran may've seen us in the parking lot when I set the firecrackers off," I said. "He thinks we'll follow him, so he uses the U-Haul as a diversion while the bones are actually somewhere else."

"That seems unlikely," Joseph said. "We went to the Lucky Seven first, remember? I think the whole setup had been planned to trick Dao, kill him at the dock."

"Lu Doc?" Abby said. "You think he killed Dao?"

"It's a reasonable guess," Joseph said. "He comes here from New Orleans to make a point. To do the killing himself."

"Doc could've hired someone to do the killing," Walt said. "Godfathers themselves don't usually pull the trigger, do they?"

"I can be wrong," Joseph said. "Why didn't Inverness or Tran kill Dao? They are both capable."

"We've seen Inverness in action," I said. "We know she is a killer. Maybe it was Lu Doc on that boat or someone else we're not aware of who wanted Dao dead."

"After Walt's conversation with Chet, guessing Lu Doc makes sense," Joseph said. "I think he's the one."

"Okay, I'll play along," Walt said. "Maybe Dao was becoming a threat to Lu Doc on this part of the coast. Doc draws Dao into this scheme, them blows him away. That sounds like something from a movie, doesn't it?"

"This whole thing sounds like something from a movie," I said.

"It is not the *Sound of Music*," Joseph said.

"Are we saying we've now figured all this out?" I said. "Who did it to who and for what reasons?"

"If so, it's the easy part," Abby said. "Now we've got to find out where those bones are, hopefully not yet on their way to the West Coast."

"We don't have a clue, not one, where the bones are right now and where Tran and Inverness went on that boat," Walt said. "We're just stuck again."

No one spoke for the next minute or so. We paced the motel room, trading places with one another. I opened the white blinds and looked at the parking lot, well-lit by a couple of bright security lights. I saw a Volkswagen Beetle with a black and white Vietnam MIA sticker on the back bumper. Then I thought about Joseph and his service during the Vietnam War.

I turned to him and said, "Can you speak Vietnamese?"

He looked at me and several seconds passed before he answered. "Yes, I was in-country long enough to learn a little. We often worked with South Vietnamese soldiers, like I told you earlier. I eventually learned some, though. Why do you ask that question now?"

"Spoken any lately?" I said.

"Not a word of it recently. But a year or so ago I was in a restaurant in Tallahassee and had a waitress from Vietnam. We spoke for a few moments. I did okay. She did not make fun of me. Not that I knew of, anyway."

"Okay, John, get to it," Abby said. "What is it you want from Joseph?"

"Let's call that number. Not us — Joseph. Maybe the person who answers is Vietnamese. Maybe part of Lu Doc's gang. See what Joseph can find out."

"Joseph will then ask about the bones, the shipment," Abby said. "Try to get some information that we can act on. That's what you're thinking? Good idea."

"That's right, I have one occasionally. If he can't pull it off, we've lost nothing. We could gain big, though."

"I need to pour that boy a Crown and water," Walt said.

"Let's wait on the Crown," Abby said. "What do you think, Joseph, about making the call? Can you do it?"

"I think so. I should be able to ask a few simple questions over the phone." Joseph looked at the phone number on the paper, looked at us and didn't say anything for a few seconds. Then picked up the receiver and dialed.

He spoke for about five minutes and nodded his head a few times and wrote things down in Abby's notepad. He hung up and explained to us what he said and what he learned. He seemed satisfied with how it all played out. He grinned just a bit.

"Mingo, give it to us," Walt said. "What'd they tell you? You were on there a while. How'd you get 'im to talk?"

"First, I asked him where he was from, he told me Long Binh. I said I was from Phu My. Both places are in the same part of South Vietnam. Down in the southern part of the country. Our Army had a big base at Long Binh during the war, but I didn't mention that. We both cussed Americans and the war."

"It must've tricked 'im," Walt said. "Did you get something we can use?"

"The exchange is scheduled for tomorrow night at nine," Joseph said. "The guy said the load won't be ready until then."

"Where?" Abby said. "Where did he tell you?"

"They plan to make the exchange at the St. Marks Lighthouse then take the bones to Mobile. From there they will go to the West Coast. I did not ask how because I did not want to push things. I assume by truck or some other vehicle. But it could be by boat."

"You said they won't be ready until tomorrow?" I said. "Did he say why?"

"No, but maybe they are still diving and pulling bones out of the Aucilla. Or there might be some other reason. I did not ask for those details, either."

"Did he mention Tran or Inverness?" I said.

"No, I did not ask him about them."

"How did you get the guy to talk?" Abby said. "What did you say to him?"

"I made up a Vietnamese name for myself and told him I worked with Doc out of Panama City, and he had given me this number a few months ago. We talked about women for a few moments. Drinking and going to strip clubs. I made the guy laugh a couple of times."

"You've always been my favorite comedian, Mingo," Walt said. "You remind me of Jack Benny. Look just like him, too."

Joseph ignored Walt and said, "I told him I had memorized the phone number, like Doc told me to. But I had not planned to see him until the shipment was loaded. Then I told him I had the name of the place and time for the exchange written on a separate piece of paper that I lost last night when I got drunk at a strip club. If I do not show up, Doc will find me and slit my throat. He laughed about that and said 'of course he will.'"

"That's good," Walt said. *"Real* good."

"Then he told you about the lighthouse?" I said.

"That's right. That is when I got the information we needed."

"You tricked 'im," Walt said. "I always said you Indians are tricky people."

"Which is it?" Joseph said. "Comedian or trickster?"

"Thought they were the same," Walt said.

"It was my Vietnamese that did it. That and a little Seminole storytelling."

"You still tricked 'im," Walt said.

"It was a good trick, though," Abby said. "Real good."

CHAPTER 27

Walt and Joseph had rented a room three doors down from us at the Lagoon Motel and around seven-fifteen the next morning, I heard hard knocks on our door that startled me out of a deep sleep. I walked to the door and through the blinds I could see Walt doing the knocking, as if he was boxing the door.

He saw me and stopped then said, "Hey, good buddy, we're burnin' daylight. Get your girlfriend up and come have breakfast with me and Mingo. Tell her John Wayne said so. Or Daniel Boone. Either way, it doesn't matter."

I opened the door wearing Mickey Mouse boxer shorts that Abby bought for me at Disney World back in the summer. "I thought they were dead. Both of them."

"No, you can't kill John Wayne or Daniel Boone. I bet they never wore shorts like those." He pointed to my boxer's.

"I don't care what you say, I love these shorts. Abby gave them to me."

"Okay, Mickey Mouse. Whatever you say. We'll meet you two across the street. Breakfast is on me. Be sure to put something over those shorts, people will stare."

"Give us a few minutes."

"Just a few. We're burnin' daylight, cowboy."

Walt left, I closed the door and turned to Abby, who was lying on her back with open eyes and a white sheet pulled almost to her chin. I loved looking at her in the morning light.

"Breakfast?" I said.

"How about making love, then having breakfast — maybe making love again. Wasn't that the plan all along?"

"I thought it was."

"Enjoy the warm sun, beautiful saltwater. Smell the saltwater. All of that earth magic of the Panhandle. That's what you promised me. We talked about this trip for weeks, didn't we?"

"I believe we did."

"Drink wine, relax. Drink more wine. We had it all figured out."

"I believe we did," I repeated.

"Now we're going to breakfast with Walt and Joseph to try to figure out how to catch some killers."

"I believe we are. We will do all of those other things soon, I promise you."

"I heard our gentle wake-up call. I heard what he said. Daniel Boone or John Wayne? He knocked like Muhammad Ali . . . I need about ten minutes."

"You got it."

Walt found the only empty table for four at The Diner, a small white cinder-block restaurant across the street from the Lagoon. The blue and white sign over the bar where customers were eating read, "Family-Owned Since 1961: Best on the Beach." A waitress with blond hair whose nametag said "Shirley" and who was probably in her early fifties, took our orders for coffee and food. The coffee came in two minutes, our food five minutes after that.

"Your order's up, hun," Shirley said, placing a plate of food in front of Walt. "Y'all's are comin' up next." She looked at Abby and nodded, then me and Joseph. Then back at Walt again. Big smile for Walt but not for us.

"Thank you, Miss Shirley," Walt said. "That sure was quick service." He tilted his head back and returned the smile.

After Shirley served our food, she said directly to Walt, "Anything else, hun?"

"No, we're good for now. Thank you much."

"You just call, if you need me. I'll be right over here. I'll come in a hurry. I promise." She walked back behind the counter where the food was being cooked.

"Walt, did you slip out of our room and meet her last night?" Joseph said. "She is most receptive to you. You are quite the charmer this morning."

"What if I did slip out last night?" He took a drink of coffee and looked over at Shirley and smiled again. "What's it to you, Mingo? I still got it. Can't hide what I have. I've always had it."

"That was last night," Abby said. "What about tonight at the lighthouse?"

"Let's talk about it," Walt said. "Now's the time."

"We can use Walt's boat, if they have not taken it or put a hole in it," Joseph said. "We can get to the Big Hole in his boat and see if they are diving. What do you think, Walt?"

"We can. I checked the tides this morning. High tide is about nine-thirty tonight. There'll be plenty of water up the mouth of the Aucilla and on the flats. We can use the boat and walk along the bank if we have to. We can get to the hole without being seen."

"You think we're going to pull this off on the water?" Abby said. "Just the four of us? How are we going to do that?"

Walt took a butter knife and spread strawberry jam on half of a big white and brown biscuit, took a bite and a sip of coffee. "Put your best idea on the table," he said. "Like I said, let's talk. I ain't got the plan, yet. Nobody does."

We were quiet and eating for the next few moments as a tall, wiry man wearing a gray tank-top and a Miller-Lite ball cap walked to the jukebox near us and played Merle Haggard's song *Okie From Muskogee*. Perfect song for Walt and John Wayne, I thought.

"Maybe they are making one more dive today or tonight or both," Joseph said. "Maybe if we can . . ."

"If we can catch the divers on the river, they can take us to the drop-off site," Walt said. "Where the other boat will be. Is that what you're thinkin', Joseph? Out in front of the lighthouse?"

"Yes, you got in the way of my sentences, but you do that a lot."

"What do you mean, 'catch the divers'?" Abby said. "Capture them?"

"That's right," Walt said. "Surprise the shit out of 'em. Threaten to kill 'em if we have to. We gotta make 'em talk. If they have the bones, they got to take them to whoever is buying. We all assume it's Lu Doc — you don't like that plan?"

"I'm not saying that," Abby said. "I guess it's as good as we got, right now."

"What if we don't see any divers on the Aucilla?" I said. "What then?" I was eating a ham and cheese omelet and hash browns. I took another bite and a drink of coffee from the heavy ceramic white cup.

"Very good question," Joseph said. "What is your answer, Walt?"

"Even if we don't see anyone diving on the Aucilla, we need to go to the lighthouse," Walt said. "As long as we can get my boat — or any boat — we can search for them. Based on Joseph's conversation with his new Vietnamese pal in New Orleans, they're supposed to be at the lighthouse."

"All right, let's say we don't see any divers but we are looking for Tran and Inverness and maybe Lu Doc on a boat in the middle of the night near the lighthouse," Abby said. "How's all that play out? What do we do, if we see them?"

"Good question," I said. "How do we do it, Walt?"

"Do you two ever run out of questions?" Walt said. "You'd never make it in the Army. We weren't allowed to ask questions."

"If we ran out of questions, our editor would fire us," Abby said.

"But first we'd get a good cussin'," I said.

"Your editor's my kinda guy," Walt said.

"We still need to answer the question," Abby said. "How are we going to do this tonight?"

"Hell, I don't have all the answers," Walt said. "Nobody at this table does. If we get out on open water, we've got to find a way to disable their boats. That I know. We'll have Mingo use his long gun. He can shoot the eyes out of a wild hog at two-hundred yards. He won't do it, but he could if he wanted to. I've seen 'im use that thirty-aught-six."

"We're not going to be part of this anymore if you're going to start killing people," Abby said.

"Oh, hell, no. Not them, their boats," Walt said. "Joseph can disable those boats from a few hundred yards. He'll hit the engines, even at night. He's got a night scope. We just gotta make sure we hit the right ones."

Joseph looked at Abby over his coffee cup and nodded his head twice. "He's right about my shooting skills."

"Then what?" I said. "Let's say we get the boats disabled, then what?"

"I got a radio on my boat, if they haven't sunk it," Walt said. "We can make our calls after we know they're on the water and can't go anywhere. We can call the Coast Guard. We'll call the FBI."

"Do you have any contacts we can notify now and let them know we might need them?" Abby said. "The Coast Guard or FBI?"

"I'm workin' on that," Walt said. "Right now, the answer is no."

"Joseph?" Abby said.

"Same answer."

"I'll make a call," I said. "We know an FBI in agent in Albany we can trust. His name is Ed Hanahan."

"Good idea," Abby said. "Ed will help."

"Okay, let's finish up here, and you can make the call from your room," Walt said.

*

Back in our room, I called FBI Agent Edward "Ed" Hanahan in Albany, who we'd gotten to know during the last few years through a couple of cases he investigated and we wrote about. We considered Ed a friend who had a deserved reputation of high integrity and decency.

Ed, as he preferred to be called, once made several arrests along the Muckalee Creek near Albany in connection with the kidnapping of immigrant girls from Central America being sold into sexual slavery. Shot and wounded during the arrests, Ed recovered and returned to work. Abby used Ed's gun to shoot and wound the despicable ringleader now in prison.

I never knew until then Abby could handle a gun, and she was a lot better than I was at it. She saved my life and Ed's that day.

Like I told Walt, we trusted Ed, and I knew he'd do his best to help us. I got a pen and the notepad at the ready, called information and got Ed's home number in Albany. I called Ed, he picked up on the third ring and we spoke for several minutes.

As soon as I returned the phone to the receiver Abby said, "Can he help us? What did he say?"

"Said he would. Here's the deal. I laid out the whole story, you heard me. Even the fact that Joseph is being framed for a double murder. He's going to call an agent he knows who works out of Tallahassee. Then get right back to us. We just need to wait."

We did. Fifteen minutes later the phone rang and I picked up in the middle of the first ring to hear Ed say, "All right, here's what I got. Listen up."

The second time I spoke with Ed was for only a minute or so and I wrote down the name of the FBI agent and his home phone number. Ed told me to call back anytime, if he could help us further.

"We got an FBI contact," I said. "The agent is Roland East who works in Tallahassee and lives in Crawfordville, not far from the Aucilla. Ed has known him for about fifteen years. Says he talked to Roland, and he'll do what he can to help us. Ed said he's expecting a call from me. Says he's a 'no-bullshit-guy,' just like Ed."

I dialed the Crawfordville number and someone who sounded like a nine-or-ten-year-old boy picked up after the third ring. The boy spoke clearly and said his father was raking leaves in the front yard and he would get him to the phone. A minute later, Agent Roland East picked up the receiver and said, "This is East. Whatta you got?"

We spoke for about ten minutes, and I gave him the full details of what had happened since we pulled Joseph out of the river. He asked a few follow-up questions about the names I gave him and expressed particular interest in Lu Doc.

"We been watching him for several months now," he said. "From Texas to Panama City. We know he's originally out of New Orleans. Came over about ten years ago from Vietnam, after the war. Probably mid-thirties at the time but moved up in a hurry. Crime-ladder, that is. He's dipping into everything — drugs, prostitution, and murder."

"That's the same thing a local detective told us," I said.

"Who'd you speak with?"

"Chet Collingsworth with the PC police," I said. "Walt Gosser, the guy from the Aucilla who's helping us, is friends with him. They're Army buddies from World War II."

"I know Chet, he's a good cop. Did he tell you that Lu Doc slit his own brother's throat and did the same to his sister-in-law?"

"No, he didn't."

"Well, we had an informant swear it happened that way," East said. "Those bodies have never shown up. He probably fed them to the sharks. None of our informants have seen the two alleged victims for months now. You're dealing with a mean — *evil* — man. We just haven't had enough on him to bring him in but we're getting close. He moves from place to place quite a bit. He's got four or five hideouts along the Gulf, based on our sources. Here's another thing, both parents were shot in the head by our troops in Vietnam, the story goes. He's been full of rage ever since. I have no reason not to believe the story about killing his own brother and sister-in-law."

"Can you meet us at the Aucilla tonight?" I said.

"No, if I tell my supervisor what you told me, he wouldn't allow it. Too thin, he'd say. But the moment you have evidence that those bones are in the hands of killers and Lu Doc, you contact us, and we'll move on it. I wouldn't get close to him, if I was you."

"It may be too late by the time they exchange the bones for money," I said.

"We'll get the Coast Guard involved if we have to. If you're certain of everything you tell me. I promise you we'll track him down on the water. Or land."

"We were hoping, like I told Ed, you folks could meet us at the river tonight and arrest these people before anybody else gets killed," I said. "That's what I'm asking."

"As of now, those killings just involve the local boys. We haven't been called into that, as far as I know. I haven't even heard about them."

"We really need . . ."

"Again, I need something solid to go on. That's just the way it has to be. I trust Ed, therefore I trust you. But if I came out to the Aucilla tonight just based on our conversation, it might be my ass in the wringer. You can call me here at home anytime and by nine tomorrow I'll be in the office. I can get to the Aucilla in less than an hour. Remember, something solid then we'll move."

"Okay, I understand, Agent East."

"Call me Roland."

"We'll be in touch, Roland. I hope anyway." I hung up and turned to Abby.

"Will he help us?" she said. "Can we count on him?"

"Of course, he will, or Ed wouldn't have called him. You know that. He said as soon as we get firm evidence that Lu Doc and the others are transporting the bones, to call him. He'll be here in under an hour. He said for us to wait and let them handle it, if we see them."

"That ain't goin' to happen," Walt said. "If we see them tonight, we'll act. They're not gonna hang around long enough for the G-men to get here and help us with this. This is on us. Everybody here knows it."

"Then what was the use of my call?" I said. "We need help, don't we?"

"Yeah, we do," Walt said, "but we're not goin' let them slip away while waitin' on the FBI to show up."

"I agree with Walt," Abby said. "I think we need to head back to the Aucilla now. What about it?" Abby looked at Walt, then at Joseph.

"I am still wanted for murder," Joseph said. "Still innocent, too. I am ready to end this with or without the help of the FBI. Been ready."

"We're burnin' daylight," Walt said.

CHAPTER 28

The drive east back to the murky and deadly Aucilla River and away from the clear, blue Gulf of Mexico took a little more than two hours as I drove Walt's truck with Abby next to me writing a summary in her notepad of everything that had happened to us since we pulled Joseph from the water.

Walt and Joseph left in the Pontiac. We agreed to meet at Walt's house on the river. I made a quick stop for gas a few miles outside of PC and saw the Pontiac race by us.

Back on the road, Abby wrote for several more minutes, stopped and flicked her black pen a few times against her chin, looked at me, didn't say anything, then looked out her window at a flock of seagulls flying toward the beach.

"Look at them," she said. "I wish we could do that and forget all about this thing we've gotten ourselves into. They have no worries. Not one. No worries."

"You don't know that for certain."

"Bet my life on it."

"We can back out anytime, but I don't think you want to. I don't. Not at this point. We both need to do what we can do help Joseph. They tried to kill him and now they've framed him for a double murder. They need to be stopped."

"No, we're not backing out of this, you know that. You know what else we need to do?"

"Yeah, we need to go to the beach for a few days when this is over. Just me and you. And not to chase after a bunch of killers." I placed my right hand on her left knee and gently squeezed. "You know I love you."

"I love you back, but there is something we need to do. We need to call Mickey. We're supposed to be back in the office tomorrow, and

182

he doesn't know what we've gotten ourselves into down here. He needs to know."

"We won't be back in the office tomorrow, that's for sure. We don't know what the hell's going to happen tonight. We don't even know where we're gonna be tomorrow."

"That's what I mean. We need to call."

"Let's wait until tomorrow. Just one more day. We may have one helluva a story for him."

"One? John, if this thing plays out the way we want it to — and we're still alive — we'll have more than one story to write. And they won't be read just by the good people in Florida and Georgia, either."

"I thought about that, too. Lots of people will be interested in this story. Think back what the archeologist said at FSU. What was his name? Lowdy . . . Drowdy . . . what was it?"

"Growdy. Dr. Zibe Growdy. I wrote his name down."

"Yeah, that one. He said mammoth bones have never been found in Florida. Said folks all over the world would be interested in these findings. Museums. Scientists."

"We will eventually find out the truth and clear Joseph's name and turn Lu Doc, Tran, Inverness and whoever else is involved in this mess over to the feds. They'll go to prison for a long time."

"Mighty confident, aren't you?" I said.

"How else you want me to be?" She placed her left hand on my right knee and gently squeezed. "You know I love you."

*

We pulled into Walt's driveway a few minutes before noon and parked behind his Pontiac. Inside the house we smelled fresh coffee as Walt and Joseph stood over the white Formica bar in the kitchen, each drinking a cup.

"Took you long enough," Walt said. "We beat you by fifteen minutes. I know my truck. It can run better than that."

"Do not listen to Walt. He wanted to make friends with some Florida troopers until I slowed him down. Had to remind him he was driving a wanted man."

"Your truck is great," Abby said. "John always goes under the speed limit. He thinks the moment he reaches the speed limit he'll get pulled over. A family tradition, he says. That's the way his dad drives."

"What a way to live," Walt said. "You two want coffee?" We said yes and Walt reached into a brown cabinet next to his refrigerator and pulled out two Army-green coffee cups that both read, "Christmas '44: Battle of the Bulge." He set the cups on the bar and poured them full.

I looked out the window over the sink and saw the thick woods that led to the Aucilla. Before this trip with Abby, when I thought of the Aucilla, I thought it to be one of the most beautiful places I'd ever seen. That still held, but now it was also one of the most dangerous.

We thanked Walt for the coffee and Abby said, "You guys got it figured out yet?"

"Well, the good news is, my boat is still on the trailer out back and seems to be in working condition," Walt said. "We checked it out a few minutes ago."

"Are you about to give us some bad news?" Abby said.

"No . . . no *new* bad news," Walt said. "The old bad news is bad enough, ain't it?"

"I'd say so," I said.

Joseph sat on one of the brown vinyl bar stools, placed both hands around his coffee cup. "I think we ought to head up the river now, just to take a look at the Big Hole," he said. "We can use your boat, Walt. There is a spot not far from the hole where we can get out and walk along the bank. We will not be seen. Same as we did before when we were on the other side a couple of nights ago."

"Fine with us," I said. "We're ready."

"When do you want to leave?" Abby said.

"Let's finish our coffee and get out of here," Walt said and took a drink and looked out the window with the rest of us.

Ten minutes later, we left the house and Walt hooked his boat and trailer to the back of his truck. He had an eighteen-foot green aluminum flat-bottom he used on the river and creeks and on the flats when the chop or waves were light. There were three seats and a twenty-five horsepower Evinrude engine, and it looked as if he'd recently painted it. Walt took good care of the things he owned.

All four of us got into the cab of the truck with Abby on my lap. Walt drove a few minutes over dirt roads and came to a small un-marked boat ramp in the middle of a cluster of cypress trees and big palm plants. Typical of other stretches of the Aucilla we'd seen the past few days.

We got out of the truck, and Walt took the straps off the boat, got back into the truck and eased the boat halfway into the still, deep-pur-ple water. Joseph pushed it off the trailer and held tight to a yellow rope that was tied to the inside of the boat. Walt parked the truck and trailer along the dirt road. Then Joseph pulled the boat against the bank and we got in.

Walt got in the back next to the engine, and Abby and I shared the middle seat. Joseph stepped into black mud, pushed us off and jumped in. We were on our way.

The engine started easily, and Walt headed down stream to the Big Hole, toward the open waters of the Gulf. Farther still was the St. Marks Lighthouse. The high sun splintered tall cypress trees causing ripples of white in the middle of the Aucilla. A metallic ballet.

Walt ran the boat slowly and said, "Here's the deal, guys. We're just a mile or so from that hole everybody's so interested in. We're gonna get close, get out of this boat, walk the bank a bit and have a look see. Got it?"

"All right, we can handle that," Abby said. "We did the same with Joseph on the other side of the river. Just lead the way. We'll be right behind you."

"Good. Hang on, here we go," Walt said, before he opened the Evinrude full. The strength of the small engine surprised me, and my head quickly jerked backwards. We held tight to our seats. Walt raised his voice over the engine. "I bought this girl in '74. She's still got it, doesn't she?"

Walt kept his boat in the middle of the Aucilla for most of the ride, but a couple of times he weaved around what looked to be big rocks just below the surface. We didn't see other boats, and there were no houses along this section of the river. Just water and trees and birds.

A few moments later, Walt pointed to the left bank and slowed the engine. He maneuvered next to the bank, turned the boat directly toward land and drove it up onto a sandy area with big pieces of brown and gray driftwood scattered about. He turned the engine off, and Joseph got out and steadied the boat as the rest of us stepped onto the bank. We pulled the boat three-fourths out of the water, and Walt took the rope and tied it around the base of a big water oak.

"All right," Walt said. "We'll use this trail the wild hogs use. They won't hurt you. Won't take long to get there. Just stay behind me. Let's move."

Walt loosened the black leather strap over his holstered forty-five as he led us away from his boat and closer to the Big Hole. I couldn't tell if Joseph had a gun underneath his jacket and didn't ask. Maybe Walt just worried about the wild hogs and other animals in the woods, I thought. No, that's not the reason he carried that gun. We were on the trail of killers.

The beaten path of black dirt weaved along snake-like about fifty yards from the water's edge, plenty big for wild hogs, deer, and panthers to use on their way for a drink from the river. We walked single file behind Walt for a few minutes and were concealed by thick trees and underbrush making it difficult, if not impossible, for anyone on the river to see us.

We were still walking when Walt spoke. "Up here a bit, we're gonna ease off the trail and head toward the river. Just keep followin' me. Won't be long."

After another seventy-five yards Walt signaled with his right hand that we were coming off the trail, and we stepped over short palm plants and around oak and pine trees as we stayed behind Walt along the thick river bottom. The underbrush was not tall or difficult to walk through. We were headed directly for the river, probably now only about a quarter of a mile from Walt's boat. A few moments later, I could see the river through a gap in several trees.

We were about a hundred yards from the Aucilla.

Ten seconds later, Walt stopped near three big oaks that formed a triangle big enough for all of us to enter and not touch the trees. Walt nodded toward the water and whispered. "They're divin' out there. Somebody is. There's a couple of boats, someone in each one. Look for yourselves. You'll see 'em."

We looked and saw the boats. I couldn't see any divers, but the boats were anchored in the middle of the river in the same way the ones were when Joseph led us to a similar spot on the other side.

"I see two boats," Abby said. "Anybody else see more than two?" We all answered no.

"Walt, do you recognize those two people?" Joseph said. "I do not."

"Hard to say," Walt said. "They both wearin' those big straw hats. Can't see their faces."

"Maybe they're doing something else," I said. "Maybe fishing. Throwing a mullet net."

"Do you see a net?" Walt said.

"No, but . . . look, look at that," I said. A diver appeared with a long object and dropped it into one of the boats and disappeared again in the water.

"It is hard to catch bones at the bottom of the river with a mullet net," Joseph said. "Not impossible but difficult."

"Y'all best listen to Mingo," Walt said.

*

Walt took a couple of steps closer to the river, and we followed him over a trail only about a foot wide, smaller than the one we used after we left his boat. We were still hidden behind a canopy of tall, thick trees and green underbrush, when we heard rustling on our right, maybe thirty or forty yards away. Somebody was coming toward us.

We couldn't see what we all heard.

It sounded like more than one person, four or five, maybe. We looked in the direction of the noise as it grew louder and closer.

"We got get outta here!" I said. "They're coming. They've seen us."

"We must try to make it back to the boat," Joseph said. "There are too many of them coming. Run the other way. *Now!*"

"Too late, just get behind those trees," Walt said as he stepped between us and the rustling of the forest-floor. The three of us backed away from Walt and toward the trees.

The ground shook.

As Walt reached for the butt of his forty-five, they burst through the underbrush about twenty yards from us. They overwhelmed him.

Their four-legged leader, with black fur and long white tusks, hit Walt probably at around twenty-miles-an-hour knocking him to the ground. His gun flew from his hand. The hog drove his head into Walt's side, and he screamed in pain. Walt lay flat on the ground and five or six big hogs ran over him as an equal number ran around him. They were snorting and kicking up debris as they ran past us, heads steady, eyes straight ahead.

The last to come through the thicket were four piglets closely following the adults. They ran around Walt and disappeared with the others. The whole thing lasted about thirty seconds.

"Can you believe this shit!" Walt said as he tried to stand. His clothes were dirty with hog prints. Blood stained his shirt on the right side above his waist. "I was lookin' high and they hit me low. FUBAR."

Walt got on his right knee but hesitated as if he didn't have the strength to stand. He didn't.

"You're bleeding," Abby said. "Hold it right there, we'll help you." The three of us eased Walt to the base of a pine tree.

Joseph ripped open Walt's dark green T-shirt and exposed a puncture wound. "You will need to get this stitched," he said. "It's bleeding. Keep your right hand pressed on it as tight as you can."

Walt leaned his head against the tree and kept his right hand on top of the wound. "Thank you, Mingo. This is some shit, ain't it? I was safer in Belgium in '44 . . . how bad is it?"

"It is a couple of inches wide and probably an inch deep," Joseph said. "We must get you to a doctor."

When Joseph said that, I noticed movement on the Aucilla. The two men in the boats had both lifted long guns near their chests as if they were ready to fire. They stared in our direction. They couldn't see us, but they must've heard Walt when the hogs came through, and now they knew someone had been watching them.

"We gotta get out of here," I said. "Those men are looking this way. They may get out of those boats and come after us."

Abby found Walt's gun lying about fifteen feet from him and picked it up and gave it to Joseph. "We gotta go," she said. "We need to get back to our boat and off the river."

Joseph placed the gun back in Walt's holster and strapped it in and said, "All of us together. Let's help him walk."

"I can walk," Walt said. "I ain't dead yet. My bell still rings."

"We know that, but we are going to help," Joseph said. "You need help. We cannot allow you to be stubborn now."

We got Walt to his feet, and I wrapped my arm around him and Joseph did the same on Walt's opposite side. Abby quickly took the lead as we hustled back to the boat. I didn't look back to see if those gunmen on the river were following us. Walt kept his hand pressed against his side, and I kept a lookout for wild hogs as we moved away from the Big Hole on the Aucilla.

A few minutes later we made it to the bigger trail and then our boat. Still no men with guns or stampeding hogs. We helped Walt sit in the front of the boat. Abby and I took the middle seat again, and Joseph started the Evinrude and pointed the boat toward the ramp where we'd left Walt's truck and trailer. Joseph opened the engine full, just like Walt had done.

At the ramp, we loaded the boat on the trailer and then drove to Walt's house. From there we got into his Bonneville and Joseph drove us toward Crawfordville, about thirty minutes north, to the Wakulla County Medical Clinic.

"Hit over the head in my own home and now a hog sliced into me," Walt said. "I been livin' on this river — walkin' these woods — most of my life and that ain't never happened. Never even shot a hog. Don't like the way they taste."

"Walt, you've experienced many new things recently," Joseph said. "It's a sign of a well-rounded life."

Walt was sitting in the front and looked at Joseph, who kept his eyes on the road. "New things? Some more of your Seminole wisdom? You can keep that. I like the old things better. You could've at least made me a drink."

"Later. We need a doctor to plug that hole with some stitches. Do not tell me you don't need them. I saw what that hog did to you."

"Okay, okay, you're in charge," Walt said. "It does hurt like hell. Maybe a drink later."

"Yes, later," Joseph said.

A doctor at the clinic closed the wound with thirteen stiches and gave Walt a dozen pain pills. He told him to limit his physical activity and come back in a week to have the stiches removed. We were back at Walt's house a little more than three hours after the hog attack.

"You promised me a drink, Mingo."

"Do not take one of those pain pills if you are going to have a drink."

"You sound more and more like my ex-wife."

We were in Walt's kitchen. He made himself a Crown and water and the rest of us had iced tea from a pitcher in the refrigerator. Walt took two big swallows from his drink. We sat on stools along the counter and talked for a few minutes about what we'd seen on the river earlier, more divers apparently taking mammoth bones from the Big Hole, and hard-charging wild hogs.

"When you finish the drink, go lie on your bed and rest. Sleep." Joseph said. "You are going to take it easy for a while, like that doctor said."

"Now you sound like my mother."

"Just do what I say. I am your mother."

"I really think you are my mother, when you keep talkin' like that. Let me tell you somethin'. All of you hear this. I'll rest for a while, but you ain't leavin' me here tonight. I'm goin' with you to finish this out." He banged the glass he was drinking from on the counter. "Don't try to pull any shit on me. We've come this far together, and I'm gonna play this thing out with you. Hog or no hog."

"I never thought that at all," Joseph said. "We are in this together, and again I thank every one of you for risking your lives for me. You try to sleep for an hour or so. We will get you up, and we will make our way to the lighthouse. We all need to rest."

"Good. I could use a little nap." Walt went to his bedroom and closed the door, as the late afternoon sun began to settle beyond the trees along the river.

"What are you thinking now?" Abby said to Joseph.

"We need to drive to the lighthouse before dark and pull Walt's boat. We take two vehicles. You and John back in the Pontiac."

"Once we get there, what then?" I said.

Joseph took a deep breath and got up from the stool and poured himself more tea and refilled our glasses. "We watch for any activity around the parking lot of the lighthouse. It could be that is where the exchange will be made and not on the water. We have to be able to surprise and disarm them."

"Let's say it's close to nine, and we still don't see them," Abby said. "What then?"

"We will take Walt's boat and get on the water. We will assume the exchange is by boat. We'll be guessing, of course. They could pull into the lighthouse parking lot a few minutes after nine and we would miss them altogether. That's the chance we take. If you have anything better, I want to hear it."

"I don't have anything better, but let's say we're on the water, out in front of the lighthouse," I said. "How in the hell are we gonna find them in the dark without running the boat right next to them?"

"Walt has a powerful spotlight he keeps in his boat. If you shine it on the moon, you can see Neil Armstrong's footprints."

"They'll be able to see us, too," Abby said. "Won't they?"

"Yes, they will," Joseph said. "We will have to act quick."

"Explain that," I said. "There may be ten or twelve or more of them with guns."

"Remember what Walt said about my thirty-aught-six? I can disable any boat within a few hundred yards without hurting anyone, if I get a clear shot at the engine. That may be the only real chance we have, if we catch them on the water. Then we call for help. There is a pay phone next to the public restrooms."

"That sounds dangerous," I said. "They will shoot back."

"All of this is dangerous."

"If we're on the water, we look for boats coming together?" Abby said.

"That's right. There are usually very few boats out here after dark. If we see a couple, it may be who we're looking for. It's all unpredictable, like smoke blowing in the wind."

"I think we should get there before dark," Abby said. "Don't you?"

"I do," Joseph said.

An hour or so after Walt went to his bedroom, he returned to the kitchen and made ham and cheese sandwiches for everyone. After we ate, Abby and I got into the Pontiac and followed Walt and Joseph in the pickup pulling the flat-bottom boat.

The descending gold and copper sun cast a glow along the Gulf as we left the Aucilla and headed for the St. Marks Lighthouse.

CHAPTER 29

Since the 1830s, the St. Marks Lighthouse has guided ships along the Gulf and the St. Marks River, and its presence has evoked both beauty and safety for generations. When I was a teenager, I went on a fishing trip to the Panhandle with my father and one of his friends, and we fished near the lighthouse, catching trout and redfish. The lighthouse stood majestically at the mouth of the river, like a sentry for an eighteenth-century fort. I became enamored of the lighthouse and Apalachee Bay, then, and have been ever since.

William P. Duval, governor of the Florida Territory, secured funding for constructing the eighty-foot tower and its twelve-foot-thick limestone base. Eighty-seven steps lead to the spiral brick tower and the lamp inside, whose light could be seen for fourteen miles. By the mid-1830s, Samuel Crosby was the lighthouse keeper who became fearful for his family's safety during war with the Seminoles and asked the territorial government to send soldiers for protection. The government refused. Then he asked for a boat so he and his family could leave. That request was denied, too.

Crosby and his family survived the war, as most of the Seminoles during that period were forcibly removed from their native lands and marched west by the U. S. government to what became the Indian Territory and is now Oklahoma. Indians called the journey the "Trail of Tears" because of the thousands who died along the way. Only a few hundred Seminoles remained in Florida, Joseph Threadgill's ancestors among them.

I wasn't thinking of any of this history when we were in Walt Gosser's kitchen that late Sunday afternoon planning how to overtake the killers we'd been following and how to prove that Joseph "Quiet Bird" Threadgill, a man we'd come to like and admire, was an innocent man.

*

We arrived at the lighthouse in two vehicles around six, while there was still some daylight. I parked the Pontiac a couple of spaces from where Walt and Joseph parked the pickup and boat. After a short argument before we left Walt's house, Joseph, concerned about Walt's strength since the wild-hog attack, agreed to let Walt drive. Walt said the Crown Royal and nap made him feel "strong like Superman." That statement ended the argument about who would drive.

We drove past an outbuilding with public restrooms, two drink machines, and a pay phone and parked in the parking lot. There were about ten vehicles there, and several people walking to and from the lighthouse, adults and small children. People smiling. Families having fun on a beautiful fall evening.

We sat at a picnic table behind the restrooms and under six large palm trees. A security light shone on the parking lot, already on with dark approaching. From the picnic table we could see anyone entering or leaving, but it'd be difficult for them to see us. We talked and kept a close watch on our surroundings until full dark finally came.

Around eight o'clock, I walked to the front of the restrooms, bought four cans of Coke from one of the machines and looked toward the parking lot before I returned with the drinks. "No signs of a van or U-Haul or Tran or Inverness," I said. "The parking lot is almost empty. All quiet for now."

"The lighthouse is beautiful up close and far away," Abby said. "What time does the entrance close?"

"It doesn't," Walt said. "People can come and go here anytime they want. The keeper's house is boarded up and the lighthouse is locked up tight. You can't get inside unless you break the iron door down. You'd need dynamite to do that. The parking lot and the bathrooms are always open."

"Perfect place for a criminal exchange," Joseph said as he looked to the lighthouse and the dark sky around it. "This is it. They will be here."

"That's right, but we got ahold of their playbook," Walt said. "I just wish those bastards would come on."

Walt got his wish.

A few minutes later we saw the headlights of a vehicle coming down the road to the lighthouse. We watched it turn into the parking lot as a few clouds rolled in and a breeze rustled the palms overhead. The same sound we'd heard outside of the Fiesta Motel while watching men load long boxes into a U-Haul.

"I'm going to take a closer look," Abby said. "Be right back."

"I'm going with her," I said.

"Watch yourselves," Walt said.

We walked to the front of the restrooms and stood next to a drink machine and out of sight from anyone driving into the parking lot. Now our three vehicles were the only ones left in the lot. The car was parked on the far side of the lot away from us and the lighthouse and as far away as they could get from the security light.

"The car looks like a BMW."

"I'm thinking the same thing," Abby said. "Could be the one Tran drove."

"Could be."

Walt and Joseph joined us just as two people got out of the car and leaned against it on the driver's side. There the security light was bright enough for us to see who they were. We were not surprised to see Tran, but we were very surprised to see who was with him.

"*Dr. Growdy?*" I said. "You gotta be shittin' me. I don't believe it. He should be preparing his next lecture. Examining some stone tools."

"That's him, Dr. Zibe Growdy. Our FSU professor. He's in this mess, too," Abby said.

"He didn't come here to teach a class. Or find old bones on the beach."

"So, this professor fellow is a big-time crook?" Walt said. "Holy shit."

"Looks that way."

"He told me in his lab he would love to have a group of students diving the river for the mammoth bones," Joseph said. "He seemed very excited."

"Very excited about the money he planned to get, looks like," Abby said. "He's obviously been in this all along with Tran, don't you think?"

"It appears that way," Joseph said. "What else should we conclude?"

"Outstanding member of the community," I said. "Dedicated to his research. Loved by everyone."

"This I wouldn't have guessed after my meeting with him," Joseph said, still staring at Tran and Growdy not far from the lighthouse. "He seemed like an honest man. I should have known better."

"You can trust some of us, Mingo," Walt said. "Don't forget that."

"The numbers keep dwindling."

"What matters now is what happens next," Abby said. "What should we do?"

"Let me approach those two," Walt said. "I'm the only one they ain't gonna recognize. I'll make up some story. A lost tourist from up north. I'll feed 'em something. Some bullshit. Let me get close to them."

"Then what?" Abby said.

"I'll get the drop on 'em with my forty-five, walk 'em over here and tie 'em up. Got some duct tape in the truck. Never leave home without it. We'll keep an eye on 'em and wait and see who else shows up. Whatta you think?"

"I don't like it, Walt," Abby said. "These are not nice people."

"I do not like you going up there alone since the hog . . ." Joseph said.

We heard a big vehicle coming, and it turned into the parking lot headed toward Tran and Growdy.

"Too late for that, now, Walt," Abby said. "They're about to make the exchange."

The U-Haul parked next to the BMW and three people got out of the cab. They looked to be wearing straw hats, same as the men we'd seen earlier at the Big Hole. The five now stood together, looking toward the parking lot entrance as if they were anticipating the arrival of others.

We saw more headlights approaching. Another U-Haul entered the parking lot headed toward Tran, Growdy, and the three others. A few minutes later, the two trucks were backed up to one another, about ten feet apart. What appeared to be a woman got out of the second truck.

"Inverness Cousins?" Abby said.

"Can't say for sure," I said. "Good guess, though. Looks like her."

"This is it," Abby said. "It all happens right here. We just have to figure out a way to stop it."

"We will," Walt said. "I'm tired of chasing 'em. So far, I got a knot on the back of my head and a hole in my side from a hog. They ain't leavin' the lighthouse, I promise you that."

"Now what?" I said. "Now there's six. Probably just as many guns."

"Let Mingo take his long gun and shoot out the U-Hauls' tires," Walt said. "Then the two of us can hold that crowd at gunpoint. Then we call your FBI contact and this thing is over, once and for all."

"We don't know if the bones are in one of those trucks," Abby said.

"What do you mean?" Joseph said.

"What I mean is, we need to see the bones and tusks before we make a call to the FBI, don't you think?"

"No, I don't think that at all," Walt said. "We gotta act. That's what I think. What say you, Mingo?"

"She's right," I said. "Agent East said we have to be sure they have the bones. Without the bones, we can't end it."

Joseph went to Walt's truck and slowly eased open the passenger door. He removed his rifle from the case and closed the door.

"From here I can shoot out any tire for a couple of hundred yards. I will not miss. Just like Walt said."

We saw the man from the first truck carry a small suitcase or big briefcase and lay it on the trunk of the BMW. Tran and Growdy looked to be standing over it, we couldn't tell if it had been opened or not.

"There's the money," Walt said. "On top of that car. We gotta act now. Can't let 'em get outta here. The bones are in the second truck . . . and there's the money."

"Let's block the entrance," I said.

"How?" Abby said.

"Park the Pontiac and truck there. At least we can keep them here. Then we call Agent East. Get the FBI out here."

"They will go right through our vehicles," Joseph said. "Those big trucks will plow them over. It will not work."

"Shoot the tires out!" Walt said. "Don't let those trucks leave. *Sonofabitch!* Let's do somethin'."

"Too much movement around the trucks right now," Joseph said. "I do not want to shoot anyone."

Now they were taking what looked like long boxes from the bed of the second U-Haul and loading them into the first U-Haul. The unloading and loading lasted for only a few minutes as Tran, Growdy, and the woman from the second truck watched the whole process. When it ended, someone from the group appeared to be walking toward us and the restrooms.

A few moments later, whoever it was kept coming.

"Who is it?" Abby said, as we remained positioned around the corner of the building near the women's restroom. "Looks like a woman. Inverness?"

"Can't say yet," Walt said. "Probably comin' over here to pee or maybe get a Coke."

We kept watching.

A couple of seconds later Joseph said, "It is Inverness Cousins. That's her. I have seen her enough to know." We eased farther behind the edge of the building and out of Inverness's sight. We heard the bathroom door open and shut.

"We'll get her when she comes out," Walt said, as he walked toward the bathroom door, and we followed him. "It'll be one less to worry about."

We waited against the white cinder-block wall next to the door of the women's bathroom. We heard the toilet flush and the water from the sink turned on and off. Then the door opened, and she walked out and saw Abby and me first.

"What the *fuck* you two doin' here?" she said. Then she turned to Joseph. "You shouldn't be nowhere 'round here. You done killed J. W. and Bubba. Cops are lookin' for your ass." She looked at Walt and said, "Y'all havin' a party here?"

"Not a party. And, no, I have not killed anyone since I returned from Vietnam," Joseph said. "You know who killed J. W. and Bubba. Tran did that. It was you who killed Ivan and Deputy Leach."

"I don't know what you're talkin' about," Inverness said. "You might still be takin' drugs, talkin' like that. Crazy Injun talk. Now get outta my way so I can get back to them over there." She nodded in the direction of the two trucks and the people standing near them. "They're gonna come lookin' for me in a quick minute. People don't mess with Lu Doc and live to tell it."

"That's your new boyfriend since you killed off Ivan?" Walt said. "Or is it that Tran fellow?"

"I ain't kilt nobody," she said. "Best not mess with Lu Doc, like I said. I'm tellin' you now, you won't come outta here alive." She took two steps to get around us, but Walt and Joseph blocked her. She stood straight and stared hard at both of them, fire coming out of her eyes. "I swear to God, I ain't playin'. Lu Doc will cut your throats 'til your heads fall off."

Abby stepped toward Inverness and said, "Where are those bones headed? They taking them to the West Coast? Did Lu Doc buy them from Tran? How's Dr. Growdy involved in this? Lie all you want, we saw you kill Ivan and Deputy Leach. We were there in the parking lot when you did it."

"I seen you before at the Clam that day. You, too." She nodded toward me. "Still askin' questions, ain't you? Well, I ain't got nothin' to say to you. To any of you. Now leave me be or you won't get out of here alive."

"You'll be talking to the police, soon," Abby said. "Charged with murder and God knows what else."

"Don't think so," she said. "If I ain't back in a minute or so, they'll be lookin' for me. Lu Doc ain't gonna let nothin' happen to me. It's y'all that should be worried. He'll fuck you up, just like I said.

"You killed your old boyfriend and now you runnin' 'round with a cutthroat," Walt said. "We know all about 'im. Tell us who planned all of this?"

"Lu Doc loves me," Inverness said. "He takes care of me. Gonna move me to California and buy me my own Bentley. He's gonna kill all y'all, old man."

She started to walk away again. Walt grabbed her around the shoulders and quickly put his right hand over her mouth to prevent her from screaming.

"Old man my ass. Never should've said that. The duct tape is in the glove box. Somebody get it. I'll tape this bitch all up."

Inverness squirmed and jerked her head, her eyes wide and full of rage, but Walt kept a tight grip on her. Like a net around a mullet.

I returned from the truck with the tape, and Walt and Joseph stuck a piece of it over her mouth. She tried to scream while they were doing it but produced only a grunting noise that likely couldn't be heard beyond the restrooms. Then they stretched her arms behind her back and taped her wrists together. She couldn't talk or use her hands. A good time to think about her new Bentley. We were all tired of her filthy mouth.

"Calm down, now," Walt said. "We ain't gonna hurt you. Just don't want you hurtin' us. We know what you're capable of, you little bitch."

Joseph kept hold of Inverness's arms as she violently shook her head and tried to lean into Walt attempting to head-butt him. Walt took a step back and said, "Easy now. You're gonna throw your neck out of joint. You look like one of those television wrestlers. Dusty Rhodes would be proud of you."

"They'll come looking for her soon," Joseph said. "We need to get her out of sight. Put her in the bathroom or the car."

"Good idea, let's lock her in the Bonneville," Walt said. "Plenty room in there. She can beat the shit out of her head against the backseat all she wants." The two men walked Inverness to the Pontiac, Walt opened the back door and guided her into the back seat. The windows were up and the doors locked. Once inside, Inverness banged her head against the seat a few times, then stopped.

"There. Tight as a tick on a bloodhound," Walt said. "She ain't goin' nowhere."

"They'll be coming for her," Abby said.

"We'll get 'em when they do."

"They might see her in the back of the car," Joseph said. "When she sees them, she will kick and try to make noise."

"We have to make the first move," Walt said. "They don't know we're here. Mingo, I want you and Abby on that corner of the building. Take that rifle with you." Walt pointed to his right toward the men's restroom. "They won't be able to see you from that position."

"What about us?" I said.

"We're gonna wait right here," Walt said. "I'm gonna lift the hood of my truck like I'm havin' engine problems. Then I'll surprise 'em with this forty-five. Mingo can do the same with the rifle, if we need 'im."

We all agreed.

Joseph and Abby walked to the side of building, out of view from anyone in the parking lot. From their position, they could see the lighthouse and the outlaws and trucks.

Walt popped open the hood of his truck, and I stood next to him and we looked at the engine as if it wouldn't start. A few seconds later, I saw Inverness in the back of the Pontiac, and she pounded her head against the seat a few times. Then she sat still in the middle of the backseat. Then some more pounding.

Walt lifted the leather strap that securely holstered his gun and said, "They'll be comin' here directly for that girl. Let's try to keep 'em away from the Bonneville. When you see 'em, get their attention."

"That won't be hard. What comes next?"

"You just follow along, and I'll tell you what to do. We'll tape these bastards up one at a time." Walt looked beyond the hood of his truck toward the lighthouse, and the men we were waiting on. "Any second now."

Anyone walking from the two U-Hauls and BMW toward the restrooms would have to pass both vehicles. We waited. But not long.

"Here comes the first sucker," Walt said. "Looks like one of 'em wearin' the big hats like we saw today on the river. We'll tape 'im up like a mummy. You ready?"

"I gotta choice?"

The man kept coming toward us. Then he stopped several yards away, cupped his hands around his mouth and hollered, *"Let's go! Time to go!"* He stayed in that spot and looked toward the restrooms waiting for Inverness to appear.

I looked at the Pontiac and saw her kick the backdoor window on the driver's side after she heard the man calling her. I assumed the man who'd come to get her could not hear the noise coming from the car. He didn't appear to look toward the Pontiac.

"She keeps that racket up, they're gonna hear her," Walt said. "We'll have to move fast. Maybe walk to the man. Here we go."

Then the man walked ten steps closer to the bathroom, hollered again for Inverness and waited. He spoke barely loud enough for us to hear. "What's takin' her so long? Lu Doc's ready to go."

A few seconds passed, and he headed directly for the women's restroom. When the man passed us Walt said, "Hey, buddy, you know anything 'bout engines? Me and my partner over here need some help. I can't tell if it's the starter or battery. Do you mind takin' a look?"

Walt's question didn't have the desired result. The man kept walking and didn't look at us. He'd come for Inverness Cousins.

"Stay here," Walt said. "I'll handle this. Just have the duct tape ready."

The man pounded on the restroom door with his right fist and hollered, *"I said let's go!* The Doc's waitin' on you. He's ready to get outta here."

From the truck, I saw what happened next. Walt approached him with the forty-five in his right hand, pointed at the man's back. He got behind him without being seen or heard. He's got him, I thought.

I heard what Walt said to the man. "Now, good buddy, just ease your hands high over your head real slow like, and I'll keep my trigger finger steady. Nobody gets hurt. Especially you."

The man's hands rose above his head, and he didn't turn around. Walt said, "That's right . . ."

Then the Pontiac's horn sounded. The noise startled me, and I turned to see Inverness in the front seat of the car with her feet pressed against the horn. "She jumped over the seat!" I said to no one. The horn continued to blare.

Things got bad for Walt.

The man who came looking for Inverness seemed to sense that Walt had turned to look at his car. Walt left himself vulnerable, and the man knew it. At probably five ten and no more than a hundred and fifty pounds, the man's quickness overcame Walt. He delivered three blows, using his opened right and left hands to Walt's face and head. Walt dropped his gun and reached to pick it up, but the man used his right leg to kick Walt hard and flush on his forehead.

Walt collapsed on the floor next to the entrance to the women's bathroom. Ten seconds earlier he'd stuck his gun in the man's back.

I ran to where Walt now lay and as I did, the man picked up Walt's gun and fired two shots into his chest.

"No! No!" I screamed.

"You're next," the man pointed Walt's gun a foot from my face. "You follow me, and you'll be like him." He nodded his head toward Walt but kept the gun in my face. Then he turned and ran toward the two U-Hauls and the others waiting for him and Inverness.

I knelt next to Walt as Joseph pulled Inverness from the Pontiac to stop the horn from blaring. Then he and Abby walked her to the bathroom with Abby carrying Joseph's rifle. Blood flowed down Walt's chest. More than it did when the hog attacked him.

Inverness's mouth and hands remained taped, and Joseph opened the restroom door, pushed her inside and closed the door. Now the three of us knelt next to Walt. It appeared that both shots entered near his left shoulder.

"I am sorry this keeps happening to you," Joseph said. "I am so sorry my friend."

Walt's eyes were open wide, and he groaned and looked at Joseph. "Don't be sorry, just don't let me bleed out, Mingo." Walt put his right hand over the bullet holes. "There's some old newspapers in the Pontiac. Get 'em. Bring the tape . . ."

Walt's eyes flickered and he moaned again, then his eyes closed altogether. His breathing remained uneven. I ran to the car and grabbed the newspapers from the backseat. Abby got the duct tape, and I folded the papers and placed them over the bullet holes. We wrapped the tape tight over the papers and around Walt's upper body a few times to try to stop the bleeding.

A few seconds after the taping, Walt opened his eyes and spoke. "This shit hurts a lot worse than what that hog did to me. I'm tired of bleeding. I'm tired . . ."

Joseph placed his right hand over Walt's forehead and said, "I know what it feels like to be shot. I know it hurts. You are not going to die."

"I will if you don't take your hand off my forehead. That's where that sonofabitch kicked me. It hurts like hell, too. A bunch of Kung Fu bullshit."

"Sorry my friend," Joseph said. "I do think the bullets went all the way through you, though. No vital organs hit."

"Feels like my whole shoulder's burning up. You owe me big-time when this is over. All of us." Walt glanced at me then at Abby.

"I'm going to call an ambulance," Abby said. "Either that or we're driving out of here and back up to Crawfordville to that clinic."

"They won't let us out of here now," I said. "We still got Inverness and they know now that we know what has happened. We're witnesses to everything."

"No!" Walt said. "You ain't doin' that. Don't call an ambulance. Let's finish it . . ."

"Walt, I don't care what you say," Abby said. "I'm calling an ambulance. It may be thirty minutes or more before they get here. By then, this thing is over one way or the other."

"You'll put those EMT's in danger," Walt said. "Don't do it. Wait until it's over."

"It will be over by then," Abby said. "It has to be. You need help."

Abby leaned Joseph's rifle against the side of the restroom and turned to go to the phone booth and I said, "Here, take this. Call him, too." I gave her a piece of paper with the phone number for FBI Agent Roland East in Crawfordville, the contact we got from Agent Ed

Hanahan in Albany, our friend I'd spoken to earlier from the Lagoon Motel. "You just tell him if they want to arrest Lu Doc and a couple other murderers to come to the lighthouse." Abby took the paper and ran toward the phone.

"Walt, John, I am going to let Inverness go," Joseph said. "Maybe they will leave then. Walt needs a doctor." Before we could answer, Joseph went into the restroom and returned with Inverness. She struggled to get away from him, trying to head-butt Joseph the same as she'd done to Walt earlier.

"I don't know about this," Walt said. "I wouldn't do it, Mingo. She may be our winning card. Ace in the hole. We best hang on to her. I'm okay, ain't gonna die here. What do you think, John?"

"I'm with Walt," I said. "Hang on to her. For now. We may have to trade her for the ambulance."

Then we heard one of the trucks start. Three seconds later the other one did. The taillights of the BMW came on. They were leaving. All of them.

"Maybe they don't give a shit about pretty little Inverness after all," Walt said. "Looks like you ain't gonna get your Bentley, little girl. That's a dirty, rotten shame."

She tried to pull away from Joseph but couldn't, and he opened the restroom door and pushed her back inside and closed the door.

"Get your rifle, Mingo. You can't let them get away," Walt said. "You may not have another opportunity to prove you're innocent. Take it."

CHAPTER 30

Abby returned from the phone and said both an ambulance and Agent East were on the way to the lighthouse. The two trucks were following the BMW out of the parking lot and back toward the entrance road. Then Inverness kicked the bathroom door a few times and stopped.

A half dozen security lights along the entrance road were now on, and we could easily see any vehicles coming and going. The BMW approached the parking lot exit, then onto the access road. The first truck moved slowly a couple of hundred feet behind the car and the second truck just a few feet behind the first truck.

We stopped Walt's bleeding and leaned him upright against the cinder-block wall of the bathroom, and he saw the vehicles on the move like we did. "Mingo, you're gonna have to move," Walt said. "You either use that rifle now or chase 'em up the road. Better do it here. No good to wait."

"I will do it right here."

Joseph positioned himself on the side of Walt's pickup and pressed the weapon against his right shoulder. Abby stood next to Walt, and I was about twenty feet behind Joseph. Inverness again kicked the door three times then stopped. All three vehicles were clearly in view.

A few seconds later, Joseph fired.

Right after that, the BMW exploded.

An orange fireball engulfed the front part of the car. Flames shot thirty feet above it. No one could survive that blast. Tran and Growdy were dead and Joseph had just killed them. Now he *was* a murderer.

"Holy mother of God!" Walt said. "You hit the gas tank, didn't you?"

"No, I hit the front tire on the passenger's side." Joseph set the butt of his rifle on the asphalt and stared at the burning BMW. He looked back at us, then again at the burning car. "Not the gas tank. I did not hit the gas tank. Only the tire. I know what I did."

"Never seen you miss," Walt said.

"I didn't miss this time, either. I did not hit the gas tank."

"Must have. Look at that car. Those men are dead."

"My shot was true. The car was moving, but I allowed for that when I aimed. Somebody planted a bomb in that car. I have seen the same kind of explosions on the streets of Saigon. Many times."

A few seconds after the blast, the last truck, the one that they unloaded, pulled around the first truck and the burning BMW and disappeared down the road. The driver pressed the accelerator hard, and we heard the roar of the truck over the burning BMW.

The first truck, the one we thought to be driven by Lu Doc, stopped after the explosion. Then a few seconds later, it slowly approached the burning car, got within thirty feet of it and stopped again. The driver got out of the truck.

He walked to the flaming BMW with a long, slender object. Like a flagpole or something used to reach and trim a high branch. The driver's side door had been blown off and landed on the other side of the road about ten feet from the car. Because of the flames, I couldn't see the driver or the passenger. Presumably Tran and Growdy.

The man from the truck stuck the long object inside the car through the driver's side, kept it there only a few seconds and pulled it out with something attached to the end of it. The brief case we'd seen them exchange earlier? That's what it looked like to me.

Abby stepped away from Walt and saw what I'd seen. "He's got the money and the bones now," she said. "It was all planned that way. Joseph didn't blow up that car. Someone else did. Lu Doc blew that car up. He's got it all, now. Lu Doc or whoever it is."

"That will not last," Joseph said.

He raised his rifle again to his right shoulder, braced against Walt's pickup, and by the time the driver of the truck was back in his cab with the brief case from the burning BMW, Joseph had fired. He set the gun down, and we watched the truck drive away.

"At least it didn't blow up," Walt said. "You better follow 'em. If he gets away, we'll never get you out of this mess. We're all in it now. All covered up in it."

"He will not get far. I hit the tire. Just like the first one."

"Let's go, Joseph. I'll go with you," I said. "We can't let this guy get outta here."

"Don't wait any longer," Abby said. "I'll take care of Walt. Go."

"We've been lucky so far," I said.

"That's right," she said. "Keep it that way."

Joseph got the keys to the pickup from Walt and gave them to me. "Here, you drive. We've got to move now. We will catch him."

Before we left, we quickly unhitched the boat trailer from the truck and pushed it out of the way. We got in and took off.

We passed the burning BMW, the flames still visible and the two dead men inside. Down a long stretch of the road, we saw the taillights of the U-Haul, moving slowly and probably a mile or so ahead of us.

Joseph placed his rifle across his lap, the barrel pointed out the window.

"He's not getting away," I said, both hands tight on the wheel.

We were gaining on him fast.

CHAPTER 31

The truck stopped about two hundred yards in front of us near a section of the road that curved south toward the Gulf. After another quarter mile or so, the road veered almost due north in the direction of U. S. Highway 98. There looked to be another big vehicle parked in front of the truck we were following.

Two U-Hauls again.

I slowed down and pulled over to the right shoulder near tall reeds and stopped adjacent to a marshy area. I rolled the window down and the breeze and smell of saltwater, for only a second or two, took my mind away from the danger we'd accepted. A few seconds only.

"Is that the other U-Haul?" I said. "You see it, don't you? The one in front of Lu Doc? If it is Lu Doc."

"I do see it, and I think it is."

"I thought they were gone for good."

"They must be working together. Everybody in the trucks against Tran and Growdy. Those are the two teams. One team is dead now."

"It was all planned. Blow up the BMW, take the money they gave to Tran and Growdy and leave with it and the bones."

"They just didn't expect someone to shoot out the tire," he said. "But now they know we are back here."

"Now what?"

"Nothing has changed. We have got to disable the truck. The one in front of us. If we can do that, that may give the FBI time to get here. If I can hit that truck, they will be able to travel only on foot."

"If you can't?"

"Then they get out of here with what they came for."

"Inverness. She's probably still kicking the bathroom door."

"Probably is."

A few seconds later, we saw what we'd seen earlier near the lighthouse. A group of men quickly unloading and loading boxes from one truck to another.

"Now they go right back in the truck they came in," I said.

The unloading and loading continued. "I do not have a good angle here to shoot. I have to move that way." He pointed to a public boat ramp across the road and about fifty yards away. "From over there, I may have a better angle."

"Go, then. They'll be done in a minute or two. They're either leaving or coming after us when they're through loading."

"I will shoot from over there. You stay here. I'll be right back."

"I'll be here."

We got out of the truck and I walked to the back of it and stood behind the bed and felt a little safer there. I could see where Joseph was headed as the activity around the two trucks continued.

"Good luck."

He nodded and ran across the street carrying his rifle low in his right hand. He positioned himself next to a group of trees just twenty or thirty feet from the road. He pressed the gun against his shoulder, the same way he did earlier when he shot the BMW and it exploded. I didn't see any people or vehicles or boats at the dock. It all looked quiet.

I waited for a gunshot. A few seconds passed and I hadn't heard one. Too much movement around the trucks, I thought. A few moments later, still no gunshot, and it looked as if they'd completed the unloading and loading of the trucks. For the second time that night. Then I saw someone walk toward the truck closest to me, the one with the tire already shot out. The person stood by the side of the truck and lifted something to his shoulder. Maybe a gun.

I knelt down behind the bed of the truck, out of the line of fire.

*

The next thing I remember, Joseph stood over me as I lay in the tall grass on the side of the road near Walt's truck. I smelled smoke and saw that the front of the truck was burning. My head was pounding and my ears ringing.

"Can you hear me?" Joseph said leaning about three feet from my face.

"Yeah, I can. But I got an awful headache."

"Had the same feeling a lot in Vietnam. You are not bleeding. You hurt anywhere? Legs? Arms?"

"Just my head."

"It will go away soon."

"Walt's gonna be pissed about his truck."

"He's always pissed about something. Do not think of him. He can buy himself a new one."

"We still gotta stop the other truck. Go. Do it. I'm okay now. We can't let them get outta here."

"They are already gone. That one good truck has left. Everybody got in it. I could not get a clear shot on the tires."

"Shit!"

"I said that, too."

"We need the Pontiac."

"Yes, we . . ."

We turned at the same time and saw two headlights racing toward us. It was Abby in the Bonneville. She parked a few feet behind Walt's truck, ran to me and knelt beside me and gently grabbed my right hand.

"How bad are you?"

"Better now that I see you."

"Anything broken? Are you bleeding?"

"Walt's truck is broken, not me. I'm not bleeding. How is Walt?"

"He's fine. We heard the explosion and I had to come."

"They fired something big at me. But the truck got the worst of it." Abby looked at the truck's mangled hood, flames shooting out from underneath it. Then she focused again on me.

"Lucky."

"Can't help it. I got you."

"Sounded like a Thumper," Joseph said.

"What?" I said.

"Thumper. That's the nickname for the M79 grenade launcher that we used in Vietnam. I think that's what they tried to kill you with. Looks like the kind of damage it could do from a few hundred yards. You were lucky. It just knocked you back several feet on your butt."

"At least I know its name. Thumper. If you're trying to kill me, I need to know your name. Now help me up. We got to find that truck."

"You sure?" Abby said. "Can you move?"

"Yeah, I'm sure." I extended both arms to Abby and Joseph and they helped me up. "Put me in the backseat."

They did. Abby drove with Joseph up front.

We left Walt's truck smoldering and drove toward the men in the U-Haul, with the money and the bones.

They were just up ahead.

CHAPTER 32

Abby pressed the accelerator hard, and my head jerked backwards and bounced off the seat like a white ball in a pinball machine. It made my headache worse.

"You tryin' to kill me back here?"

"No, somebody else is trying to. I'm trying to catch up with that truck."

"I feel like the Pinball Wizard."

"Just hang on tight," she said. "This shouldn't take us long."

"I got a shortcut for us," Joseph said.

"Where?" she said.

"There's a dirt road coming up on your left. Take it." He pointed across the dashboard and five seconds later, Abby slowed and made the turn.

"Where's this take us?" she said.

"We will beat them to the highway," he said. "It cuts off a few miles, then intersects with the lighthouse road. The same one they're now on."

"Not if they took this shortcut, too," Abby said. "They could have."

"Probably they didn't," Joseph said. "Even if they know about it, it is narrow and full of potholes. Big potholes. Might not want to take a truck down it. It is possible, though, that I'm wrong. We shall find out."

Once on the dirt road, Abby kept her speed around ten miles-an-hour. I could've reached through either one of the back windows and pulled leaves off of trees. The kind of thing I would've done as a boy and enjoyed it. She couldn't avoid hitting some of the potholes, big ones too. I used my right arm and braced myself against the back of the front seat. This helped some, but it was an awful ride.

Without any street lights along the dirt road, thick darkness covered the woods. A Bob Dylan line came to me: *"Darkness at the break of noon/Shadows even the silver spoon."* In an instant, it was gone.

"Another two miles or so, and the road bends to the left," Joseph said. "After that, there is a big, big pothole in the middle of the road. I suggest you veer to the right to avoid it. That intersection we are heading toward is just beyond the pothole."

"What do you want me to do at the intersection?" Abby said.

"Block it."

"What?"

"Drive the car to the middle of the road and stop it," he said. "We'll get out and take our positions in the trees, out of sight, along the road. We will wait in the trees."

"This only works if we beat them to the intersection," Abby said. "Right?"

"That's right."

"You're not worried about other cars?" I said.

"I would be, but usually this time of day there are very few," he said. "We have got to stay lucky. There are too many things to worry about, so don't worry about any of them."

"I'll do my best," I said.

"Me too," Abby said.

"Think of Panther and not what might worry you," Joseph said. "I know that's difficult. Always think of Panther."

We were quiet for the next few moments. I kept my focus through the front windshield and Abby eased to the right shoulder, a couple of tires in the weeds, to avoid the pothole Joseph warned her about. We were close to the intersection.

She leaned over the steering wheel and reminded me of the way my father used to drive on long trips when he grew tired from several hours on the road. She was focused. Joseph kept his rifle on his lap, barrel pointed out the window. The same way he did when we were together in Walt's truck. His head motionless, eyes straight away. The look of Panther.

Then Joseph said, "There's the road that runs to the lighthouse. You see it?" He pointed again over the dashboard. "Just up ahead."

"I do," Abby said. "I got it."

"Drive to the middle of the road and park," he said. "Just a little more luck. That is all we need. No worries."

She drove a little faster, maybe twenty or twenty-five, hit a couple of small potholes, then stopped when the dirt turned to asphalt. We all looked both ways. Nothing coming. She drove to the middle of the road and parked. We got out and jogged to the side of the road, Joseph with his rifle in hand, and stopped behind a line of trees. My head felt better, my thoughts were clear again.

"We can't be seen from here," Joseph said. "If they decide to go through Walt's Pontiac, that will give me time to hit a tire. The truck will not leave this spot."

We waited and watched. A few moments later, a vehicle approached heading toward the lighthouse. I saw it first and said, "Look, there's traffic tonight."

We watched the headlights get closer to Walt's car. The oncoming vehicle stopped about thirty feet from the Pontiac. It looked to be a big four-door sedan, maybe an LTD Ford. The driver got out and placed a red flashing light, the kind the police use, on top of the car. Someone else got out from the passenger side. The men didn't appear to be wearing law enforcement uniforms, but I wasn't certain.

"Cops?" Abby said.

"Could be," Joseph said, his rifle leaning against an oak tree. "The kind without uniforms."

I took five steps toward the men for a closer look and realized who it was. "That's Ed. Ed Hanahan from Albany. The other guy must be the agent from Crawfordville."

"We're still lucky, aren't we?" Abby said.

"Must be," Joseph said.

"*Ed!* It's us," I said. "We're coming out." We walked toward the big car with the red light on top and Ed and the other man met us halfway.

"Didn't expect to see you," Abby said. "But we're sure glad you're here."

"You two are just havin' all the fun down here in Florida, aren't you?" Ed said. "I just didn't want to miss out." He smiled and used his right hand to tap the thirty-eight he kept in his shoulder holster.

Ed introduced us to Agent Roland East, and Abby introduced Joseph to the two FBI men. We explained the situation to them about the U-Haul. "Joseph, you hang around with these two, there's gonna be trouble," Ed said. "Wherever they go, they find it."

Before Joseph could answer, we heard the sound of a vehicle coming from the opposite direction, coming from the lighthouse. A few seconds later, we saw the U-Haul.

"That's them," Abby said. "Your shortcut worked, Joseph."

He said nothing and kept steady eyes on the oncoming truck.

The U-Haul stopped a couple hundred yards or so from the Pontiac and the LTD, and kept its headlights on. At least three men got out of the truck, walked to the front of it and looked toward us.

"You think Lu Doc is one of them?" Roland said. "Were you able to get a positive ID on him?"

"We're not certain, but a lot of evidence points to him," Abby said. "I think your man is down there." She nodded in that direction.

"Be careful, they got a Thumper," I said.

"Thumper?" Ed said. "What the hell's that?"

"A M79 grenade launcher, like what the Army used in Vietnam," I said.

"We are out-gunned, then," Ed said. "That's not standard FBI issue. You guys head back into those trees and let us handle this. *Don't* get in the middle of this." He looked at me than at Abby. "I know you two. Do what I say."

"All right," she said. "No argument from us this time."

"Joseph, make sure they stay behind those trees with you, would you?" Ed said. "I don't trust those two. Never will. They can't just write a story, they got to get right in the middle of it when it's happening."

"Yes, that's one thing I've learned about them, too," Joseph said and he pointed toward the tree line we'd come out of. "But they did save my life. We will do what you say." The three of us jogged back into the woods.

I stood next to Abby with Joseph a few feet behind us. We were maybe fifty yards from the two parked cars on the road. We watched the U-Haul and the men who'd gotten out of it.

Ed and Roland hustled to their car, opened the trunk and put on bullet-proof vests and removed two shotguns. They stood behind Roland's car. Walt's Pontiac now separated the two FBI agents from the violent men in the U-Haul.

"How are they going to stop that Thumper?" I said. "What would you do, Joseph?" Thirty seconds passed and Joseph hadn't answered. Abby and I kept a straight lookout. Didn't turn around to look at Joseph.

I tried again. "What do you think? How do you defend against a grenade launcher?"

Still no answer.

Thirty more seconds passed, and I turned around.

Joseph was gone. His rifle leaning against an oak tree.

We looked in the direction of the U-Haul and didn't see him. He'd cut through the trees, he's going after the men in the truck, I thought.

Then we heard that familiar screeching, high-pitched sound from a couple of nights ago along the Aucilla when he seemed to effortlessly dispatch those two men chasing us on the trail. The howling paused for a few seconds, then started again.

The return of Panther.

The armed men in the U-Haul stood behind the opened doors. A few moments later, someone fired the Thumper and the trunk of Walt's Pontiac exploded, orange flames coming out of it and extending into the night sky.

"Ed and Roland better get the hell outta there," I said. "They can't handle that. They better get outta there. We warned them."

Then another round from the Thumper. This one landed in the middle of Roland's car. I couldn't tell if Roland and Ed were hurt, but I did see what happened next at the U-Haul.

Joseph had looped around the truck and came behind unseen and unarmed. There were two men behind the driver's door in firing positions, with their backs to Joseph. The one to his right fell quickly from repeated blows from Joseph to the man's head and neck. The one on the left turned and experienced the same fate.

It was the same way he'd handled the racist biker at the Lucky Seven.

They both were lying on the ground when Joseph eased behind the truck and to the other side. We couldn't see what happened over there. But the next thing we saw, was Joseph in the front of the truck waving us on.

CHAPTER 33

Ed and Roland handcuffed the three men lying in the road next to the truck, and a few moments later they gained consciousness, one by one. The men who tried to kill us. We stood several feet away from the truck and watched the FBI agents work.

The backup help Roland had called arrived in the form of four patrol cars from the Wakulla County Sheriff's Office. Two of the cars were used to transport the suspects to the jail in Crawfordville. The two others remained with us along the lighthouse access road.

"You wanna take a look inside?" Ed said as he stood next to the U-Haul. "Maybe find what you've been looking for these last few days?"

"We're not going to say no to that," Abby said. "After what we've been through, you might say we deserve it. At least Joseph does."

The U-Haul contained thirteen wooden boxes, all looked to be about the same size. They were about six feet by three feet and probably two-feet deep. The boxes were not locked and were easy to open.

They were full of tusks and bones pulled from the bottom of the Aucilla River at the Big Hole. All this killing and framing Joseph with a double murder was connected with these giant mammals, or *mammuthus columbi,* that once lived in the Florida Panhandle and were hunted by Paleolithic man

"How old are these bones anyway?" Ed said. "Got any idea?"

"Maybe fifteen thousand years old," Joseph said. "On one dive I found old tools, knives, and other things used by hunters probably to skin these animals. That part of the river may once have been a watering hole for them. There the hunters waited."

"How deep of water were you in?" Roland said.

"Thirty or forty feet," Joseph said.

"Must be a different world down there," Ed said.

"On that river bottom, I found a time machine," Joseph said. "These bones will re-write the history of Florida and America. The discovery puts human in this area centuries and centuries before what is now accepted. That's what we believe, now."

Roland looked at the three handcuffed men and the two burning vehicles and said, "Well, they sure caused one helluva mess tonight."

*

After we looked at the boxes full of bones, Roland found a metal fire-proof briefcase in the cab of the truck. It remained intact after the explosion that killed Tran and Growdy inside the BMW. Like the long boxes, it was easy to open. After a quick preliminary count, Roland estimated around four hundred thousand dollars.

"This group got the money and the bones?" Roland said. "Is that the way it all went down? That's what you saw? It seems like somebody got screwed over, right?"

"That's about right," Abby said. "There was an exchange made at the lighthouse. Two U-Haul trucks pulled in and boxes from one were loaded on the other. During the exchange, we saw what looked to be that briefcase."

"Who got screwed?" Ed said.

"You'll find two bodies back there in a blown-up BMW," I said. "One's a Vietnamese guy who ran a fishing charter in Panama City. His name is Harry Tran. Or that's what we know him by. The other is probably an archeologist from FSU. Dr. Zibe Growdy. They had the bones and traded them for the money."

"That's a helluva an odd couple," Ed said. "But this is Florida. Some wild shit can happen down here. We should never be surprised."

"Then these guys, the ones that Joseph took out, blew up the BMW and took the money they'd just given them?" Roland said. "I get that right?"

"You got it," I said. "They blew up Walt's pickup, too. It's back there near the lighthouse. Joseph said they used the Thumper. It nearly blew me away."

"Well, I'll be damned," Roland said.

"And then some," I said.

Roland then turned to Joseph. "We didn't see how you did it, but you did it. Thanks for risking your life for ours." The two men shook hands.

"As I have said before, they did the same for me," Joseph said tilting his head toward Abby and me. "They pulled me out of the Aucilla after these men shot me in the head. My luck still holds because of those two."

From the north we heard a siren, and a few moments later an ambulance stopped suddenly behind Roland's LTD, still smoldering from the Thumper's blast.

"Anyone call an ambulance?" Ed said.

"I did at the lighthouse," Abby said. "Walt needs them. I called them the same time I called Agent East. They need to get Walt to the hospital. I'll let them know how to find him."

Abby explained the situation to the ambulance driver, who then drove the vehicle off road and around the LTD, the Pontiac and U-Haul. A few minutes later, the ambulance was transporting Walt to Tallahassee Memorial Health Care.

"We need to follow that ambulance," Joseph said. "Walt will not die, but we need to be with him at the hospital. He has risked his life for me, the same as you two."

"We can see Walt tomorrow," Abby said. "We're all just hanging on here, barely. We need rest. Peace. They're taking Walt to Tallahassee Memorial. They'll probably sedate him on the way."

"Give me a number I can reach you later tonight," Roland said. "I'll call the hospital for you and get an update. He'll get good care there. I've got a couple of good sources there who've helped me in the past."

"Okay, we'll do it that way," Joseph said. Roland gave Joseph a pen and a small black and white notebook that he wrote Walt's phone number in.

"I'll call you as soon as I know something," Roland said.

"We still got Inverness — Inverness Cousins — back at the lighthouse," I said. "She's taped and inside the women's restroom."

"Which side was she on?" Ed said.

"Both sides," I said. "She killed her boyfriend and a Jefferson County Sheriff's deputy and ended up with these men you're hauling away. Said she was Lu Doc's girl. He was going buy her a Bentley. Make her queen of everything. Queen of the world."

"We'll see what Lu Doc has to say about that and a lot of other things," Roland said. "I'll send one of these deputies to get her." Roland talked to a deputy who followed the same path in his patrol car that the ambulance had taken to the lighthouse.

Abby turned to Ed. "We need a ride to Walt's house. Can you help us out?"

"I think we can arrange that. Since you three are the vigilantes who seemed to have captured one of the most god-awful criminals on the Gulf coast."

"Walt, too," she said. "He's part of this team."

"We'll get you out of here, but I need you to come by the sheriff's office tomorrow morning in Crawfordville," Ed said. "Say about ten, if you can. We're going to need a full statement. Then you can head up to Tallahassee to see your friend."

"We can do that," Abby said. "Walt had a car and a truck before tonight, but neither are fit to drive now. John's car is at Walt's house. All we have is our legs, and we're tired. Awful tired."

"We'll take care of it," Ed said.

Roland instructed the remaining deputy to take us to Walt's house. He and Ed drove the U-Haul, with its cargo of bones, to the sheriff's office in Crawfordville. Less than an hour after Joseph had knocked out the men firing weapons from the U-Haul, we were sitting again at Walt's kitchen counter.

Finally, it was over. Some fishing trip it had been. Should've gone to Disney Land. Maybe a weekend in Atlanta.

I poured myself a long Crown Royal, certainly Walt would approve, and found a bottle of Chardonnay, opened it and poured Abby a glass. Joseph drank the rest of the iced tea from earlier that day.

We sat at the counter for several minutes and didn't say much. All three of us exhausted and relieved. We felt safe for the first time in three days. Agent Roland East called and told Abby that Walt was in "good" condition in the hospital, didn't need surgery and would likely be released in a few days. We raised our glasses and toasted Walt.

After we finished our drinks it was around ten-thirty. Joseph slept in Walt's bedroom, and we took the guest bedroom. I opened the window near the bed and a cool and clean breeze came through. I could hear the rustling of Walt's big palm plants in his backyard.

It reminded me of the palm trees at the lighthouse, wind-blown just moments before Joseph shot the BMW's tire and the car blew up killing Tran and Growdy inside. That was the last thing I thought about before I fell asleep with my arms wrapped around Abby.

We woke up together about eight o'clock and in the same position.

CHAPTER 34

About eight-thirty that Monday morning, thirty minutes after we were supposed to have returned to the *Albany Chronicle* newsroom, I called our editor, Mickey Burke.

For the next ten minutes I explained to him how our weekend getaway along the Florida Panhandle played out. We'd told him where we were going before we left Albany. He asked a few questions during my story, had me repeat a few parts. Specifically, the ones about us seeing Harry Tran murder J. W. Wingfield and Bubba Fanning, and Inverness Cousins murder Ivan Wingfield and Deputy Dwight Leach. And seeing someone murder Jerry Dao, the owner of the Lucky Seven. Probably Lu Doc.

"Goddamn, Maynard! This is a helluva story. I'm going to send a photographer down there to work with you two. It'll probably be Tommy Clarkson. We'll need plenty of art. He'll bring some money for you to stay in a hotel for a few days. Meal money, too. You'll have something for tomorrow's paper, right? Helluva fuckin' story."

"We will. We're headed up to the Wakulla County Sheriff's Office in Crawfordville to answer their questions. Ed and the other agent want us there. After that we've got to check on Walt Gosser. He's in a Tallahassee hospital."

"I'll send Clarkson to the sheriff's office. He should be there by eleven-thirty or so."

"Okay, we'll be on the lookout for him."

"This is gonna be picked up by the AP, you know that don't you? This sonofabitch of a story will fly all over the country. Maybe farther . . . goddamn, what a story, Maynard."

"We talked about that. There's going to be a lot of interest in this, not just because of the killings and the organized crime aspect of it.

From what we've learned so far, these are new scientific discoveries. People all over the world will be interested."

"You just call me if you need something. I want you two down there at least a few days. After that, we'll see. There's a lot we can do with this. Follow-ups, features. We'll need to stay on it. We'll cover any criminal trials as well."

"Okay, I got it. All of this after we caught a few fish Thursday afternoon."

"Just like goddamn Ernest Hemingway."

"Abby will like that."

"Tell her I said it and tell her great work. You two stay in touch with me. Stay safe down there, Maynard."

"Thanks. We will."

I told Abby what Mickey said, including the reference to Hemingway, one of her favorite writers.

"How many times did he say 'goddamn'?" Abby said.

"His usual. I lost count."

"I bet he wants a story by this afternoon."

"You know he does. Here's the best part. He's sending Tommy Clarkson with some money to put us up in a hotel a few days, so we can do a few follow-ups. He wants a lot of art."

"More time on the coast. That could be dangerous."

"Don't even say it. Maybe we can have some fun this time," I said.

"I bet his eyes lit up when you told him the story. His head weaved all around while he was smoking his Marlboros and drinking coffee. Ashes falling all around his desk. One day he's going to burn down the newsroom. I can see him now. Happiest man in the world. Newspaper ink, like blood in his veins."

"He'll be tap dancing all day and into tomorrow. Two or three gin and tonics at lunch."

"We've seen that look before," she said.

"After we visit Walt, we're going to have find a hotel, do some writing, and call it in to the paper."

"Wish we had a typewriter," Abby said. "Maybe Joseph or Walt has one. If not, we'll just write it long hand. Around a thousand words ought to be plenty."

"If that much."

"We'll get quotes from Ed and Roland, maybe the county sheriff. And Joseph. We can talk about the follow-ups tonight over some good food and wine."

"Sounds like a plan," I said. "A good one. It's going to be time for you and me to have a little fun."

"That's why we came down here."

*

Joseph cooked eggs, bacon, and hash browns, made a pot of strong coffee, and we ate in Walt's kitchen with the bright morning light filtering through the windows. Birds were singing under crisp blue skies. A few minutes later we left in my car for Crawfordville, and it was the most relaxing drive we'd had since we drove down from Albany last Thursday.

We met Ed and Roland at the sheriff's office. They found an empty room in the back with a long white table and black folding chairs. The room had nothing on the walls but chipped gray paint, and a blue water dispenser in one corner and a coffee pot in another. Roland lit a Winston and poured everyone a cup of coffee in large white Styrofoam cups. The three of us sat across from the two FBI agents.

They asked us questions for about forty-five minutes, then we signed statements authenticating what had happened the last few days since we pulled Joseph from the Aucilla. They used a tape recorder and both agents took notes with black pens on big yellow notepads.

Abby told them we planned to file a story later that day, calling it in over the phone to one of our editors at the *Chronicle*. We then asked Ed and Roland questions about the arrests they made, getting quotes on the record for our story. We didn't have a tape recorder and never used one like some reporters did. We believed they could make a source nervous. Even when you put away your notepad and pen, people seemed more relaxed and gave you more information for a story than they would otherwise. We always relied on good notes, though, and double and triple checked what was said during interviews.

Roland said he made a few phone calls earlier that morning, including to FBI agents on the West Coast, and after estimating how much the mammoth bones in the truck weighed, their street value for traditional medicine and other uses might have been more than a million dollars.

"Can you believe that?" Roland said. "All that money for grinding up bones?"

"Yes, I can," Joseph said. "It is animal magic. I understand it."

Earlier that morning they'd questioned Lu Doc, the other two men, and Inverness Cousins.

"What did you get out of Lu Doc?" Abby said.

"Same thing that's in that cup," Roland said, pointing to his empty coffee cup. "Nothing from nothing leaves nothing, as someone once said. We gave Doc his one phone call, and he said a team of lawyers is flying in from New Orleans. Since then, he's said about as much as a dead man."

"What about the other men?" she said.

"Different story there," Roland said. "We identified the two others, both refugees from South Vietnam. Said they were hired out of Mobile. Both of them were eager to talk. They've worked for Lu Doc before this weekend and they both got criminal records. Minor stuff. Drugs mainly. They spoke fairly good English. So far, they haven't asked for a lawyer. They've confessed."

Roland showed us the names, ages, and addresses of the two suspects on a piece of paper and the criminal charges against them. We both copied the information. "Can you tell us anything they told you?" I said. "Any quotes we can use?"

"Anything else we give you two has to be off the record for now," Ed said. "There are a lot of things we need to confirm before we can give you more to print. I know you two appreciate the complexity of all this — you've seen it up close."

"We understand," Abby said. "Off the record, what did you get from the two men?"

"They said Doc had a buyer for the bones in San Francisco," Roland said. "The plan was to drive the truck to the West Coast. Delivery was scheduled for the end of the week. We got an address from them — but they said they didn't have any names — and we've contacted our office in San Francisco."

"So that was the plan all along?" I said. "The market for these bones is the West Coast?"

"That's what they said," Roland said. "For medicinal purposes and as an aphrodisiac. They said that, too. Both suspects said the same thing. We interviewed them separately. They'll go to prison for a long time but not quite as long as they could have, since they're cooperating. We'll start with attempted murder. They admitted to firing the grenade launcher."

"How do Harry Tran and Ivan Wingfield and Deputy Dwight Leach play into all of this?" Abby said.

"We're still off the record," Roland said.

"Until you say otherwise," I said. "What about Jerry Dao and the FSU professor. Zibe Growdy?"

"It's just going to take some time to pull all this together," Ed said. "You understand that. We want to sort out how exactly it all happened. And who did what when."

"What do you think at this point?" I said. "Walt still doesn't know who hit him in the head in his own home."

"This is based on what Inverness told us," Roland said. "She didn't request an attorney, either. Not yet anyway. She confessed to killing Wingfield and Leach but hasn't said anything about Walt Gosser. She's been charged with double murder. Probably other charges later.

"We saw all of that," I said.

"We just don't want to release that to the public yet," Roland said. "We're still working with her. There's more we think she can tell us. This is complicated."

"We've been saying that for the last few days," Abby said.

Here's what Roland told us they got from Inverness. During one of Joseph's dives at the Big Hole, Ivan and Inverness were having sex along the banks of the Aucilla and saw Joseph putting the big bones in his boat. She said Joseph didn't see them.

Ivan was already pissed because a few weeks before that day, his grandfather, J. W. Wingfield, owner of the Bearded Clam, told him he was dying of cancer, and Ivan wouldn't inherit the store or the land. Ivan was jealous of Freddy "Bubba" Fanning and thought he'd be in the will because J. W. often spent a lot of time with him. More time than he spent with Ivan. Ivan convinced Deputy Leach to help him with his scheme. That wasn't hard to do. Leach could be easily swayed by Ivan.

"Ivan wasn't excited about his future job at the state nature preserve?" Abby said sarcastically.

"Not according to Inverness," Roland said.

Roland continued his story. Ivan had known Harry Tran for a few years and often bought marijuana from him, sometimes three or four pounds at a time. Then Ivan sold it to folks he knew along the Aucilla. The two had met through a mutual friend who was in the drug trade, Inverness said.

"Inverness told us she'd been seeing Tran on the side and sometimes had sex with him on his boats," Roland said. "Tran traded cocaine for the sex. She said Ivan knew and didn't care."

"She spoke with pride about her full range of experiences along the Panhandle," Ed said.

"Sounds like Inverness stayed pretty busy around here," I said. "Happy little mermaid."

"Wait, it gets better," Ed said. "Or worse, depending on your perspective."

Ivan told Tran about Joseph and the bones, then Tran and Ivan and a few men Tran hired, dove the Big Hole and found the bones. Tran knew Jerry Dao and knew that Dao could contact Lu Doc, who might be interested in buying what they found. Dao was the go-between for Tran and Lu Doc.

Like the FBI agents said, this was complicated.

Jerry Dao was the man who owned the Lucky Seven, the titty-bar in Panama City where Joseph did to a biker what he'd done to the men on the river-trail and the ones in the U-Haul not far from St. Marks Lighthouse. Panther struck hard those nights. And it was Dao who was shot dead, we know because we saw it, at a fishing dock by a man in a boat.

"According to Inverness," Ed said. "Lu Doc swung the deal with Jerry Dao and Tran knowing all along he was going to kill Dao. He was concerned about Dao moving in on some of Doc's territory. Drugs, prostitution, gambling — selling animal bones. Everything."

"You think that was Lu Doc who shot Dao?" I said. "We saw all of that."

"Probably. If not, someone who Doc ordered to do it," Roland said.

"This is more than just *complicated*," I said.

"Right. We don't have it all pieced together yet, like we said," Roland said. "It's going to take some time. But it'll all flush out if we have to take that sonofabitch to trial. We hope, of course, he confesses for a lesser sentence before it gets to that point."

"Let me finish it out for you," Ed said. "Inverness . . ."

"Let me guess," Abby said. "Sweet little Inverness screws Lu Doc, too."

In a wonderfully fake southern accent, Ed said, *"Well, I declare Miss Sinclair, you mighty smart for a lady. Mighty, mighty smart."*

No comment from Abby.

"She finally found true love?" I said.

"You can say it that way if you want to," Roland said. "That girl was cussin' up a hurricane last night. Still cussin' this morning. Said Lu Doc promised her a Bentley and a house on the Pacific Ocean. A trip to Europe. She wouldn't stop talking to us about how she'd shoot Lu Doc, if she got the chance. Said she had a weeklong romance with Lu Doc, but true love doesn't always last."

"But she did confess to killing Ivan and Deputy Leach?" Abby said. "That's what you said?"

"Sure did," Roland said. "Won't be any trial for her for that."

"I know we're still off the record here, but what about Dr. Zibe Growdy?" Abby said. "How does he play into all of this?"

"We're still working on that, too," Roland said. "Inverness couldn't help much. Other than that Tran and Ivan met him at FSU to show him some of the bones. We'll know more about his connection soon, I hope. We have to interview some of his colleagues and family."

"They did the same thing Joseph did," I said.

"What's that?" Roland said.

"They went to Growdy for an expert opinion," I said.

"Reckon so," Roland said. "Now Growdy's dead."

"Growdy wanted the money," Abby said. "It's always about the money. Most of the time, anyway."

"Anything else for the record?" I said.

"No, but you two got enough for tomorrow's paper, don't you?" Roland said.

"We do," I said. "We'll be checking in with you and Ed as this thing goes on."

"You know how to find us," Roland said. "Call us anytime."

"We will," Abby said. "Thanks for everything."

"Thank you," Roland said. "It's your team that put Lu Doc behind bars. The FBI thanks you."

On the way out of the sheriff's office, we met our photographer from the *Chronicle*, Tommy Clarkson, and spoke with him a few minutes. He took mug shots of Joseph, Roland, and Ed and then he left for the Aucilla River and the St. Marks Lighthouse. He planned to return to Albany that afternoon and have some of the pictures developed for tomorrow's story.

He gave us the money that Mickey sent, enough for us to spend a few nights in the area, conduct some more interviews for follow-up stories, and have some good meals.

It was almost noon when Joseph, Abby, and I left the sheriff's office in Crawfordville and headed for the Tallahassee hospital to visit Walt. I didn't want to tell him both his pickup and Pontiac had been blown up. We'd leave that up to his friend, Mingo.

I could hear Daniel Boone cussing now.

CHAPTER 35

We walked into Walt's hospital room in Tallahassee unannounced as a tall, slender, and attractive black nurse stood over him checking his blood pressure and pulse. He wore a white gown and was propped up on a couple of pillows and looked good for a man who'd been gouged by a wild hog and shot twice, all in the same day.

He introduced us to his nurse, Kathleen Rose, and she said hello in a strong, comforting voice but kept her focus on the things she was doing for Walt.

"I told Miss Rose not to let y'all in if you came up here. You're bad medicine, all of you. Don't want to see any of you again. Ever. Didn't I, Miss Rose? They just sneaked in here like they always do. Worse than damn criminals, they are. Never trust that sneaky Seminole. Never."

She was reading the blood pressure gauge and didn't look up. "That's what he said earlier this morning. He warned me about you three." She played her part well.

She reminded Walt what a doctor had told him earlier. Rest for a few days under hospital care, and he'd be released soon. The gunshot wounds didn't require surgery, just stiches. They both made a clean exit out of Walt's left shoulder, like Joseph had said. As long as there's no infection, full recovery shouldn't be long.

"I will check on you later, Mr. Gosser," Kathleen said. "I hope your friends don't hurt you. I see why you don't trust them."

"I asked you to call me Walt."

"Okay, Walt. Hope they don't hurt you."

"You know I don't trust these people. They're dangerous. All of 'em. Everyone of 'em."

The nurse said goodbye and left the room with her brown clipboard. She gently closed the door behind her.

"I think she's in love with me," Walt said.

"I thought the waitress in PC was in love with you," Abby said.

"Both of 'em are. It's just my sweet nature."

"No surgery," Joseph said. "Very good news. I think I recall saying that to you at the lighthouse. The bullets went in and out. Walt Gosser, a man who lives a charmed life. A man all the women love."

"And I think I recall almost getting killed for you," Walt said.

Joseph grabbed Walt's right hand and in a low voice said, "Thank you, my friend. Thank you for everything."

Walt nodded his head, looked at us, and no one spoke for a few seconds.

"That's good news," Abby said. "Good news that you're going to get out of here soon, and we have more good news about last night."

"You gonna give me the details, or am I gonna have to read about it in the papers?" Walt said.

"Nobody else got shot," Abby said. "Them or us. Joseph took care of the men in the U-Haul, and the FBI agents arrested Inverness and Lu Doc. They're in the Wakulla County Jail. And we'll have a story in our paper tomorrow."

"What about the BMW that exploded?" Walt said. "After Joseph shot it."

"Those two are dead," Abby said. "Harry Tran and Dr. Zibe Growdy. Lu Doc blew up that car. They put a bomb underneath the car with a timer on it, according to some preliminary FBI work. That whole gang turned on one another."

"Mingo is no longer a wanted man," Walt said. "That's a good thing."

"It is," I said, "but there's something else you need to know."

"Let me guess," Walt said. "The FBI said we could keep the money in the brief case, sell the bones and keep that money, too. Am I right? We'll be rich, all of us."

"No, that's not it at all. Not even close," I said. "Joseph has something he wants to tell you." I looked at Joseph, and I knew he didn't want to tell Walt about both his truck and car being destroyed by the grenade launcher. I knew I wasn't going to tell him, neither was Abby.

"Walt, I want to do something for you since you helped me," Joseph said. "I want to buy you a new car to show my appreciation. You risked your life for me. For us."

"New car? I don't need a new car. Got a truck and a car now. Both in great shape. I love both of 'em. Just buy me a fifth of Crown, and we'll call it even."

"You're going to need something to drive when you get out of here," Joseph said, "because your pickup and Pontiac were both blown up last night. You cannot drive either one of them."

"Blown up? I'll be a dirty sonofabitch. I did hear few explosions after the BMW. How?"

"Vietnam-era M79 grenade launcher," Joseph said. "Known as Thumper. They were effective during the war, and they seemed to work just fine at the lighthouse last night. It made a mess out of your Ford and Pontiac."

"I can't wait to tell my buddy Chet this story. I've already talked to him at the PC Police Department and he's on his way here. He wants to hear the whole thing from me. He'll be sorry he missed all the fun last night."

"Detective Collingsworth was a big help to us," Abby said. "We never would've finished this thing without him. We've taken some bad people off the streets, and they're going to go to prison for a long time."

"Those boys sure came to play," Walt said. "Like I said, I heard it all when it happened. Man, I loved my truck. *Really* loved my big Bonneville."

"They came to play with big medicine," Joseph said. "They will play no more. I am sorry about your car and truck. That's why you'll need something new to drive."

"Well, shit, Mingo, I always wanted a new Cadillac."

*

Over the next several days, Abby and I wrote five follow-up stories connected to the mammoth bones and the violent people who shot Joseph, framed him, and killed others but were arrested on a dark road near the St. Marks Lighthouse. All the stories were picked up by the AP and received national and international attention because of the new scientific discoveries found at the bottom of the Aucilla River.

As a result of their ongoing investigation, the FBI learned that Dr. Zibe Growdy of FSU, one of the nation's top archeologists we were told, was a compulsive gambler and had amassed debts of about fifty thousand dollars to Jerry Dao, the now-dead man and former owner of the Lucky Seven. This was confirmed when agents raided the bar and found a safe that contained a black book with a record of Dao's illicit businesses.

Plus, according to Inverness, who never got her trip to Scotland or California, Tran had told her about Growdy's gambling debts to Dao. Growdy agreed to help Tran dive for the bones in order to pay off his debts, she said. Tran had offered Growdy fifty thousand for his help.

Just the amount he needed.

Walt spent four nights in the hospital and made a full and quick recovery. I wasn't surprised. The man was tough. Joseph didn't buy him a Cadillac. He tried, but Walt wouldn't let him. Walt bought himself a new Ford pickup almost identical to the one destroyed by Thumper. He promised us a ride in it the next time we came to the Aucilla.

We stayed at a bed and breakfast in the little village of St. Marks after we visited Walt in the hospital and Joseph returned to his home on the Aucilla. From there we wrote stories on an old, black Royal typewriter Joseph loaned us and dictated over the phone to our editors in Albany. We managed to have some fun, too.

The night before we returned to Albany, Joseph invited us to his house on the river and cooked trout, hush puppies, and cheese grits, and we split two dozen raw oysters. After we ate, the three of us sat on white wicker chairs about twenty feet from the water, where Joseph's boat was docked. The Coast Guard had recovered it and returned it to Joseph.

It was a cool evening, and we wore light jackets as the wind blew and the white moon rose high, the sky clear and crowded with stars. The same kind of night sky we'd seen since we'd arrived at the Shell Island Fish Camp almost two weeks earlier. We sipped Chardonnay, and Joseph had coffee.

We talked steadily for several minutes about what we'd experienced together and what the future might be. Joseph said he'd decided to do something he'd thought about since he'd returned from Vietnam. Visit Johnny Kicking Horse's family at Pine Ridge Reservation in South Dakota. Johnny died in Joseph's arms in Vietnam, a tragic story that he shared with us after his nightmare in the chickee.

Joseph said that, a few months back, he'd bought a book that made him think of Johnny called *God is Red: A Native View of Religion*. The book's author, Vine Deloria, was born near Pine Ridge Reservation.

"That book touched me. Changed me, even. I've read it three times and each time I've learned more. Each time I think of Johnny Kicking Horse and my own family and all Indian people."

He said he planned to try to contact the family the next day.

Then there was a lull in the conversation. The quiet was shattered by a high-pitched squeal from the other side of the river but not far away. The sound lasted a few seconds, stopped and began again. Thirty seconds later, it was gone for good.

"What was that?" I said. "Was that the old Seminole monster, Stigny?"

"You mean *Stikini*," Joseph said. "No, it was not him. Don't worry."

"What then?" Abby said. "If not the monster?"

"Co-wah-chobee," Joseph said slowly. "Panther is speaking to us from the other side of the river. He sees us, but we can't see him. The Creator's favorite animal. Always remember that. Never forget."

"We're safe then, aren't we?" I said.

Joseph leaned forward on his chair to get closer to us and said, "Yes, we are safe again. All of us."

AUTHOR'S NOTE

The first time I fished the Florida Panhandle near the St. Marks River and the St. Marks Lighthouse, I was probably fourteen or fifteen and it was the early 1970s.

I believed then, and still do today, that those saltwater flats are some of the most beautiful and inspirational places in the world. I've fished there many times since then.

Throughout *Aucilla Bones*, I refer to historical events and places, but have taken a few liberties, specifically with the land adjacent to the St. Marks Lighthouse.

I was inspired to write *Aucilla Bones* after my friend, Lon Sweat from Tallahassee, took me fishing on the Aucilla several years ago. Lon told me about the accidental discoveries made on the Aucilla in the early 1980s by diver Buddy Page, a former Navy SEAL who served in Vietnam.

After that trip, I read about Page and mammoth bones and other artifacts that have been pulled from the Aucilla since then. And I thought it would make a great adventure for Maynard and Sinclair.

Thank you for following my series. I appreciate the opportunity to tell my stories. And I appreciate every reader. I started the series five years ago based on my time as a reporter for the *Albany (GA) Herald* in the early 1980s. I wrote for two other newspapers in the Southeast throughout that decade.

And thanks again to my editor Rosemary Barnes of Atlanta who has edited and improved all five books. Her insights are invaluable.

My wife, Phyllis, is a teacher and published poet and her work, *Chasing Hemingway*, is available on Amazon as well. We live in the country in Fayette County, Georgia, and often tell our stories around the campfire with our two dogs Bear and Mercy and cats Lucy and Nigel, and the sounds of owls and coyotes.

To leave a review on Amazon, go to my product page, click on Customer Reviews and share your thoughts with other readers.

Made in the USA
Middletown, DE
11 February 2020